THE POET

OF

BALDUR

THE POET OF BALDUR

ANDREA BIANCA DA SILVA

The Book Guild Ltd

First published in Great Britain in 2021 by
The Book Guild Ltd
9 Priory Business Park
Wistow Road, Kibworth
Leicestershire, LE8 0RX
Freephone: 0800 999 2982
www.bookguild.co.uk
Email: info@bookguild.co.uk
Twitter: @bookguild

Typeset in 12pt Adobe Jenson Pro

Printed and bound by CPI Group (UK) Ltd, Croydon, CR0 4YY

ISBN 978 1913551 452

British Library Cataloguing in Publication Data.
A catalogue record for this book is available from the British Library.

To Aaron and Isla – you're both my favourite.
Mario, Natassja and Jurgen – my best friends.
Mom – my hero when I was little, my hero now.
And lastly, Hubert – we did it.

ONE

A VISITOR IN THE DARK

"Stay still," it whispered to him in the dark.

James opened his eyes, but there was nothing there. He was lying in his bed, the covers desperately clinging to the hard mattress, leaving his skin exposed to a cool draught of air. He glanced at the window, tightly shut, with only a sliver of moonlight seeping through the shutters.

All he could see was a bare wooden floor with a few items of clothing laid out across a rickety chair and a small, dark wooden chest. He was sure he'd heard something, but nothing appeared out of the ordinary. The room was barely two large paces across and little more than four paces long.

It was starting to get chilly. Autumn was approaching. James reached over to the floor to pull up his bedsheet, grabbed a handful and pulled it up, turning over in the process. That was when he realised it was lying next to him.

James screamed and the thing pawed at him, but he threw himself out of his bed, out of its reach. Its hands were almost human, but in the dark, many things could pass for human.

James was lying on the floor when it thudded onto his chest.

"Stay still," it hissed again. James wasn't listening. He twisted and turned, scrambling for the door. A damp, pale hand grabbed James's wrist and held it there, leaving him with one hand free. The held wrist began to tingle, as if he'd placed it underwater so hot, at first it felt cold. James felt forced to look up into the creature's face and when he did, he screamed again.

The creature had a long, grey face and crimson lips. It reminded James of a story he'd heard as a child, about the women in the hills who had died during childbirth. They were ghosts – shadows who haunted the moors, crying out for their children. It was said they had pale, almost porcelain skin and blood-touched lips.

"How will you learn if you're not afraid?" it whispered. It took hold of his other hand and straddled him so he couldn't move. James tried to throw the thing off him, but he couldn't move. His spine dug painfully into the wooden floorboards as he fought against its weight.

"What are you?" he screamed.

"…but you will be afraid." It ignored him; its warm breath smelled of damp earth. "Oh yes, you will be afraid."

"I… I am afraid," James admitted. He could see the creature's eyes now – they were cloudy, like those of a blind man, but somehow he knew it could see him. It leaned in closer, its white eyeballs rolling in its head, flitting from James's wide open eyes to his twitching hands. Its red lips parted into a broad smile.

"I will come again for you, James Fiddick," its voice was unsettlingly feminine, "and when I leave, I'll take your heart with me."

James panicked and bucked, trying to throw the creature off of him, but he met no resistance, only air. It was already gone.

He searched around the room, his breath coming fast and hard, his heart beating heavy in his chest, and with each beat, he felt a burning pulsing in his wrists. There was only shadow and quiet. It was as if it had never been there. He looked down to find burn marks shaped like fingers wrapped around his wrists.

James stood quickly and moved over to the shutters and found them latched. He checked the door and saw that it too was locked. He didn't need to search the room to know that the creature was no longer there, because there was simply nowhere for it to hide. He got back into bed and lay there for a long time, shaking. He didn't fall asleep again until he could see a thin sliver of light slip through a crack in his shutters, and the last thing he heard before sleep took him was the tolling of the town's church bells.

*

The winding cobblestone roads that led through the heart of Dasdaya were uneven and layered in grime from horse dung and the contents of slop buckets, but James knew how to avoid getting his shoes soaked. He would keep his eyes on the ground, watching for murky puddles, and he wasn't afraid to leap over large patches of foul-smelling water. He knew to stay away from the green, moss-covered stones, which were slippery and could quickly have him lying face down, covered in the Weavers knew what.

He arrived at the tavern just as the air was beginning to warm, passing by Bradan, who swept the streets with a broom that was nothing more than a wooden handle with a few wiry bristles on the end of it.

James stopped for a moment to watch Bradan scrape his stick against the hard, dry ground. James tensed with every grating motion.

His stomach growled and James rubbed it, his thoughts turning once again to the visitor the night before. He had heard of people who, having eaten something foul for dinner, had experienced lucid nightmares, but it had felt real.

Maybe that's what everyone thinks when they go mad, he thought. *Maybe it all feels real to them too.*

By the time he had listed everything he'd eaten the day before in his mind, Bradan had noticed him staring and he gave James a dark look. Bradan was young, with dark eyes and deep lines on his forehead, which made him look as though he was always frowning. He wore an orange and white tunic, a uniform that clashed with his red hair but was a requirement of all servants of the King – even those such as Bradan who would never step foot inside the castle walls. James knew he'd be seeing many more orange and white-clad servants in the days to come, shuffling quickly through the city, preparing for the King's Parade.

It was the time of year when a procession of knights, performers and members of the court would soon appear to the public, following along the main route into Dasdaya, waving to the public and officially marking the end of the summer months. It was tradition for the King to appear at the very end of the procession, in a magnificent white carriage with his family crest, a blue crane of house Coleridge, proudly displayed on banners that draped across the front quarters. A hand would even appear from the carriage at times, waving to the crowd briefly before being drawn inside, but everyone knew that it didn't belong to the King. The King was safely locked up in his tower, and it was said that he hadn't left it since he was a young man.

Bradan was only a couple of years older than James – nineteen at most. Next to him, James felt washed out with his mousy brown hair and pale skin. Bradan was tall and imposing, whereas James had always been short and thin. Before he turned away, James caught a quick glance at the fine black lines on his inner wrist that marked Bradan as an Uringi. James went to push the tavern doors open, but his eyes must have lingered for a moment too long, because Bradan had caught him looking.

"If you weren't a Katyaya, you would know that the Uringi don't like it when you stare," he said, clearly disgusted.

James knew that word – all Uringi knew it. It meant something close to "deserter", but it also meant "dirty". It was what the Uringi called those who turned their backs on the clans, the small bands of Uringi who still openly practised magic.

"I am not Katyaya, Bradan, and I am barely Uringi. I don't do magic," James explained, but this only seemed to make Bradan more angry.

Bradan shook his head. "If you aren't Katyaya, and you aren't Uringi, what are you?" he challenged.

"I am busy, Bradan." James cut him short as he pushed open the tavern doors and was greeted with the smell of beer and stale sweat.

The tavern never seemed to empty, and although it was barely past midmorning, there was already a group of men staring down empty beer mugs. One of the men laughed while another made a revolting hacking sound before spitting onto the floor next to him.

James decided to make his way to the kitchen to begin scrubbing down the pots from the night before. Soon he would have to begin preparing for tonight's meals, and that entailed hours of washing, chopping and grating before the cook came in and threw it into a large pot. Everyone in the tavern would eat the same thing – there was never any choice – but it was usually something warm and hearty.

The door to the kitchen swung open and James heard the voice of an old man.

"They say that he has come again." He heard a snippet of a story before the door shut behind Bella, the serving girl, as she came in search of a mop.

"What do you mean, he's back? How could a character from a children's story return?" someone asked as the door swung open again.

Something about the first voice had piqued James's interest. It had a warm, oaky quality to it. James decided that he wanted to hear the rest of the story, so he stopped scrubbing, threw his rag into the basin of hot, soapy water and made his way into the dining hall of the tavern, where a fire burned in a large hearth. Here, an old man sat at a table surrounded by three companions. His face was long and sharp, with high cheekbones and dark shadows beneath his eyes. His hair fell down against his face, making it difficult to read his expression unless you were standing very close to him. There was a boar's head peeking out from the stone brick wall behind him, and the room smelled of beer and onion with just a hint of smoke.

The old man paused for dramatic effect, giving James time to find a seat, slipping in beside a woman nursing a young child.

"There are many who claim he was never just a legend – not really," the storyteller continued. "Some men call him the devil, while others have named him a saint." At this he chuckled, though it was a hard and mirthless sound. "He is nameless, shapeless, a creature that can swim through shadows and steal men's souls from their chest. They say that you would not even know that you have met him, this creature, until his sharp fingers are wrapped around your neck – and even then, they say that you pray for death to come for you. They say you beg for death before you beg for air." The man stopped then and took a long drink from the mug he held in his hand.

"Some call him the fool," another hollow chuckle, "but the man who crosses his path earns that name. He is to be feared," he nodded his head as if in agreement with himself, "that is to be sure. Some say even the Weavers fear him – the *Weavers*." The listeners' eyes all went as wide as a nest of waking owls.

A large man stumbled into the tavern, and, stopping to listen to the story, he blocked James's view. He shifted in his seat so that the storyteller came into view again. James didn't want the teller to see him, but he wanted to make sure that he could see his face. A story wasn't as good if you couldn't see the teller's face.

"It is whispered that he is just a bogeyman," his eyes glinted in the firelight, "that he steals children to bring back to his lair, but he is so much more than that. Yes – yes, so much more than that." The old man was obviously enjoying the attention he was getting, and the story took on a theatrical flair. His fingers danced along with his words, as if they were partners in a ballroom.

"He is a shapeshifter. They say that every hundred years, he is reborn into the world, and it is on the night of the autumn festival that he takes his first breath."

A few members of the audience gasped, remembering that tonight was the first day of autumn. James smiled, realising that the old man must have been aware of this. It was as enjoyable watching the man perform for his audience as it was hearing the story.

"You might meet him on a lonely road back to your village. You might think you are alone – just you and the moonlight – and you will turn a corner and see a man sitting by the roadside. As you pass, he will do nothing, say nothing, but he will watch you closely, and you will feel the hairs on your body stand on end."

His voice grew quiet now. He had the ability to make himself heard over the crowd, but it was intimate enough that it gave the story an air of secrecy.

"Once you've passed him, you will breathe a sigh of relief, thinking that the danger itself has passed, but this is not so. He knows, you see – he knows your heart. He knows your home. When you reach your front door and see a warm light shining from within, you will already have forgotten his face. You will go inside, take off your heavy cloak and slip into bed, stretching your toes and relaxing into the heavy comfort of its safety, and you will breathe out deeply, thinking your day is done. That…" he paused, "is when he will come for you."

He took a deep drink from his mug. The listeners were quiet, but other patrons in the tavern had grown rowdy. The old man waited until they had settled before he continued. This gave James a moment to think about what he'd said. Yes, the fool coming for his victims in their beds brought up an image from last night. The memory of him waking up next to the creature flashed violently in his mind, like being hit in the face with a bucket of water.

"Why do they call him the fool?" a young woman with mousy brown hair asked. The listener smiled. This wasn't the first time he'd been asked that question.

"Have you ever seen a fool perform for the court?" the teller asked no one in particular. A few people shook their heads. James smiled. It was unlikely any of these people had ever seen the inside of the castle. The old man reached into his pocket, pulling out three small balls. He began to juggle.

"A fool's face is painted into a frozen smile, and he's made to dance and sing and juggle. His job is to entertain the court, and there are those that are so good at it that you'd think they were born to be fools. There are some that are so good at it that you can't tell the difference between the fool and the man behind the mask. Those smiles are frozen permanently to their faces, and you can never really tell what sorts of thoughts are hiding just behind their eyes. To the world, this sort of man is nothing more than a fool, and there is no man more dangerous than one who can fool the whole world."

The crowd appeared unsettled, and some visibly shifted in their seats.

"James!" a woman wearing a dirty red apron called to him, motioning for him to follow her into the kitchen. James sighed, got to his feet and made his way through the growing crowd.

"Back to work," he whispered to himself, looking back one last time to see the storyteller take a long sip from his mug. Just before the door swung closed behind James, he heard the speaker continue.

"His trade is children, they say…"

James wasn't able to hear any more than that. Once he was in the kitchen, he pulled up his sleeves and plunged into the hot sink of dishes.

*

A few hours later, when the rush had ended and James was able to make his way into the dining hall, he saw that the speaker had left. The fire was starting to burn down and the room now smelled of smoke and sweat. Only a few people still lingered, some talking softly with each other, enjoying the silence of a late night spent with family and friends, while others stumbled around, making gaudy remarks, unable to hide the fact that they had drunk too much. James saw an older man emptying his bladder over a smouldering ember that had tumbled out of the bonfire's circle. It sizzled as the stream of yellow urine washed over it. The man chucked to himself, then stumbled and wet his trousers. James decided that it was time to leave, so he pulled his cloak around him, emptied a mug of warm cider that was left by the bar – warm cider that burned all the way down, giving him the courage to face a night in his bed and the thoughts of cold hands around his neck. Then he began his journey home.

TWO

THE LADY AND THE WARRIOR

Without the moon lighting his way, James was finding it hard to see much more than a few yards in front of him. He was still lightheaded from the cider, and his face burned from the cold, but he was warmed from the exercise.

A shadow moving just beyond a hedgerow caught his eye, and when it moved, he realised the shadow was cast by a young woman. She watched him from across the street, shadows covering her face so that only a glimpse of her profile was revealed as she stood, motionless. She looked as if she was waiting for something. The cloud cover shifted ever so slightly and he could see her face more clearly; her skin was pale and her dark hair fell loose around her face.

Her feet were barely touching the edge of the street, but as he passed her, she was suddenly in the middle of the road. He felt her hand before he saw it, slapping into the side of his face, and then she was out of reach, on the sidewalk, watching him. His hand moved to where she had hit him, and he could only look at her, confused.

Before he could move, or speak, she was on him again, and this time, she landed two solid blows – one to the side of his face and the other to his stomach – before she slid out of reach again. Wind escaped his lips as he doubled over with the last blow. For a second, he thought he was going to vomit.

"What… are… you doing?" he shouted as he gasped for air.

He turned once again, angry and confused, when he saw the smile on her lips – a taunting sneer that made him fearful.

"Who are you?" he asked weakly, licking his lips. "What do you want?" He spat out some of the blood that was pooling in his mouth. He hated the taste of blood.

James saw her move towards him again and he threw an arm out blindly to block the attack. He caught her wrist for only a few moments before she twisted her body round completely so they were back to back. Her elbow slammed into his kidney and dropped him to his knees. He let out a yell of pain as his kneecap made contact with the stone street. She laughed, and the sound grated at him.

"Do you want to die in the street like a dog?" she asked him before landing a blow to the back of his neck, fireflies exploding in front of his eyes. This time he didn't hold back the contents in his stomach.

"I'd rather not die at all – if that's an option," he croaked between retches.

Surprisingly, the woman waited until James was done voiding his guts before pulling him to his knees. She helped him up by the crook of his arm, and he pulled away from her. He caught a look of what might have been pity in her eyes.

"Fight back." She spat.

"Who are you?" he asked again, spitting blood with every syllable. The sour taste of vomit remained in the back of his throat. The beating was giving her no more pleasure, and she now seemed angrier than when it had begun. She showed her mood with the sharp of her elbow, striking him hard across the face. He felt the skin on his cheek open up and warm blood spattered out in front of him. Light exploded behind his eyes.

"Call me Dalahan, for I will be your end," she said. He felt another blow land on his shoulder and felt the sharp pop as the joint was dislodged. The searing pain almost blinded him, and he struck out blindly, but she was always one step ahead of him.

Just before the pain became unbearable, she turned in, pulling his arm forward between them and, at the same time, pushing the flat of her hand into the space between his limb and his shoulder blade. It snapped back, and James gritted his teeth to stop himself from screaming in pain.

"Useless," she sneered as he dropped to his knees once again, wincing. He tilted his head up and watched her slip back into the night, catching a glimpse of a wandering tattoo that slithered up her right arm and disappeared under her shirt. Then he was alone.

By the time he had stumbled home and gotten into bed, various parts of his body felt strange to him – his face was so swollen, his cheeks and lips didn't feel like they belonged to him. He didn't think anything was broken, but he was vaguely aware that the alcohol would be working to dampen the full force of the beating he had received, and he knew he would feel the brunt of it in the morning. The good news, he thought, was that he was in too much pain to worry about the cold, strange creature returning to his bed tonight. For some reason, that thought was comforting enough to allow James to fall into a deep sleep.

*

By morning James could feel every bruise and cut that riddled his body. He lay staring at his ceiling for a few moments, listening to the distant ringing of bells, gathering the strength to get up, knowing that more pain would follow. It was raining and he thought about standing outside to let the water cool his burning skin, then decided against it when he saw the clock beside his bed. It was getting late and he had work to do. He washed quickly with a cloth and a few cups of cold water hastily emptied into the small bucket in his room before getting dressed and stepping out into the street.

The usual horde of people were making their way up and down the streets of Dasdaya. A woman with bright red hair and a dirty, brown apron was hanging strips of fish on lines that ran from one pole to another, posted outside a small shop with a misspelt sign that read 'fresh caugt daily'.

An old man with white eyes sat on the steps of an old factory building, his hands cupped in front of him, begging. People passed without seeing him, but his head turned with each passing body. James wondered if he could see shapes and shadows, the way some blind men did.

His eyes are too white, James thought, realising the old man was probably only able to see darkness.

"You are staring." The old blind man spoke, making James jump.

"You can see me?" asked James.

The man turned his head, as if listening, but his eyes never came to rest on James. "Someone is always staring," the old man said. "People like to stare. Few like to help." Then he smiled a mischievous, childlike smile. "I like to say that every now and again. See if I can catch someone off guard."

James smiled, and the old man motioned for him to come closer.

"Are you strong enough to help an old man to his feet?" the man asked, reaching out a hand for James to steady him. The man's hands were clammy, and he leaned heavily on James's arm.

James grunted as he took the weight, and the old man chuckled, wobbling first and then standing up straight.

"You are very kind," the man said to James. "I need to make my way to Maud's hostel up town and I didn't think I would make it to my feet."

James heard the bells begin to ring again, signalling midday, and he realised he was going to be late.

"I don't have time to take you all the way, but I can take you as far as the river," said James.

The old man shook his head in the affirmative. "I don't want you to be late," he said, "just take me as far as the end of the street. I don't like to walk this block alone. They throw fish guts onto the walkways, making them slippery and dangerous."

The old man locked his arm with James's and together they made their way slowly up the street. Every now and again, James would navigate them around someone hurrying along with a basket or barrel, or stop the old man in time to avoid being covered by the slop that most people threw out into the street. More than once, someone nearly knocked them both over.

"You are too kind, too kind, the Weavers will bless you." The old man patted James's arm as they finally reached the end of the street.

"Are you sure you're going to be okay?" James asked, aware that he was now going to be really late, but not wanting to leave the old man to the throng of the crowd to find his way alone.

"I'll be just fine, thank you, thank you," the old man said, reassuring James with a wave of his free hand.

"Okay… if you're sure…" James let go of his arm, still unsure about leaving the man.

"You've done more than enough. It was nice to meet you." The old man smiled widely.

"It was nice to meet you too," James said as he turned away, trying to figure out the fastest way to the tavern.

*

When he arrived at the tavern, he hurried to the kitchen and quickly filled a large pot with water, bringing it over to the large fire and settling it onto a hook that would hold it until the water boiled. Once it was hot, he used a metal rod to remove it from the hook and bring it over to the basin, where he poured it over the dirty pots and pans that were waiting for him in the sink. He began to scrub, his hands turning pink in the hot water. That was when he saw the finger marks begin to appear on his forearm, and his skin began to burn, as if the hot water had irritated an old wound.

James removed his hands from the water and stared at them for a long time. The marks on his wrists had faded by the next day and he was sure he hadn't had any marks on his forearm from the fight with Dalahan.

He threw his hands back into the water, hiding the evidence among the soapy bubbles in the water.

A particularly stubborn black mark was testing his resolve and he doubled his efforts, determined to remove it.

The Weavers will bless you, he remembered the old man saying. He'd heard that often. Old people loved to say it, as if the Weavers were their personal bankers of goodwill.

He rubbed at the burns on his arm again, wincing.

He'd also heard of Weavers visiting the world in human form, but they were supposed to be chained to their looms.

That was the point of them – they were meant to weave the destinies of men, and stories of them visiting Dasdaya were hundreds, if not thousands, of years old. James shook his head, focusing once again on the pot in front of him.

"James!" A voice broke through his reverie and he looked up to find Beth, the old, plump cook taping her foot impatiently at him. "Where are the potatoes?"

James jumped, then nodded, heading over to the mountain of potatoes that were piled high on the long wooden table that stretched from one end of the kitchen to the other. He picked up a knife and began peeling, his fingers working nimbly, as if he had been born peeling potatoes. A handful of minutes later, he had a pile of naked vegetables building next to him, all ready for the pot. The noise of the tavern drifted into the kitchen every now and again, like a smell on the wind, and for the first time, his thoughts drifted away from the old man, the Weavers and the stranger in the night, and settled back into the comfortable rhythm of the manual task in front of him.

*

By the time the tavern had emptied, it was so late that dawn threatened to spill over into the world. James tidied the kitchen, hung his apron on the hook by the back door of the tavern and slipped out into the night. He drew his coat closer to his body and put his head down, walking quickly.

He was so busy thinking about the old man that he almost didn't see her. The figure slipped in and out of the shadows like she was made of water. He could see nothing more than a silhouette, all curves and temptation, leaning against a dirty brick wall. For a moment, James feared it was Dalahan, the woman from the night before who moved like quickfire, but this one was different. She had something strange about her, as if she were a drawing without thick, bold outlines. They were murky, making it easy for her to blend in with the wall behind her. He couldn't see her face. His eyes were drawn down to her breasts. Two pale mounds that were cupped by a thin cotton dress that fell to her knees and yet clung to her body, wantonly, as if it were something alive and hungry. His eyes worked their way up to the nape of her neck. That place where all things were possible.

He tried to lick his lips, but his tongue stuck to the roof of his mouth. He could smell something strange in the air and saw her bring a cigarette to her mouth. Her face lit up ever so slightly and he saw her breathe the smoke through thick, wet lips. His mind felt as if it had been too long underwater, drowning in a stagnant pond, and as he drew closer, he felt a sort of electricity in the air. He was just a few steps from her now, but for some reason, she didn't come into focus – not in the way that he knew she should. He could tell that she was smiling, but he wouldn't have been able to describe the shape of her lips. He could imagine what they would feel like on his own, however, and he wanted that more than anything. She moved, like silk, onto his path, and then she was close enough for him to smell her. She smelled of something sweet, of something earthy. She smelled like forgetting, and he wanted that. Without saying anything, she sidled up to him, leaning her body into his. Her lips parted, bright red and promising.

As James leaned in closer for a kiss, he felt something push him from the side, forcefully out of the way. He looked up, irritated and groggy, as if he were waking from an afternoon nap. Dalahan stood in front of him, fierce with anger. Instinctively, he brought his hands up to protect his face. Dalahan pulled a knife from the belt around her waist and James saw his partner recoil in fear.

"Keep away from her," he shouted protectively. "I told you before, I'm not going to fight you."

"I don't want you to fight me," Dalahan spat. "I want you to fight *her*." She motioned to the woman standing with her back to the wall. James looked to one woman, then the other, confused. Then Dalahan handed him the knife. The young woman whimpered and James felt his face flush with anger.

He turned the blade and pointed it to Dalahan, unsure whether he would actually be able to use it, but he hoped the threat alone was enough to scare her off. "I don't want to hurt you, but please just leave us both alone," he said.

Dalahan laughed at him. "Were you really going to stick your tongue in her mouth just now?" she asked James, and then she made a disgusted face. James kept the blade between himself and Dalahan, but her tone confused him. There was something too familiar in it.

"That is really none of your business," he said again, hoping he sounded more confident than he was feeling.

"Can't you smell her?" Dalahan asked again, and this time, blood rushed to James's face.

"What?" he asked.

And then he heard the hissing. He turned to see what had made the sound, and the woman suddenly came into focus – but it wasn't a woman. It looked more fish than woman. Where the beautiful woman had stood, now there was a sallow, black-haired creature with fingers much too long for its hands. Its eyes were an ice blue, and James could now clearly see the blue veins running along its arms; a sour smell emanated from its body.

This thing continued to smile at him and small, sharp teeth glinted at him from below her upper lip.

"She's a wraith," Dalahan said simply, bored with just a hint of glee as James stood slack-jawed and mortified.

"I-I…" he stammered, turning his gaze from the thing to Dalahan. "…she looked like… something else." He blushed, not knowing what to say.

Dalahan exhaled sharply, rolling her eyes and motioning for him to return her knife. He did, his face burning with shame.

"Get out of here," she hissed at the thing, "bitch."

The wraith turned for once last glance at James, and he could have sworn it winked at him before turning sharply and undulated down the dark stone corridor nestled between two buildings. It moved like a snake would if it suddenly grew legs but was unsure how to use them. The odour began to fade the moment the wraith was gone.

After the wraith left, the street felt darker, and James's eyes shifted from corner to corner, trying to see if there was anyone or anything else hiding in the shadows.

"You let her go," he said, not sure what he was expecting.

Dalahan snorted. "Not much love lost between you and Miss Long Legs, is there?" Her smile was taunting. He must have looked hurt because she added, "I will find her another time. I thought you'd seen enough for one night."

He nodded, grateful.

"What's a wraith doing in Dasdaya?" he asked, wondering how many he'd unknowingly escaped on his way home from work in the past. He travelled these streets often, and sometimes he'd passed pretty girls who might have been just that – pretty girls – but suddenly he wasn't sure.

"Wraiths haunt places abandoned by the holy." Dalahan ran her fingers along the dark stone walls.

"This place was once a monastery. You can still see some of the old mortar peeking through where the stone has crumbled away. They didn't bother to break the entire building away – not that it would matter much. The ground, once hallowed, was abandoned when they started hanging monks because of they were praying to the wrong god." Dalahan shook her head in disgust. "It's all in the luck of the draw, isn't it? Whether we believe what the King believes? Well, they drew and lost – the ground bled and the wraiths answered their cries. Once abandoned, men tried to buy this ground, but the few who succeeded were fodder for the wraiths. They might breed where holy men are slaughtered but they are not picky with their victims. They'll kill just about anyone."

"How do you know all of this?" James asked her.

James was becoming very familiar with Dalahan sighing in his company.

"I know this because I have to know this," she threw her hands up, "and you will have to learn before you get yourself killed. By a wraith." She said the last few words slowly, as if he were a child and didn't have the kind of common sense that other children had.

"What do you mean I will have to learn?" James asked.

This time, Dalahan really smiled and her eyes lit up with the joy. "I am here to take you home, James Fiddick," she said. The difference in her manner was alarming, and it forced an uncomfortable laugh from James.

"I'm sorry, but after what just happened in the alley – are you suggesting—"

"No," she cut him off quickly, and he noticed that she was flushed, "you are of the Uringi. I am taking you home to your brothers. To Migdasha."

James's heart sank. "I'm sorry – I'm not going anywhere. You have the wrong person."

"No, I don't." Her tone wasn't softened by his refusal. "James, I have been watching you for months. I know who you are, and I want to offer you a home and a job," she said.

He rolled his eyes at this. "I have a job," he replied.

"I have seen where you work. Are you afraid you are going to miss the tavern?" she mocked. "Are you going to miss having small children gape in wonder at every fire dancer you produce – oh wait…" She stopped. "…you don't do magic – at least not in front of anyone. You sweep." She wasn't finished. "I can offer you more than that. And most importantly, what do you have to lose?"

"I don't even know you. How am I supposed to trust you? Look at me – you did this!" He pointed to his face, which was still swollen and blue from the night before, and she grimaced.

"I am sorry, James," she said, and for a second, she looked genuinely ashamed. "I didn't want to hurt you."

He gave a hollow laugh at this, and the look of anger on Dalahan's face returned.

"Listen," she said, "I was just doing my job." She had the decency to blush, then she went quiet.

He'd had enough. "I'm not interested," he said, pushing passed her. He expected her to stop him, but she didn't touch him.

"Please." Her voice was surprisingly gentle.

James hesitated. Then he sighed and turned back to her. "What's the job?" he asked.

"Come with me to Migdasha tomorrow and I will tell you everything," she said. The glow had returned. He started to laugh, but she held his eye. "Please," she said again.

"Dalahan, I—" James started, but his companion pulled her face and burst out laughing. The look on his face made her stop short.

"I'm sorry, James. I didn't mean to laugh. My name isn't Dalahan. Dalahan a character from a story book…" she trailed off, as if expecting him to catch on and join in her laugher. When he didn't, she continued, "…he's the bringer of death?"

James wanted to roll his eyes at her, realising that she had been mocking him when she told him to call her that.

Her eyes softened, and she smiled with something like remorse painted across her face.

"My name is Anna," she said.

James didn't say anything for a moment and then finally he nodded. "I don't do magic, Anna," he said.

She smiled, but it faded quickly. "Then we will teach you to use a sword," she replied.

THREE

THE BROTHERS

James dreamed that he was standing at the base of a pyre, watching Bradan burn, but Bradan wasn't screaming.

"What are you?" he asked James, as his flesh fell away from his skin. Someone in the crowd was tapping the ground with a stick.

"I am Uringi," James answered softly, trying not to draw attention from the crowd. This was difficult because they were all staring at him.

A piece of Bradan's cheek had come away, exposing the teeth behind, making it look like he was smiling.

The tapping grew louder.

"Uringi can do magic." Bradan taunted him as his eyes bulged from their sockets.

The tapping grew more urgent.

"I don't know how," James called back. "I never—" And then the dream was gone. He was awake, staring up at Anna.

"I did knock," she said without the slightest guilt. "Are you ready?"

It took a moment for his head to clear before he remembered why she was there.

"The job," he said, rubbing his eyes and swinging his legs off his bed.

"I…" Anna looked down at her feet then turned a dark shade of red. "I'll wait for you outside." She left, shutting the door behind her and leaving James to wonder what had made her so uncomfortable. It was then that he looked down and realised he had gone to sleep without any clothing.

*

Once James was dressed, he packed a bag containing a few items of clothing, and he and Anna left the bustling city of Dasdaya quickly, stopping only shortly to purchase two rabbit nests from a small, bald vendor. The rabbit nests weren't actual nests, nor did James think they contained much rabbit. They were half-loaves of bread with the filling scooped out, filled with a meaty substance and then smothered in gravy. They had devoured every morsel before they reached the city limits. It was after that, that they set off again. James never felt more sheltered than the moment he stepped foot out onto the road that led him past the great city gates.

He and Anna walked for the first few hours in relative silence, sharing a few words only when they stopped for water along the river. On the outskirts of Dasdaya, they passed narrow farmer's fields, separated by bleached, stacked stone fences. These were lands that sustained the residents of the great city, but just beyond those, the flat land turned into hills, with nothing but winding rivers to break up the green expanse.

When they had walked for half a day, the sun at its peak, Anna suggested they stop and have something to eat. James had brought nothing with him, but Anna had cheese and bread in her sack, and they shared it between them. Sitting on the grass beside a small lake, James took a deep breath, his lungs filling with fresh, clean air. Tiny white and yellow daisies poked newly blossomed heads up from among the grass.

Anna lay herself down in the grass and flowers, her long black hair splayed out behind her head. She had her eyes closed, seemingly enjoying the combination of warm sunshine and the cool autumn air. The last hour before they rested had been a gradual climb so that they were looking down over the foothills. James could smell lavender in the air.

"You said you were Uringi." James spoke.

Anna opened one eye. "I did," she said.

"Can you do magic?" he asked.

For the first time since they met, she smiled a genuine smile and turned to lean on her elbow. "Of course I can," she replied. "Why don't you?"

The words could have sounded harsh, if she hadn't chosen her tone so carefully.

It wasn't the first time James had been asked that question, but he had never answered it honestly before.

"Both my parents died when I was young. If my uncle knew magic, he didn't teach me," he said, shrugging his shoulders.

Anna nodded her head and they sat in silence for a few moments.

"What can you do?" he asked her, and once again she smiled.

"We don't have much further to go." She got to her feet, then caught the disappointed look on his face. "I promise, I'll show you soon enough."

They set off again, and sure enough, it wasn't long before they began to descend into a valley, with a shadow in its centre. Anna gave James a few minutes to take in the view.

"Migdasha," Anna said, pointing out a crooked building in the middle distance, which was no less daunting for its odd shape. It looked like a building that had been designed by a blind builder who had had the concept of a building described to him but he had never actually seen one, or indeed fully grasped the concept. With that being said, it was still impressive, and the closer James got to it, the more impressive it was.

Migdasha soon loomed over them, beckoning and warning, with two towers jutting out at odd angles from the tall structure. And it was tall – so tall, in fact, that James had trouble getting a feel for the whole place, even though they were still a good few minutes' walk from the front door. At least, he hoped there would be a front door. It looked like something out of a children's book.

Anna hadn't said anything for at least an hour, but as they neared, she seemed to perk up a bit. He wondered for a moment whether he'd be expected to climb a turret on a rope. A quick glance to the east and he could see a great lake in the shadow of a mountain range. Travel far enough in that direction, he recalled, and you would come to Aventias, one of the five counties that made up Gedeon, the kingdom after which its largest city was known, and the land of the winds. To the north-west lay Fiachra-Rádha, he remembered now, a barren desert that was home to nomadic, barbaric tribes that bartered people for coin. Just a bit further south from their present location was Morvoren, a strange, dark land that birthed rumours of women who would take a corpse to bed for the right price. Ancasta lay furthest south and was the last of the counties. Ancasta was said to be flooded for the better part of the year – so much so, in fact, it was said the nobles built entire cities under the lakes that appeared during the long tides of winter.

Turning his attention to the valley again, he realised that Migdasha looked like an old church, with turrets that were worn and straining against the passage of time. It was a strange paradox that the building looked both impenetrable and as if it could topple over from old age at any moment.

There was indeed a front door. It was enormous, made from wrought iron, and stood in front of them, cold and unwelcoming. He didn't see a keyhole. James stepped aside as Anna took hold of a large brass knocker and announced their arrival to everyone inside.

James realised, just as the final boom echoed within the building, that he had no idea what to expect when the door opened.

For a few minutes nothing happened. For a moment the anti-climax was almost comical. They were just standing outside of this dark fortress, built in the middle of what might have otherwise been an ordinary meadow, waiting for someone to open a door and – what? Turn him into some kind of wraith-destroying warrior? Suddenly, James was unsure why he had agreed to come in the first place. He nearly turned and started walking back home.

Back to what? he thought.

He didn't hear keys finding their way into a lock, but of course that wouldn't have made sense considering there was no keyhole. Apparently, there was no need for one, because moments later the door was opening and light was filtering through to the other side. On that other side stood a small, stocky man.

The small man came to barely above James's waist height and he was wearing what looked like a very uncomfortable formal tunic and a stiff, white ruff around his neck. He had a face James might have associated with a schoolmaster or even a barrister because of the pinched lips and the look of disdain in his eyes, but there was something about him that didn't quite fit. James couldn't put his finger on what it was. The smaller man stepped aside and a large one with bright red hair stepped forward and grabbed hold of Anna, lifting her up into the air.

"Phoenix, put me down." Anna giggled.

"We were getting worried when you didn't return last night," Phoenix said; his voice was somehow comforting, like a crackling fire in winter.

"I'm sorry. It took a bit longer than I thought." She grunted, and Phoenix put her back down on her feet. James wondered if he was the "it" that had taken longer than she thought. He briefly wondered whether he should be insulted, but suddenly Phoenix's hand reached out and nearly swallowed his own in a meaty grip.

"Welcome, James." Phoenix vigorously shook James's hand. He had a warm, friendly smile and James liked him immediately.

"Thanks," James replied, a little uncomfortably, taking a step through the door. It was promptly closed behind him. He offered his hand to the smaller man but only received a cold look in return before the doorman scuttled off, down the hallway, into the depths of the house.

Phoenix laughed. "No need for formalities. Humbert's a domovoi," Phoenix said.

"A what?" James asked.

Phoenix laughed again, deep and long. "A domovoi. He's like a dwarf" – they heard a loud clatter from inside the house, as if something had been violently thrown against a wall – "except he takes care of the house. You know, cleans and cooks and generally does everything you'd expect from a good woman." He smiled cheekily at Anna.

"You know he doesn't like that," she chided.

Phoenix shrugged, but as the candles in the hallway flickered, his eyes went wide. "My bathwater is going to be cold tonight, isn't it?" Phoenix looked somewhat dejected.

"He's a house spirit," Anna explained to James, "and don't be fooled by his size – he's dangerous when he wants to be." She motioned towards the candles, who were still dancing as if agitated.

"It's… he's… what's doing that?" James asked. The candle flames rose like an audience offering a standing ovation, and Anna moved swiftly to put out a small fire that had caught onto one of the long, heavy curtains that draped across a large window. She reached it just in time and snuffed it out with her deft fingers.

"*His* name is Humbert," she corrected him, "and yes."

"Why keep him around if he's dangerous?" James asked.

Anna and Phoenix gave each other a look that James didn't quite understand before Anna spoke. "He protects this house. He's been here since they laid the foundations. If Phoenix would just stop goading him—"

"Come with me, I am going to show you to your room." Phoenix ignored her and made his way up a large, elegant, winding staircase that led up to the first floor. From there, a long hallway split into the east and west wings of the house. As they reached the top, Phoenix turned left and they passed two doors before he stopped in front of a white door, turning a large, silver doorknob.

The door opened to a large room, lined from floor to ceiling in rich, blood-red draperies. The four-poster bed was adorned with intricately woven pillows. The room was ten times the size of James's entire room back in Dasdaya. There was a large fireplace, already lit, in the centre of the room, and a soft, dark blue rug was laid out in front of it. The room also contained a large tub, which was situated in front of two very large windows, looking out across the lake.

"Make yourself at home," Phoenix smiled, "but don't take too long. We meet in the library in ten minutes."

"Wait," James called out, and Phoenix turned back to him, his eyebrows raised as if in a question. "This is mine?"

Phoenix gave a quick nod. "Ten minutes," he reminded James, and then he was out the door, shutting it softly behind him.

James was alone in his room. He was almost afraid to lay his travel sack down on the floor in case he dirtied it. Then the moment passed and he threw his things onto the bed, pressing his hands down onto the soft throw and feeling how inviting it was. He realised then just how tired he was.

There was a small stand next to the bath with a jug of water and a washcloth, and he used this to wash his face. The water was warm, which surprised him. Once his face was clean, he walked over the windows and noticed two small handles that allowed him to push open what he realised were two glass doors, leading out to a balcony.

James wandered onto the balcony looking down onto a lake that shimmered with stars, reflected from the clear night sky above. He felt the chilly air embrace him, then stood for a moment and took in a long, deep breath. It was never this quiet in Dasdaya – there was always someone in the streets, yelling, fighting or singing, stumbling drunkenly through the streets. Here, the only thing he could hear was the wind. Then he heard a soft knock on his bedroom door.

"It's me again," he heard Phoenix saying. "I'm here to take you to the meeting."

Reluctantly, James turned his back on the view and closed the balcony doors before crossing the room and opening the door to the hallway. Phoenix was leaning up against the wall, just underneath a portrait of what looked like Humbert, the domovoi.

"That's strange," James remarked.

"What is?" asked Phoenix, as he started to walk down the hall.

"The portrait of the domovoi – it looks just like him… but… not…" James's voice trailed off. There was something so odd about the painting, as if the domovoi's features were lengthened, reshaped ever so slightly, to look just a little more human.

Phoenix laughed a deep, chesty laugh. "That is not a portrait of the dwarf" – somewhere in the house, pots clanged and something made from glass was shattered – "it is the original owner of Migdasha. The domovoi is supposed to take on the appearance of the owner of the house. The actual owner died many years ago, but technically, the house still belongs to him, so the domovoi still looks like him."

James nodded, ignoring the imagined fingers that tickled his spine and raised the hairs on the back of his neck. As he walked away, he could feel the dull, brown eyes of the painting following him.

They took a right turn and then a left before coming to a dark green door. When Phoenix opened the door, the smell of cinnamon and warm bread filled James's nostrils, and his mouth filled with saliva.

The room was lined with dark, wooden panels, some filled with books, others with knickknacks of sorts, and five, large, overstuffed chairs were placed in the centre, surrounding a table that was piled with food. He saw large, golden brown breads popping up from between cuts of cured meats and soft, creamy cheeses. There were thick cinnamon rolls coated in a honey glaze, and large jugs of something warm, steam curling up and out of clay pitchers. James was sure that was where the smell of cocoa was coming from. Anna was already seated at the table.

"Have a seat, James. And please, have something to eat too."

James didn't wait for another invitation. He picked up a plate and piled it high with cheese, two warm rolls and a large, pink peach, topping it off with a mug of dark, creamy hot chocolate. When he bit into it, the peach's skin broke and juice dripped down into his lap. His mouth was filled with the sweet flavour, and it was enough to lift his mood and clear some of the fatigue of the long journey.

"We still waiting on Evan?" asked Phoenix.

Anna nodded, but just as she did this, the door opened and a slim, dark-haired young man walked through the door. He looked to be around the same age as Phoenix – maybe nineteen, if that.

"James, I'd like you to meet Evandor – but we call him Evan." Evandor was at least a head shorter than Phoenix, and the second man seemed to tower above his friend in more than just stature. Evandor reached out a hand to James and he shook it. As he pulled it away, Evandor smiled and wiped peach juice onto his trousers.

"Sorry about that," James said with a mouthful of cinnamon roll.

"I should be the one apologising – you must be starving after such a long journey," Evandor said.

"She out here tonight?" Phoenix nodded towards the window and the hills outside it.

Evandor smiled again. "She is," Evandor replied, but he didn't offer anything else. James noticed that he carried a small staff in his hands.

The others had the decency to wait until James had sated his hunger and quenched his thirst. When he couldn't eat any more, Anna rang a small bell, and Humbert waddled in and cleared the table. He was fast and efficient, and paid them very little attention. For the most part, Phoenix and Evandor spent time whispering among themselves, while Anna waited patiently, saying nothing.

Once the table was cleared, their mugs were filled, James with the same dark cocoa and the others with something lighter and smelling distinctly like alcohol. Phoenix and Evandor ceased their secret meeting and they huddled just a bit closer together. They waited until the door was shut behind Humbert and then Evandor began to speak.

"You probably have many questions," Evandor said to James, "but let's start with why you are here." His light brown eyes were kind but tired. "We have a lot to tell you, and I am afraid it is going to be a long night."

"James, we brought you here because you are Uringi. As you might have guessed, so are we," Evandor continued, and the other two nodded. "Each of us is from a different county in Gedeon."

"I am from Fiachra, the land of the Cinder Forest and the Red Desert." Anna spoke, and as she did, she tapped her fingers on the dark, wooden table, and suddenly a small dancing figure sprang to life out of nowhere and began to twirl, on one leg, graceful and beautiful along the table's edge. James took a sharp breath, watching it bow down low.

"I am from Ancasta," Evandor spoke now, "the land of the great lakes and rivers." As he spoke, another dancer appeared, this one made entirely of water, and the two joined, never touching but always in sync, twirling to music James couldn't hear.

"I'm from Ancasta." Phoenix spoke now, and with his words arose a wind, forcing the two to join together, and they snuffed each other out. Phoenix had used the air itself to accomplish this, but there was little theatre in the way that he did it, or perhaps the theatre was in the simplicity of it. "The land of the sky towers and the great birds."

They were quiet for a few moments, watching James.

"You aren't expecting me to put on a show, are you?" he said. "I told you – I don't do magic."

Evandor looked confused for a moment. Anna said nothing.

"But you are Uringi," Evandor said, not unkindly.

James didn't say anything.

Phoenix looked to Anna. "If he can't do magic, how's he going to fight?"

"Woah…" James shook his head, turning to Anna. "You didn't say anything about…" Just as he was admonishing her, he realised that she had indeed said something about fighting.

Then we'll teach you to use a sword. Anna's words came back to him and things slowly started to slip into place. He looked around him as if taking in for the first time just how opulent this house was – just how expensive it was to maintain.

He hung his head, realising for the first time why he was there. "You are mercenaries, aren't you?" he said quietly, angry at himself for not asking this question sooner. When no one replied, he looked up.

"No, not exactly," Anna began, but he heard a hesitation in her voice that was all the proof he needed.

He got to his feet. "I think I'm done," he said, unsure if he was more frustrated with himself or the three that sat before him.

Evandor raised his eyebrows. "Already? We haven't even gotten to the bad stuff yet."

James laughed, but he was cold and tired. He thought of the journey back home. He wondered if he still had a job.

He reached the door and heard Anna.

"Stay one night and I will pay you two gold Kilns."

This made him pause. He hadn't even seen that amount of money in his life.

"One night?" He turned slowly, not sure if he should believe her.

"One night," she replied.

He considered for a moment. With that money, he wouldn't need to go back to the tavern right away. He could live on that amount for months. And not just live, but live comfortably. He might even be able to afford a room with a wrought-iron bath and have soft, warm towels brought to him each evening.

"I want payment up front." He tried his luck.

Anna got up and began digging in one of the many pockets that lined her vest. She pulled out two gold coins and handed them to him. He closed his fingers around them, feeling their weight. The weight felt good.

"You just have to listen to us. Then you can decide whether this is the right place for you," Anna said.

He went to take his seat. This time, the weight of the money made him feel much more at home. He took a long sip from his mug.

"So what are you, if you aren't *exactly* mercenaries?" he asked.

"We are the Keepers of the Dark," Anna said. With that, Phoenix gave a long, hard guffaw. "And we're here to bind the fool."

FOUR

THE STORY OF THE FOOL

"Phoenix, you promised not to do that," Evandor said.

"She's trying to resurrect ghosts," Phoenix put his hands up, "it's not enough that we're just about chasing a ghost – now she wants to turn us into some children's version of the Knights of Valore." He took a big sip from his mug, washing down a large chunk of jam-smeared bread that he'd been hiding somewhere under the table.

"The Knights of what?" James asked.

"The Knights of Valore," Evandor explained, "were a band of rogue nobles sent to protect Gedeon from the fool, when he awoke from his slumber and began slaying children in their sleep."

"I've heard of the fool," James said, turning to Anna. "Phoenix is right – he's just a children's tale."

Phoenix made a grunting sound, and Anna returned it with a dark look. "How about you let me finish and we let James decide what he believes?" she asked him.

James tried to remember snippets of the stories he'd heard as a child, but all he could recall were broken images and a lingering dread, the kind all children feel when they talk about monsters in hushed tones. Every now and then, someone reinvented the story, turning it into the sort of tale the old man told back in the tavern, but most shared a similar element – you never actually found out what the fool was. That was what made him scary. He was just a monster.

"He's some sort of banshee, isn't he?" James ventured.

"Close," said Anna, "he is a death spirit, but he doesn't wail to warn of death." She shifted in her seat. "Not a whole lot is known about him, but he pops up in children's stories all over the capital city of Dasdaya and the four surrounding counties. In Fiachra-Rádha we call him Righul. Our old women warn the children about him during the midsummer months when the air gets so hot and dry that fire is a constant danger." She spoke with the warm familiarity of someone who missed home.

"During these months, the old women say that you can see Righul dancing through the Cinder Forest if you look closely through the mess of smoke and old elm leaves kicked up by the fire's breath. Children who wander too close to the forest at night are in danger of running into Righul and being set alight.

"In Morvoren he is the spirit of the nightshade who roams the forest of Baldur. He is a poet and a killer."

"He would be in Morvoren," Evandor chuckled.

"…but it's hard to tell whether they love him or fear him more," Anna continued.

"Morvoren is a dark place." Phoenix nodded.

"In Ancasta he is little more than a water sprite, albeit a powerful one," said Evandor. "When the waters rise, they say he wakes from the depths of the Alhar and swims the length of the county looking for prey, as if the winter months have bound him in some way. Each year, the outer villages listen out for reports of drowning or disappearances so they can track Old Telhac along the way."

"They act as if drowning isn't common in a county that is made up of lakes and rivers and ocean," said Phoenix.

"It isn't, though, is it, Phoenix? They are trained to swim before they can walk," Anna argued.

"Of course they are," he said defensively, "but accidents happen, just as they do in Fiachra. And besides, he's not the only monster they say haunts the waters of the Great Lakes. Your children are taught to fear thirst above all else, are they not?" he said to Anna. "Yet how many are found delirious, wandering the desert half naked, with bloody lips, crying for water but no longer able to keep it down?"

"Children in Fiachra are taught to fear slavery above all else," she said bitterly, bringing an end to the argument.

Phoenix swallowed his retort. "In Aventias we know him as the great bird, the traveller from the north. Many still believe he carries the spirits of the dead to the great Pentoc – the Other World," Phoenix said.

"In Dasdaya, you are right, he is a children's story," Anna said to James. "Here, he is the fool and children are his trade. Strangely, the city is the only place in the whole of Gedeon where only the children are taught to fear the fool."

"What is strange about that?" asked James. "He's some sort of bogeyman, isn't he? Why should anyone other than children fear him?"

"She doesn't believe it's a children's tale." Phoenix nodded his head in Anna's direction.

"Neither does Evan," she replied almost petulantly, picking up her mug and taking a sip.

They all turned to look at Evandor. "All stories have some truth to them," he said simply.

"How can you believe it's anything more than a children's story?" asked James incredulously. "Have you seen the fool?"

Phoenix nearly spat his tea back into his mug. Evandor smiled.

"No," Anna's voice was firm, ignoring the others, "but I'm not the only one who believes. The King believes too."

Phoenix snorted loudly.

Anna frowned. "The King has seen him—"

"The King once believed his old nursemaid to be of the Effluvium so he had her skinned," Phoenix added.

"What's the Effluvium?" James asked as Anna opened and closed her mouth.

"Ghoul lovers," Evan explained.

Both Anna and Phoenix pulled their faces in disgust at this.

James had heard of the ghouls of Morvoren. They were rotting corpses that fed on human flesh. They carried disease and it was said they brought a plague to Dasdaya in centuries past. It was one that took years to flush from the city. He has also heard of ghoul lovers.

"They give their bodies to the ghouls. The ghouls feed on them slowly, sometimes for years before they finally give in to rot or disease," James said, recalling what he knew of them. "But, why do they do it?" he asked, disgusted.

"They say it gives them visions," Evan answered. "It allows them to tell the future."

"Doesn't do them any good, though, does it?" Phoenix derided. "For some reason, the moment they enter into one of those ghoul dens, they become so intoxicated they can barely speak. Even if someone tried to help and remove them by force, they end up crawling back only days later. The ghouls don't have to try very hard to fill those dens up either, do they?"

The others nodded in agreement.

"So?" asked James. They all turned to him questioningly. "Was she a part of the Effluvium?" he asked.

"Who?" Anna asked.

"The nursemaid?" James added.

"No," Anna snapped, "of course not."

"The King is mad." Phoenix got up to stoke the fire. It was getting dark outside.

"Everyone knows that," Anna said.

"But you believe that the fool appeared at his bedside one night and told him that he was going to die by his hand?" Phoenix's tone made it clear he wasn't expecting an answer to this question.

Anna pulled her legs up onto the large chair in the corner of the room, looking angry.

Evandor cut in. "Whatever he saw scared him enough that he chose to lock himself up in Warenhai Tower for the past twenty-five years."

Everyone in Dasdaya knew that the King had not left Warenhai Tower in almost three decades, but James had never heard this story of the fool. He had heard rumours, of course, of assassination attempts and the like, but he had come to believe what everyone else in Dasdaya believed – Gedeon was no better or worse off than before the King shut himself away. The children went hungry. The men died ploughing barren fields. Over time, the King was forgotten. He had been a poor king when he took the throne and he remained a poor king with the throne standing empty.

"What do you believe, Anna?" James asked.

"I believe the fool came to the King when he was a boy." She sounded certain. "I also believe he's returned."

"And what does that have to do with us?" James asked.

"This is where it gets really good." Phoenix smiled.

Anna glared at him but continued anyway. "Because we need to stop him," she said.

James laughed, then realised she was serious. His smile began to fade.

"She believes we're knights, James." Phoenix laughed again while James felt a faint fluttering in his stomach. "She thinks we're the Knights of Valore, returned to slay the fool."

Anna didn't get the chance to reply. The knock at the door was so faint they almost didn't hear it. The sound of Humbert's footsteps echoed softly towards the front door. They could hear him speak in his hushed monotone. Someone answered with a softer voice but with an urgency that brought Anna to her feet. She was at the door when they heard the footsteps return. This time, there were two sets.

The fire cast a warm glow throughout the room, but everything beyond the door was in shadow. The footsteps came to a stop outside the door and Humbert emerged from the shadows.

"You have a messenger," he drawled before he disappeared into the darkness, his footsteps echoing once more down the passage. From the shadow, a little boy emerged.

"Welcome, Thomas?" Anna's words were both a welcome and a question. She moved aside as the boy entered the room. The boy could not have been more than ten years old, but his face was lined and worn, like a field worker who spent too much time in the sun. His dirty blond hair threatened to spill over his face and he wiped it away hurriedly with earth-stained hands. He nodded to Phoenix and Evandor. His eyes shifted over James, as if to acknowledge his presence, before they moved to Anna once more. He blew into his hands and rubbed them near the fire.

"Would you like something to drink?" Anna asked, but the boy quickly shook his head.

"I must get back." He was already moving towards the door, but James caught the look of longing as his eyes shifted back towards the fire. It lasted only a moment, then it was gone and his expression was all business. "I came to tell you that we are holding the Sepultura Bellator in Dima's honour tomorrow, at midday." He motioned to Phoenix and Evandor.

A strange look came over Anna's face. She pursed her lips and went to put her hand on the boy's shoulder, but he quickly shrugged it away. Phoenix was staring off into the fire while Evandor had his eyes trained on the boy.

"It is a great honour for the Skyburiow family," the boy said, almost frigidly.

"How is Penhallurick?" Evandor spoke softly.

"He is with Lacey and Thalbir." This seemed to answer Evandor's question and he was quiet again.

"I will walk you out." Anna moved towards the door.

"No need." The boy held up a small, weatherworn hand. "I know the way." He walked out of the room and it was only moments before they heard the front door slam.

The room was quiet for a few moments after the boy had left. Anna was looking at the door as if expecting someone to walk through it, but there was no one there. She touched her hand to the back of her neck, rubbing at something that looked like a tattoo carved into her skin. Finally she looked up and gave James a faint smile. It was almost eerie.

"It's getting very late; I think it's time we get some rest. Tomorrow we leave for Balhatchett," she suddenly looked very tired as she walked out the door.

"But wait – I still don't understand what we're doing here?" he asked.

"We still have a lot to explain," Anna replied. "I promise, you'll get all your answers soon."

Evandor and Phoenix began heading for the door.

Evandor turned around just before he slipped out. "Get some rest, James. Tomorrow is going to be a difficult day for all of us."

FIVE

MIGDASHA

James lay in his bed for a long time before realising that he wasn't going to fall asleep again. Memories from the past few days wove into his dreams and created half monsters that hid just beyond the firelight of his conscience. He listened to the wind outside the large, glass windows to his right and opened his eyes. He had left one of the glass doors open, just enough that the curtains billowed as it entered the room, filling his lungs with cool, crisp autumn air. Somewhere far away an animal, maybe an owl, screeched.

James got out of bed and stiffened when his feet touched the cold, stone floor. He pulled his cloak from the post on the bed and wrapped it around his shoulders. Then he slipped on his shoes, opened the door, turning the handle softly so as not to alert anyone in the house that he was awake, and slipped out of his room, closing the door behind him.

Out on the landing he realised he didn't need a lantern to see by, and, looking up, he realised why. Large skylights allowed moonlight to pour into the hallways, giving him a view of a night sky full of stars.

James looked to his left, then to his right, trying to figure out which direction he wanted to take first. He wasn't really sure what he was looking for, only that he wanted to get acquainted with Migdasha without the lingering presence of Anna, Phoenix, Evandor or indeed the creature Humbert hovering over him.

He decided to head right and began making his way past a hallway of closed doors. He thought that many of them must be rooms, much like his own, and didn't want to chance walking in on one of his companions and waking them, so he ignored these doors. When he reached the end of the hallway, he saw another dark, wooden door, but this one was circular with a heavy, round handle. He hesitated for a few moments and then turned the handle, quietly, pushing against the wood until it gave way.

He smelled the room before his eyes adjusted enough to see inside – it smelled of old books and dying embers, as if a fire had been lit in the hearth. James sought out the fireplace and it didn't take long before he found it. It was a lumbering, kingly hearth with the head of a wolf peering out over the top. The wolf was carved from dark wood, with amber eyes that stared James down as he approached it, slowly. He reached out a hand and touched the cold surface of the wolf's mane, stroking it, letting his fingers become acquainted with its lines. The wolf didn't seem as fierce once he'd petted it, become familiar with it.

James found a pile of wood stacked up high beside the hearth and it took a few minutes for him to get a fire burning. After he was done, he wiped his brow and turned back to the room to take it in with the help of the firelight.

His work was not wasted – he could now see that the room was much larger than he first thought, but the light was not able to reach all the corners of the room, which meant that most of the room was hidden from him.

James had always loved the smell of books, and he'd kept an old copy of *The Traveller's Tales* with him when he was a boy. It was an old book written by someone who'd explored all five counties of Gedeon, and the book was a memoir of sorts. James had always skipped the chapter about Ankou, the old man who carried wagons of the dead and turned a person's hair white if he looked at them. Maybe it was because the drawings of Ankou always depicted him as faceless, with long, grey hair and a pointed chin. James never liked those drawing either.

James began to cross the room, the thick carpet muffling his footsteps. His toes sank into the soft expanse and James wriggled them for a moment before continuing. He saw a ladder that reached up to the tops of the highest bookshelves and he began to climb each wrung, one by one, scanning over titles as he moved. Some were long and sounded as though they were written with only one intention in mind – to put the reader to sleep. He came across a book titled *Orwil Binder's Laborious Ponderings on the Pedagogy of Permutations*.

When he stumbled across a book called *The Massacre Dasdaya Forgot* by Penrose Tyme, he picked it up and began to leaf through it. On the cover of the book was a woman with wild, red hair and a mouth that was too big for her face. It gave her a wicked look. After a few minutes of scanning through the first few pages, James was fairly certain that the woman on the cover of the book was Leanan-Sidhe, a witch that had brought a plague to Dasdaya. James didn't get far enough into the book to read how she accomplished this, but it was believed that, during the great plague, she began bathing in the blood of her victims to make her more powerful.

The bodies soon piled up across the land, not only calling attention to her deeds but also spreading death and disease throughout Dasdaya. Men built great pyres throughout the city to burn the bodies and the fires crept underground, causing the roots of great trees to set alight and begin to smoulder.

When the pyres died down, they didn't realise it still burned beneath the ground. One day, a wind swept through Dasdaya from Aventias, and in minutes, Dasdaya was burning once again, but this time, the men had no control over it.

He slid the book back onto the shelf, in between a large leather-bound diary of a man who enjoyed painting boats, and a small, tattered copy of *The Astronomer's Axiom*. He climbed down, nearly reaching the bottom when his eye caught the glint of gold from a small book bound in black leather. He drew it from the line of tightly stacked books and turned it over in his hands. Golden stencilling, like clouds, wafted across the front and back cover of the book, as if a stiff wind has been used to decorate the book. It was the name on the front of the book that caught James's attention: *The Weavers: Beasts or Gods of the Loom?* James couldn't find the name of the writer on the cover and there were no pictures in the book, except for an etching of an old loom on the first page. James leafed through the book, coming to a stop when he saw something that caught his interest.

The room in which the four Weavers sit, quietly, behind four looms, is painted white. The only sounds that can be heard are the shuttles clanking as the machines unravel the spools of weft. They speak to no one — not even each other. They are the Weavers of the destiny of men. Another sound interrupts the noise of wood slamming into wood — that of a chain rattling as one Weaver stands to take up the roll. His long fingers spin the sheet deftly into a long tube and it is placed in a wicker basket beside his station. Another life is done. He wastes no time, returning to his loom and starting over. Even if he wanted to leave his place, he could not. The sound of the rattling chain comes from the shackle around his ankle, and it is forged from the bones of the Weavers who came before him and strengthened with the steel of the sword used to slay them.

The question before us is whether these creatures are indeed gods – creators of our destiny – or blind beasts, tasked with recording lives on wooden looms and little more.

James stopped reading. His eyes strained with the effort of trying to see the words with nothing more than the firelight to guide his way. Every time he turned a page of the book, the page's shadow would make it difficult for him to continue and he had to take a few minutes to turn the page this way and that to get it at the right angle to see by.

He'd heard some of what the writer was describing before. He knew the Weavers as gods of sorts, and he had heard of their great looms. The shackles were new to him.

He closed the book and slipped it back into place, then took the couple of steps down the ladder to the ground, his feet sinking down into the soft carpet. He wondered for a moment if Humbert would object to his bringing a blanket and spending the night on the floor. He glanced at his hands, noticed they were grey with dust and quickly changed his mind.

He took a few moments to wander around the quiet of the library, enjoying the warmth that was quickly spreading through the room. He was beginning to feel the length of the day in his bones and he decided that he had done enough exploring for the night. He picked up the bucket of sand that stood beside the hearth and emptied it out onto the fire, turning it into a smouldering pyre. The room became dark and somehow felt colder with the lack of light. James turned the door handle and stepped out into the hallway, glad for the moonlight that filtered down through the skylights.

He made his way to his room and slipped into bed, closing his eyes as the soft covers fell around him.

He closed his eyes and fell into his sleep.

SIX

THE LAST REFUGE

When he woke, James took a moment to stretch, expecting to have his feet thump against the rough wooden post on the foot of his bed, but instead there was nothing but soft down and a warm quilt as far as his limbs could reach. He opened his eyes and saw the first light of the morning slipping through sheer curtains on windows overlooking a valley. He had left a shutter open the night before – just enough to let in some fresh air, and that had paid off. He breathed in the clean, cool air deeply, nuzzling down into the covers and closing his eyes.

He wasn't sure for how long he fell back asleep, but the sound of someone tapping at the door woke him. He opened his eyes again, somehow expecting Anna's stern face to greet him, telling him he was late for something or other, but it was Humbert.

"I've been sent to wake you," the creature croaked, looking downright jolly. James wondered if the domovoi was always this cheery in the morning.

The small servant disappeared and James was left to get dressed.

When he reached the bottom of the stairs, Anna was already waiting, ready to go. She handed James an apple and some bread, which he took and immediately began eating. The apple was bright green and tart, making his mouth water the moment he bit into it. The bread was freshly baked and still warm.

"We're already late," she said, throwing items into a sack and heaving it over her shoulder. "Evandor and Phoenix have just left. They will meet us there."

The air outside was biting and James's breath turned to mist every time he exhaled. As they set off down the valley, James felt the walk from the day before in his muscles, but this time, they travelled for only a couple of hours before they reached the edges of a forest and immediately broke through the treeline and delved into its depths.

The trees began to lean in closer as their feet crunched along the floor, disturbing a peace that he was sure could only be found this far from the crowds of the city. Nothing moved here, and even the wind seemed to be holding its breath.

Waiting – that's it, James thought, *it seems as if they are waiting.*

Anna gave him an impatient look as the distance between them widened and James suddenly realised that he was slowly falling behind, so he took a few swift paces to keep up, ducking to avoid a low-hanging branch. The trees continued to lean into the path, looming over them. Anna didn't seem to mind this as she strode with a determined look on her face, speeding up slightly. James realised that they had almost reached their destination.

Anna was moving more frantically now, her boots turning the fallen leaves on the ground to dust. As the trees begun to encroach in on them, James was forced to follow right behind Anna, as there was no room to walk beside her. It began to grow dark well before sundown as the light struggled to break through the trees. As the shadows grew larger, James felt something begin to follow them, as if it had suddenly stepped onto the path behind him. He stopped suddenly and turned around, but there was nothing there except the trees, ever silent, watching. He could no longer see where their footsteps had marked the ground, and he wondered if he would ever find his way home again if he lost Anna in this place. He looked up, trying to catch a glimpse of the sky – anything that would give him an idea about where he was. Something that would make him feel less as if a great monster had swallowed him whole, closing in on him, tightening his chest until he found it difficult to get a proper breath.

Anna's impatient huff made him jump and he realised that she was waiting for him. He quickened his pace, but this time every footstep was like a drumbeat in his chest. They were too loud for this place, and James couldn't swallow the feeling of growing anxiety that had settled itself in the pit of his stomach. He concentrated on the way that Anna's hair bobbed with her every step until he suddenly gasped with pain. Something had cut at his face, and he was about to call out to Anna to stop when he opened his eyes and realised that he had walked directly into the branch of a tree so large he couldn't see past the topmost leaves of its tallest branches, and yet it was stooped so low over the path that it could have hid him from view if he took only one step to the right.

Again he heard Anna sigh in exasperation. "We are almost there."

He didn't have to look at her face to know that she was getting frustrated. "I… I'm sorry." He could feel a thin line of hot blood drip down his forehead into one eye. Trying to ignore the sting, he tried to wipe it away and forced himself to look through his one clear eye so that he wouldn't lose Anna again.

Anna turned around and caught sight of him. Her face softened and she nearly smiled. "You look ridiculous." She pulled a clean rag from her travel sack and handed it to James. "Press down hard. The bleeding should stop soon."

He did as he was told, and sure enough, in a few minutes, he could open his eye. He shoved the rag into a pocket and followed Anna again in silence.

*

He could hear a child's voice in the distance. Anna was still in front, now using her sword to move the branches that barred her way forward. James wondered why she simply hadn't cut them down, since she probably walked this way many times before.

In fact, James thought as Anna waited impatiently for him to step in front of her sword, which was keeping the branches from swiping at his body and legs, *why hasn't someone cleared a path here at all?*

The child's voice was unmistakable now; but it was followed by another and another. James knew that the sounds were getting closer, and this meant that they had almost reached their destination.

But why would anyone live in these woods? he thought. There was barely enough space for him and Anna to walk one in front of the other; there was no way they could have built any sort of home in this forest.

Again the sounds of children sounded just behind the low-hanging branches which formed a barrier just in front of them. Anna stopped, forcing James to halt so abruptly that he bumped into her, causing her to grunt as he reached out his hands to stop himself from falling over her.

She turned and glared at him, and he instinctively took a step back, bumping his head against one of the branches that they had just ducked under.

She put her finger to her lips, indicating that he should keep quiet, so he simply rubbed the bump on the back of his head and gave her an annoyed look before wincing in pain as he ran his finger over a small bump. It wasn't bleeding, so he pulled his hand away and watched as Anna pulled out her sword and turned the blade so that its tip reached just below her nose. For a second he thought that she might cut through the branches, and he wanted to ask her why she hadn't simply done this the first time she had entered this place, but she must have realised that he was about to speak because she gave him a warning look. He shut his mouth and watched as she turned her eyes to the sword. He nearly laughed out loud at the way that she looked at the item, but he knew better than to giggle at Anna when she was holding a sharp object.

She started lifting her hand, and once again James thought that she was stroking the blade affectionately, but when she pulled it away, he saw what looked like a small ruby on the very tip of her finger. His eyes widened when he realised that it was blood.

Her eyes flitted over to him and the look on her face made him take a step back; he winced once again as he knocked his head on the same branch. He put his hand to the back of his head – this time a spot of blood marked the place where his fingers had met his skin.

Anna smiled and his face turned red again, this time in anger.

"What are we doing here? Where is this place you are taking me?" She remained silent, but he wasn't quite done. "Either you tell me what we are doing here or I am leaving."

Anna grabbed his hand, and he would have jerked it away if he hadn't heard the child's voice again.

"Who is that?" He was more frustrated than angry now. Anna was wiping the blood from his finger, and for a moment he thought that she was showing some sort of remorse for dragging them both into the forest and getting them lost. He changed his mind when she smiled.

He watched as she took both hands – the one that was now marked with his blood and the one stained with her own – and rubbed the leaves on either side of the path affectionately.

"I am making you welcome here by mixing my blood with yours," Anna said.

He was just about to turn his back on her when suddenly he heard the branches rustling, and in the quiet of the forest this noise seemed to come from all around him. He turned back to Anna and saw vines, leaves and branches unravelling themselves like a ball of snakes, and the space in front of them began to open. He could now clearly hear that there were children on the other side of the barrier, but he was mesmerised by the shifting, writing and turning of the forest before him, which was suddenly alive and moving. The breath on the back of his neck was no longer there, but the memory came back to him like a ghost and he wondered what kind of place this was; this place where the forest breathed, moved and was home to the sounds of children. A small child came running past them, carrying a basket with bright red flowers hanging over the sides, and James called out to her, but she weaved through the forest like she was born to it, and she was gone as quickly as she had appeared.

"Do we follow her?" James asked.

Anna laughed, but it was just a shade darker than was normal. "I wouldn't," she said.

James frowned at the way that she spoke those last two words, and when he turned to her, he could see that her eyes were focused on something up ahead. He couldn't see anything except a slight murmur that emanated from the bushes just in front of them.

"He's coming," she said.

"Who's coming?" he asked.

She put her hand to her lips, motioning for him to keep quiet. James turned once more to the path and saw a pair of human eyes staring back at him. The eyes were the only part of the creature that was human – the rest was covered in black fur with a canine shape that reminded James of the wolves that sometimes wandered out of Baldur Forest. Wolves that had grown rabid and hunted men in the winter. They were supposed to be the size of horses. His hand reached out for Anna, attempting to shield her, while his left hand went for his knife.

"I think the boy is about to do something foolish." The hound spoke. His voice wasn't quite human, and it resonated deep in James's chest, each syllable beating like a drum against his breast.

"I think he already has," Anna replied. She slapped his hand away.

"What is it?" James spoke softly, hoping only Anna would hear, but the hound turned its head to the side, its eyes narrowing.

Anna laughed, but it was strained, uncomfortable.

"I am Cerberus." The hound spoke, turning his head ever so slightly, as if he were talking to a small child. There it was again – the voice that beat against James's chest. "I am the guardian of Balhatchett."

Then the hound grew quiet, watching him. James suddenly wondered if he was expected to introduce himself. He could smell the familiar scent of dog.

"Cerberus is a hellhound," Anna stepped forward and whispered in his ear.

James swore softly; his hand moved back to his knife, but as he reached it, he felt Anna's hand was already there. She was standing so close he could feel her breath against his back. He let her pull his knife from the sheath, slowly, and Cerberus watched them both, unmoving. He was nearly as big as James, but it was the animal's eyes that unsettled him. James had been right the first time – they were human – and in the hound's head, they looked oddly out of place.

The animal continued to bar their path.

"What does it want?" James asked, then quickly changed his tone. "*He.*" He cleared his throat. "What does *he* want?"

"I want blood," Cerberus said.

"Blood," Anna said. "We either offer it to him willingly or he'll take more than his share. That's the deal."

"But we've already given blood," James said. "Isn't that what we did back there?"

"That was to allow you to enter Balhatchett. This is to make you welcome here," Anna replied.

"I'd rather not," tried James.

"You don't have a choice," Anna said.

The moment the knife bit into the skin, deep red blood filled the path that was engraved onto her skin and fell in thick droplets onto the ground beneath them. She wiped the blade onto her slacks and turned to James, holding out her hand for his. He clenched his fist at the thought of being cut open and looked over at Cerberus once more. He hadn't moved. James placed his hand in Anna's and turned his head so he wouldn't see her make the cut. He felt a sharp pain, then a deep, dull ache. When he clenched his fist, he could feel his hand was wet with blood.

Cerberus said nothing as he stepped aside, clearing the path for them.

"Welcome, James Fiddick," Anna said solemnly, "to Balhatchett, the home of the forgotten."

SEVEN

THE BOY WHO FELL

"You are late. It is almost time," a blond boy of about seven scolded them just as they crossed through the hedges. He was unkempt and just dirty enough to give him a mischievous look.

"Where is Penhallurick?" Anna asked the boy, running a brush that she'd pulled out of her travel sack frantically through her hair.

"He has gone ahead with Phoenix and Evan," the boy said, giving James a curious look. Then he was gone, his small feet carrying him away from the cottage, leaving James and Anna on their own.

"What is going on?" James turned to her while she re-tied her cloak so that it no longer hung crookedly over her left shoulder. She wouldn't meet his eyes when she spoke again.

"We are attending a Sepultura Bellator," she said, her voice clipped, "a warrior's burial."

"A burial?" asked James, looking down at his own clothes, which were dirty and smelled of sweat and earth. He wiped his hands on his pants, hard, trying to run off some of the muck that naturally attached itself to every part of the body while on the road. The only burial he'd attended before was his uncle's, but he didn't think it was right to show up to one with dirty hands.

He looked up to find Anna watching him.

"You could have given me a bit more warning," James said, wishing he had packed a clean set of clothes, but as it were, he had nothing in his travel sack but some water.

"There's no warning I could have given you that would have prepared you for what you are about to witness," Anna said, before turning away and moving quickly towards the crowd of children that stood, waiting, before a stone monument in the distance.

"Wait, what?" James called after her, but she only sped up.

What is going on? James thought to himself.

James had to jog to catch up with Anna, but she didn't turn to face him. She kept her eyes on their destination, which was a field with yellow flowers that swayed with a light wind. They had to pass through the eastern edge of Balhatchett to reach it, following one of the many stone pathways that littered the small village. Cottages lined the western edge of the village, stopping just short of a forest that hugged it on its northern tip.

But they didn't head towards the cottages. Instead, Anna and James followed a stone path that led towards the field where more than fifty children stood, waiting before a raised platform of stone. A boy stood on the platform. He was waiting to speak. James could see a handful of adults scattered, like buoys, their heads floating just above the crowd.

The speaker was a boy of about twelve, with golden blond hair and fine features. His cheeks were smattered with dirt, but he stood with his chin raised, proudly looking down at the crowd with pursed lips.

As Anna and James made their way forward, the children cleared a path for them, allowing them to move towards the front. James could see Phoenix and Evandor standing just to the left of the obelisk, but their heads were bowed and they didn't meet his eye. As Anna waded through the crowd, the smallest children reached out and touched her, gently, not quite grabbing onto her cloak. She returned these gentle greetings with her own, touching their cheeks or wiping away a tear as she moved ever more closely towards the front. A few of the children were looking towards James, and he could see their puffy eyes and the streaks that their tears had made against their muddy faces. A little girl of about five, with blonde hair that formed a curtain over her face, was rubbing her fists against her eyes, sobbing quietly. James smiled kindly at her, wondering if he should stop and say something to her, but something about the size of the crowd made him unsure of himself. Then the crowd closed around her, and James and Anna reached the front.

A young boy of about ten stood beside Phoenix. His face was ashen, his lips shut tight in an effort to maintain his composure. He watched as James and Anna took their places next to Evandor. Phoenix looked up and nodded his head to James, but he didn't speak. Phoenix then turned and whispered something to the boy, who gave a curt nod and then turned back to the speaker.

James turned to the front just as the speaker began the ceremony. James could now see that they were standing beside a small cairn, with grey stones that covered a burial mound.

"Dima was a soldier," the speaker began. With a voice that was barely breaking, the declaration was childlike, but although he spoke to a large crowd, he didn't have to raise his voice to reach those at the back; the only sounds to compete with his words belonged to the small ones who stood with their heads pressed against the sides of the bigger children, seeking comfort from their touch.

"We fight a war," the twelve-year-old speaker continued, "and he fought bravely." With this, the speaker gave a nod of respect to the young boy standing beside Phoenix. James wondered whether the child was related to the dead. He hoped they weren't burying the child's mother or father.

James turned to watch the crowd. He noticed a dark-haired child muffling his tears with the sleeves of a torn coat.

Another boy, probably around nine, was shifting from one foot to another. His face was pale and so heavy with grief that it formed a knot in James's throat, but he was clearly not looking for comfort. He wiped at his face often, his eyes refusing to give away the fact that he was crying. James would have believed this if he hadn't seen a glimpse of a tear caught on the wool of this clothing. He suddenly realised that the boy was holding a red flower in his hand, and he was standing with the bigger children, who nearly hid him from view with their size. The boy furrowed his brows as he caught James staring at him, and James quickly turned to face the speaker.

"...there will be time to weep when this all ends," the speaker continued, "when we win this war, we will reclaim all that we have lost. Children weep. Children seek comfort when they have been injured, or beaten, or" – he turned to the small boy with the red flower that had caught James watching him only moments before, and his tone softened, but only slightly – "when we have lost one that we have loved so very dearly." The speaker turned to the rest of them, his face hardening once again. "But we are not children, are we?" The last few words burst from him, catching James off guard. He heard the crowd cry out, a sound that was all the more unsettling for the quiet that had come before it. Then he saw it. The coffin.

It was too small to be the child's mother or father. It was too small to be an adult.

"Anna – what is going on?" James leaned in, whispering into her ear, but she shook her head, silencing him.

"We are soldiers, are we not?" came the shout, and again the children answered with their war cry. The ones that could no longer hold in their sobs simply poured them out into their battle cry.

"Soldiers?" whispered James, loud enough that a few children turned their head to him. A little girl *shushed* him with an angry finger to her lips.

"What is this?" he said, louder, daring Anna not to answer him. He noticed that his jaw was tight and stiff from clenching it for too long.

Anna looked uncomfortable, but she answered him. "There will be time to explain, *later*." She stressed the last word.

James didn't hear what the boy had said, but the crowd roared back in return.

James caught a glimpse of the blonde little girl, her face contorted with her cry, her tears now drying on her face.

Something moved inside of James, slipping from a shadow into the light. He wasn't sure if it was anger or fear.

"These are not soldiers." James almost laughed, but he had already been admonished once and he didn't want to risk another scolding.

Anna turned to him, and this time her face softened. "No," her voice was so low, he could just make out what she was saying, "they are not soldiers."

"We will not face our enemy like children; weeping and begging to be allowed to go home," the boy at the makeshift pulpit began again, "we are more than that. We do not cry, because it shows them that we are weak. We are silent because this is the power that we hold. The power that they cannot take away from us. The time will come when we are no longer helpless – no longer lost. The time will come when we will stand on the battlefield, victorious. And all that we have lost will be but a bad dream. So let us show Dima that we are more than the children that they tried to stamp out. Let us show him that we are stronger than them all, that we will fight in his name – in the names of all those that we have lost, and when the time comes for victory, we will make sure that the world remembers their names once again."

Anna turned to James, her eyes searching his eyes, trying to convey something that perhaps she couldn't bring herself to speak. She turned instead to the hills just below the field where they stood. The hills rolled on towards the mountains that cast a shadow across a valley that was dotted with small, white stones. The light from the sun seemed to make the entire valley shimmer, like moonlight across a lake. For a moment James wondered what Anna was trying to show him. And then it was as if the white stones came into focus. The shadow within him shifted again, stretching, waking, angry.

They are graves, he realised. *They are the graves of these children.*

Anna spoke softly as the cold realisation seeped through his skin, making the hair on the back on his neck stand on end. "They are the forgotten ones," she said.

He almost didn't hear the boy as he spoke to the crowd of children standing before him.

"Our silence is our power. Let us show Dima our strength."

The silence that followed seemed to touch each grave as it rushed along the ground, over Balhatchett and out across the home of the forgotten.

EIGHT

THE BIRTH OF A KNIGHT

"I am leaving tomorrow," James said. After spending the journey to Migdasha in silence, James was still as angry as when they had just started out. He began throwing his belongings into his travel sack. He didn't have much to pack, but he knew it was half a day's journey into the heart of Dasdaya and he wasn't looking forward to covering that distance with a storm brewing outside. Anna was standing at the foot of his bed, and he could tell Evandor and Phoenix were standing just outside his bedroom door because their shadows betrayed them. For some reason, this seemed to irritate him even more.

"I understand that today was difficult for you." Anna's voice was hoarse and she looked tired. For a moment, he almost felt sorry for her, but he remembered the size of the coffin they slid into the ground and this was quickly replaced with irritation.

"How old was he?" James was trying not to shout.

"James—" Anna started.

"How old?" His jaw was clenched.

"He was fourteen," Anna answered, swallowing as she said it. "He was killed by a Babau in Baldur Forest." Her voice trailed to a whisper as she stopped talking.

"I don't want any part of this… this…" James continued, his teeth clenched, refusing to give Anna the satisfaction of asking what a Babau was.

But Anna wasn't looking at him – she was staring down at her feet. He didn't want to be cruel, and he knew that what he wanted to say was going to hurt her. Whatever was going on at Balhatchett, Anna didn't deserve cruelty.

"I am leaving in the morning. I am not who you think I am," he said simply, then turned to the door, where he could see Evandor and Phoenix peering through a crack in the frame. "I am not who any of you think I am." He wasn't sure if that was insulting. He rubbed his eyes. He was tired.

"It is alright to be angry—" Anna started, but James cut her off.

"Who are you to tell me what is alright?" he snapped.

"—but why leave?" she finished, ignoring his biting words.

"Perhaps I'm not as comfortable asking children to die for me," he spat at her, and she winced.

For a second he thought she might cry, but her face turned hard. "I have never…" she started, but her voice faltered.

"These children don't belong in a war, Anna. What are they? Your idea of the knights returned? Is this how you intend to save Gedeon?" With every word, his anger flared. "You are sending children to the slaughterhouse so that you can chase your bogeyman? Your fool?"

Anna didn't reply, but neither did she turn away. "I…" She tried again and then stopped. A moment later she turned and walked out of the room.

James made a deep, guttural sound of frustration. "What is going on here, Evandor?" he asked the empty room, knowing he was just outside of the door. "I don't want to contact the city guard, but it doesn't look like I have any choice. These children need to be taken care of. Living on the streets would be better than being recruited into some twisted war."

"Do you believe that?" Evandor asked quietly, his voice barely making it over the threshold.

"What?" James did not disguise the irritation in his voice. "Believe what?" he asked again when he got no response.

"That they are fighting a war," came the reply.

James waved a hand in the air, as if swatting away the thought. "Of course not," he said, more loudly than he intended. "I don't have a clue what is going on here, but someone needs to put a stop to this."

"How would you do that?" Phoenix stepped into the room. There was an edge to his voice. It infuriated James. He bit back a reply.

"How would you protect them, James?" Evandor interjected as he came into view.

"Uhm, I don't know..." James exaggeratedly stroked his chin. "I might not send them chasing after bogeymen or have them guarded by the local village mutt."

For the first time, James was uncertain whether Phoenix might actually hit him. Phoenix stared down at him and he stared back, his fury filling him with something close to bravery. Phoenix looked away first, turned his heel and followed in Anna's footsteps. It was only Evandor left standing at the threshold of the door, and unlike the others, his face was soft and he didn't speak. Something about the way he tilted his head, the certain kindness in his eyes, unravelled something deep in James's chest, and he felt the rage seep away, replaced with a weariness he thought he'd never shake.

"Before you say anything more," Evandor spoke, "before you decide to leave, I want to show you something. We are leaving tonight – by tomorrow morning, you will have your answers, and if you decide to leave…" he hesitated for a moment, "no one will stop you."

"Would you stop me now?" James challenged.

Evan tilted his head to one side, eyeing James carefully but saying nothing. "A few hours. I promise, you will see Balhatchett – and Migdasha – in an entirely new light."

James wasn't sure if he wanted to nudge at all that Evandor was choosing not to say.

After Evandor was gone, James was left to pass the next couple of hours on his own. He ignored the knocking on his door when he was called to dinner. He sat on the edge of his enormous four-poster bed and ran his fingers across the lace quilt.

So much luxury, he thought, growing angry. He got up and began to tear the bedding off the bed, throwing it to the floor. The sheets were rich and heavy, and when he was done scattering the pillows across the carpet, he turned to the bath with its ornate, gold legs. He turned it over, roaring as it turned over to lie on its side. Not sated, he began to grab at the drapes that hung elegantly around the bed. They made an unsatisfying *flump* as they fell to the ground.

Still it was not enough to put the shadow that had begun to stir inside him to sleep. He sat down, exhausted, with his knees in his arms and his back against the bed, staring up at the fireplace.

A little while later, he heard a soft knocking at his door. He got up and went to wrench the door open, ready for an argument whether the visitor was inviting one or not, but he found nothing but his dinner on a tray, set outside on the floor.

He deflated a little and picked the tray up, bringing it inside the room. A thick stew with a small load of bread caused his mouth to fill with saliva, but he was still too angry to eat.

He placed the tray on the bedside table and went to sit down again, trying to ignore the smell wafting up and filling the room.

A few moments later, he went to fetch the tray and placed it in front of him. He broke into the bread and felt its warm weight against his palms. He shoved a large piece into his mouth and began to chew. Then he dipped a piece into his stew and watched as it soaked up the rich, brown sauce. It tasted as good as it looked. He continued to scoop up his stew in this way, not bothering with his knife and fork, until there was nothing left in the bowl. Then he placed the tray aside, guiltily, out of his eyeshot.

It wasn't long before he heard another soft knocking at his door. This time, he felt more tired than angry.

"James, are you awake?" It was Evandor.

James got up and walked over to the door, turning the round handle and opening it to find Evandor smiling kindly at him from the other side. If Evandor noticed the mess James had created in the room, he didn't say anything about it.

"It's time," Evandor said. "Dress warmly."

James had been debating whether he was going to follow them and was not able to come to a decision.

"Are you ready?" Anna asked from down the hallway, to no one in particular. She shut her bedroom door, and as she moved, he caught a glimpse of a sword's hilt at her waist. She turned and it was gone, hidden by the folds of her cloak.

James took a breath, returned to his room to pick up his cloak and travel sack, and followed Evandor out, closing the door behind him.

Phoenix stood at the bottom of the stairwell and passed something to James as he moved towards the door. It was a dagger with a deep brown hilt. James pulled the dagger from the hilt and saw a delicate bone handle. There were no other identifying marks, no engravings or decorations.

"Will I be needing this tonight?" he asked, turning it over. It felt strange in his hand.

"You might," Anna replied, then passed through the open front door behind Evandor and Phoenix, not waiting to see if he was following.

James sighed, almost resigned, and then followed them out into the night.

It wasn't cold enough to force James to draw his cloak close to his skin, but it was cold enough to remind him that winter was on its way.

They moved quickly, passing the quiet lake, out towards the heart of Dasdaya, heading west. They travelled for a couple of hours in relative silence before the country roads began to take on a worn feel, indicating they were on the edges of another city.

James recognised the city they entered just after midnight. Beleage looked empty, but James knew that within the dark, hulking buildings on either side of the narrow streets slept hundreds of people. This was one of the smaller cities on the outskirts of Dasdaya and only a couple hours' journey from Migdasha. It was a poor city, and it looked it, with buildings that were old and near collapsing still being occupied by people looking for shelter from the cold.

Just like Dasdaya, the streets seemed to zigzag around the buildings. Beleage looked as if it were built in a hurry, and it most likely was, in sections and patches to fill the needs of a rapidly growing population.

The city was so quiet that the four of them seemed to take up more space than they did. The empty streets were disconcerting – there was always someone wandering about in Dasdaya, whether it was a constable or a cutthroat. The chances of running into no one after drifting through the streets for a good half an hour were slim, but it seemed that here, the streets were deserted.

James was so lost in trying to find someone – anyone – that it took him a couple of seconds to realise that Anna had grabbed on to his jacket, attempting to pull him backwards. They others had slowed down – not stopping, precisely, but they were now moving with purpose. Anna gave James a hard look and then gave a short nod in the direction of a cold, concrete building to their right. There were no lights on, even though the street was poorly lit with too few low-burning gas lamps.

The building looked as if it were once a factory of some sort, but if that were the case, its good years were far behind it. It had the look of a building that had long since been forgotten. The roof was inching down, collapsing slowly in on itself, weighed down by damp, pests and years of neglect.

Phoenix motioned to Evandor and they both started moving towards the building. Anna nudged James's arm, expecting him to follow, but he wasn't sure he wanted to.

"What's in there?" he muttered as quietly as he could.

Anna frowned for a second, as if she didn't understand, and then something dawned on her. "It isn't in there – look up," she whispered back, and James followed the broken line of the side of the building upwards to the sagging roof. He didn't know how he had missed it the first time. Something was scuttling along it, moving quickly – too quickly for a human. It cleared the roof of one building in seconds and had nearly reached a red-brick building next door. It was there that he saw the creature scuttle into a hole in the roofing, dragging something behind it. The sound the thing made along the tiles was similar to the sound a crab makes walking along stone. James could hear a click-click-click of something sharp, interspersed with something else – a whimpering.

"The child is still alive," Anna hissed at the others, and they picked up the pace. This time James received a sharp nudge and she didn't wait for him to start moving before she made towards the building. Phoenix and Evandor were the first to start climbing the side of the building – an easy task if you were practised at it, but James was not. Anna went after them and James took up the rear. He found handholds and footholds, and began inching his way upwards, trying his best not to look down. By the time he had reached the top, he was breathing heavily with the effort, and his three companions simply stared down at him, impatiently.

"Quiet." Anna held her finger to her lips, then turned and headed for the same entrance they had just seen the creature use to enter the building. Not for the first time tonight, James wondered whether he had made a mistake in agreeing to come; then he thought of the sound the child had made when it had been slid over the roof tiles like some piece of meat and he pushed himself forward, following the others.

The entrance was little more than a hole in the roof, a part of which had caved in from rot and neglect. Careful about where they were placing their feet, the four peered through. After travelling in darkness, James's eyes did not have to adjust to the dimly lit warehouse, and it quickly became clear what they were dealing with.

The floor was covered in creatures that moved and writhed like maggots. No part of the floor was visible through the mass of their slick, pink bodies, moving under and over each other. They looked human, with arms that were too long and faces that stretched down to their chests. What should have been fingers were dagger-like blades that stretched out from their hands and made a clicking sound as they were tapped together, hundreds of them, in irritation or anticipation – James couldn't tell which. Their mouths were gaping, searching, swallowing.

"What are we…" He wanted to ask about a plan but smelled fire and realised that Anna wasn't wasting any time.

James' eyes went wide, thinking that Anna had just made them all easy targets by giving up their location with her firelight. When she saw the look on his face, Anna shook her head quickly.

"They don't have eyes – they can't see us and they are afraid of fire," Anna said, then started climbing down the same beams that must have supported the creature, which was making its way through the bodies. The girl in its arms was still struggling, which was a good sign.

"Everything is afraid of fire," James retorted, still unsure how he was going to save anyone from the mass of creatures that had begun to raise their blind heads, sniffing at the air.

Can they smell us? James wondered.

"They can smell it," Evandor answered, reading his thoughts. "They are *very* afraid of fire."

Anna slid down a beam, hit the floor and started running. James watched as the bodies parted like water. As they moved, something else came into view – children, at least thirty of them, looked to be sleeping, but the way they were angled suggested something was wrong. A boy of twelve lay on his side, but his head facing an impossible direction. Some had their eyes open, but they didn't blink. James felt his heartbeat quicken.

How many bodies do you have to see before you begin to see them even when your eyes are closed? he wondered.

He spotted the young child that had been brought into the warehouse by the creature. He could see now that she was a little girl of no more than five. The child was dirty and her clothes were a mess of blood and dust.

The creature that held her looked like the others – shaped like something human, but it would only pass as such in the shadows; it wasn't quite complete. In the light, it was easy to see it was something else.

The creature stood tall, its arms hanging past its knees. It stood over her body, shielding its face from Anna's fire. All around her, the creatures scuttled for the shadows, but this one held its guard, as if it were stubbornly fighting for its prize. For a moment James thought that these things would escape into the night, through the windows that lined the walls of the building, but looking closer, he realised that they were boarded up, probably to prevent sunlight from getting in. That was probably why the creature had brought the girl in through the hole in the ceiling. With nowhere to go, they pasted themselves to the walls of the warehouse, as if they could be absorbed by the building. They ended up looking like macabre witnesses to a show, with Anna as the star. James was grateful for the fire. He had his dagger ready in his hand, but he was unsure whether he had the courage to use it. Anna, on the other hand, stood fiercely wielding her torch, holding her ground only a few feet from the creature.

"Check for survivors," Phoenix yelled out, and he and Evandor began to wade through the piles of small figures strewn across the dirty, wooden floorboards.

James turned back to Anna, who was still facing the creature. She wasn't advancing, but she wasn't backing off either, and the two of them stood facing each other, only feet apart, the body of the little girl between them like a porcelain doll.

James followed Phoenix's direction and began to sift through the bodies. The creatures threw their heads back and began to howl.

More than once, James had thought he had seen a small chest rise and fall with breath, but it had only been the light of the fire causing this illusion. Each time he reached out to grab at a child he thought might still be alive, he bit back a gasp as his hand brushed their cold skin.

They were circling Anna and the creature as they meticulously checked each body, but it wasn't long before the creature began to lunge at Anna, testing her resolve. She didn't flinch. James wondered how the creatures were sensing Anna if they couldn't see.

The small girl that lay between them started to stir, and he saw Anna's neck muscles tense. The girl had straight, light brown hair, and when she looked up and saw what was standing over her, she began to cry. She then turned her head and saw Anna, and her eyes lit up. She whimpered and started inching towards her, her arms outstretched, wanting to be picked up, away from the monster that had stolen her from her bed. She stopped crying then, but she could not get close enough for Anna to reach her.

Anna took a tentative step forward, and instead of moving away, the creature simply moved in closer to the girl, as if daring her to make a move. It opened its mouth and a long, red tongue slipped from between its lips. Its mouth curved into what looked like a smile, but its eyes were dark and unmoving.

"I found one," Phoenix called out, and James forced himself to turn to look. Every time he looked towards the massacre, more details became clear to him. Evandor was frantically making his way through the bodies, but he was gentle, as if not wanting to disturb their sleep. It was a respectful urgency. As he did so, he could hear a clicking coming from the furthest corners of the room. He could hear the anticipation in it. Phoenix was holding up a small boy with bright, yellow hair. The boy had buried his face in Phoenix's chest and was crying softly. The boy held a hand close to his chest, as if protecting it. When James looked closely, he saw that only the last two fingers on his left hand remained, while the rest looked as if it had been gnawed off.

"They ate it," James heard the small boy cry into Phoenix's chest. "I asked them to stop, but they kept going. It hurts." Phoenix made a small, reassuring sound.

"There is no one else." Evandor returned to their side. "I have checked twice."

"Check again," Phoenix ordered, and Evandor turned and made his way through the bodies. James could now see that most of the bodies were incomplete. He could see a boy of about eight with his tongue poking out through a hole in his cheek. He could see a pretty girl of twelve with the insides of her thighs eaten away.

His grip tightened on his blade as he turned back to Anna. The little girl was looking around, confused.

"Please," the girl begged, turning from Anna to the monster. She was still crying. "I'm cold. Please I want to go home."

The creature that loomed over her turned its head to one side, as if trying to hear something. It stared down at the girl and then at Anna's fire, and slowly took one step back.

Anna lowered her head and took a step forward, challenging the creature. She was about two feet from the girl now and could almost reach down and touch her.

"Is there anyone else?" she shouted over her shoulder. Evandor had just returned from his third check and shook his head.

"Just a boy," shouted Phoenix.

"Get him out of here," she yelled back, not taking her eyes off the creature in front of her.

"It's time to go," Evandor called to James, and they started making their way back up the wall, towards the ceiling. A noise like hundreds of insects scuttling over dry leaves began emanating from every corner of the room, but nothing moved towards them. Getting out of the building proved to be more difficult, especially as Phoenix now carried the boy. A low-hanging beam would allow them to gain access to the hole from where they entered, but they weren't able to reach it from the ground.

"Hold the child," Phoenix barked at Evandor. "I'll break a window."

The boy whimpered as Evandor took hold of him but quickly quietened down. Phoenix wasted no time as he walked over to one of the large factory windows that lined the back of the building and pulled at the wooden x that barred entry. After a few moments, James heard the wood sigh and groan as it came away. Then Phoenix took a step back, placed his palms facing outwards and his body shook as a small blast of air slammed into the glass, bringing it crashing down at his feet.

Evandor was out of the warehouse first. Before he slipped over the threshold, he passed the boy to Phoenix and then took him back so that Phoenix could cross over. Then it was James's turn.

"What about Anna?" James said, not wanting to leave her behind. She was still standing her ground, and neither her nor the creature had been able to reach the child.

"Trust me, you don't want to be here when Anna is done with the place," Phoenix shouted back, offering a hand to James, but he didn't take it. When he turned around, he saw Anna take another step towards the creature and it took another step away. He knew that was Anna's chance to grab the girl, and that was exactly what she did. The little girl immediately buried her head into Anna's neck, hiding her face from the creatures that stood watching them. She tightened her arms and legs around Anna and shook quietly.

Anna held on to her with one hand, and with the other, she let fire drip down like running water from her fingertips. Each drop of hit the ground and fizzled out very quickly, but it was still quite a sight.

James was just about to crawl through the window, confident that they had more than enough time to get away, when suddenly the creature lunged and then scuttled into the safety of the nest that had been formed within the shadows of this huge space. The light flickered and James saw the little girl Anna was holding onto so tightly slump back, a long, thin line of blood appearing at her neck. Her porcelain face was bared to the world.

Anna looked down, a look of utter disbelief colouring her face. The girl limp in her arms. She lay the girl on the ground, trying to put pressure on the wound, but blood began to pour through her fingers. Eventually it slowed and then stopped altogether.

The sounds coming from the shadows seemed somewhere between hissing and applause. Anna lifted the little girl and pulled her into her arms. She didn't turn to look at the creatures; she simply made her way to the exit. When she reached the window, James lifted his arms up to take the girl and Anna passed her to him, silently, not catching his eye. The light left with Anna and the creatures filled that space, wasting no time in pulling flesh from the little bodies.

Anna lifted herself out of the warehouse and into the cool air. The little girl weighed very little and James could smell the faint scent of lavender in her hair. He held her body close to him, trying to shield her from the cold air, not caring that it didn't make any difference to her now.

Just as James began to turn towards the street, he saw Anna place both palms against the wood panels of the building.

Thin veins of light began to spread from beneath her fingertips. They looked like small torches shining from each finger, but a few moments later, they began to writhe and move as if they were living. It was then that James realised that they were snakes, made entirely of fire, and it didn't take long before there were hundreds of them, all slithering deeper into the building, setting everything they touched on fire.

The flames spread and the creatures began to panic. The little girl's killer was lost in the noise, but James warmed at the thought that one of those screams would belong to that creature. The bodies of the children would burn with the monsters, but it was a better burial than being eaten by them. For some reason, the flames began to eat away at some of the anger that had been building in James since the Sepultura.

The companions made their way into Beleage. Anna was now holding the little girl and Phoenix carried the boy.

Once they were a safe distance away from the building and onto the streets, Anna calmly handed the little girl's body over to Evandor, took a few steps away, got down on her knees and began to wretch into the street. James could smell burning flesh and ash began to fall like snow, carried by the wind.

"We need to keep moving," Evandor said gently, offering Anna his hand to help her up. She took his hand and got to her feet, wiping her mouth on the back of her sleeve. She took a few moments to calm before taking the water pouch Evandor held out to her and cleaned her hands. The water turned pink as it washed the blood down into the street.

They moved quietly, the stone streets lit up by the fire only a couple of blocks away now. The smell of smoke was heavy in the air and they could hear people begin to take notice and shout for help. A few began to pour into the streets carrying buckets of water. It quickly became clear that fires in these parts weren't uncommon. James just hoped the fire would do its job before they put it out.

A man in a blue uniform and a stiff top hat that marked him as a constable was walking briskly towards them, but his eyes were focused on the fire behind them.

"Hey…" James called out to the constable but cut off what he wanted to say next when he saw Anna hold the little girl's body tighter to her own, as if trying to shield her, and take a ninety-degree turn into an alleyway. Phoenix quickly followed and Evandor slipped in behind them. James was left standing in the middle of the street, his mouth partially open.

"What are you doing just standing there?" The constable shouted, suspiciously.

James hesitated, not sure what to do.

"Go find a bucket!" The constantly motioned to him like someone trying to shoo a dog. James turned quickly and ducked into the alley along with his three companions while the constable continued making his way towards the fire and the crowd that was gathering there.

"We shouldn't be hiding, we should be telling him what happened," James hissed, his voice low.

"Be my guest," Phoenix snorted.

"It would do more harm than good," Anna started to explain.

"Are there more of these things?" James nodded at the little girl, but they knew he was talking about the monsters.

"Dasdaya is crawling with them," Anna replied.

James felt a sudden, overwhelming panic. "We need to tell someone," he said urgently.

"He really believes that." Evandor spoke quietly. "Anna, he won't believe us until we show him the truth."

"Show me what truth?" James gritted his teeth.

Anna swallowed hard, thinking, then handed the child to James. He hesitated, then took her gently into his arms.

"The boy stays here, with Phoenix," she said softly.

"I don't…" James wanted to explain that he didn't understand, but Anna was already heading out of the alleyway onto the street.

The little girl felt heavy in his arms. Heavier than she should have been.

"Go and explain, James." Anna motioned in the direction of the constable. "But make sure that you bring her back." She nodded her head at the body of the little girl in James's arms. James frowned before turning and walking out onto the street. Evandor followed him, but Phoenix stayed behind.

The fire was already amassing a small crowd, but most stood only to watch. The constable tried in vain to quench it with small, wooden buckets of water, but the fire was too big and burned too hot. Eventually he gave up and wiped his face with a white handkerchief that he pulled from his coat pocket. Then he noticed James standing across the street, out of view of the crowd, holding the small child's body.

"You don't want to be putting out that fire," James called.

The constable looked as if he were about to turn his attention away from James, when his eyes shifted to the blood on the girl's clothing and hands, and the fact that she wasn't moving. He began to cross the street, making his way over to James.

"Hey – what did you—" he started, but James cut him off.

"It wasn't me – it wasn't us," he explained, feeling Anna and Evandor standing beside him. "There were creatures in that building – there were hundreds of them – and children too." The constable's eyes went wide, and James wasn't sure he was explaining himself right. He looked hopefully at Anna, then at Evandor, but they were silent.

"We tried to save them, but they were already dead – most of them, anyways," James went on.

The constable looked around them, at the crowd mesmerised by the fire, and back at the three companions.

"There might be more of them in the city," James continued. This time, the constable went for his baton, and pulled it free from his belt. He motioned the three companions away from the crowds, crossing the street to the darkness of the alleyways.

"I think I understand," he said as they entered the same alley where Phoenix carried the boy, but they were well hidden by the shadows. "Did you get anyone out alive?" the constable asked.

James nodded, and Evandor made what sounded like a choking sound. James turned and saw Anna shake her head, ever so slightly, but he decided to ignore this. If they weren't going to get help, he would, he decided.

"Phoenix!" he called out, looking around him and seeing nothing but waste scattered across the stones of the alleyway and crates piled against one wall. "Phoenix, come out, it's okay."

Phoenix stepped out from behind the crates, the boy lying still in his arms. His eyes were dark with rage. "What have you done?" His words were directed at James, but he was looking at the constable.

"He can help us," James tried to reassure Phoenix.

"I can – I can help you all," the constable stated. "What happened wasn't your fault. You will take no blame for this." He slipped his baton back into his belt. "I can see the boy is hurt – I will make sure he is well taken care of. We're aware of this problem in our city, and I am grateful that you were there to help him, even if you couldn't save the little one." He smiled kindly as he spoke and reached out to stroke the little girl's hair.

Relief washed over James, and for the first time since meeting Anna, he felt like he could breathe again.

"Give him the boy, Phoenix," James said.

"No," Phoenix replied, a dark look crossing his face. James was confused for a moment and looked to Anna, but she looked almost scared. She gave Phoenix a pleading look.

"What do you mean, *no?*" James said. As he spoke, he saw the constable draw his baton again, but Phoenix only shifted the boy to leave one empty hand free.

"This isn't the time for games, Phoenix." Evandor spoke this time. It sounded like a warning, but his voice was soft. Phoenix nodded but made no move to hand over the child. Then James felt the air begin to stir. Phoenix's fingers were moving quickly.

"Right, that's enough – hand over the child." The constable took a step forward, reaching out his hand as if to accept the child, and then grabbed his throat. He started coughing, but it was as if he couldn't catch his breath. Then it stopped. James knew Phoenix had given him a warning.

"You're going to get us all arrested." James said.

"I'm not sure that is going to cut it, my friend." Evandor spoke again. James suddenly realized that Evandor was not trying to convince Phoenix to hand over the child – he was telling him to attack the constable.

"I won't arrest *you*, boy," the constable spoke, "if you free the child from him."

James was still holding the little girl, and he didn't want to lay her on the ground. He also didn't want to fight Phoenix. He looked helplessly at the constable for a moment and was surprised at the look of irritation that flashed across his face.

"You think you're going to be safe from them if I don't take him back?" the constable asked, his smile gone. "They will eat you alive. I've seen it." This time, he smiled widely, but there was fear behind his eyes.

"Take your hand from your belt or I'll do worse to you," Phoenix spat.

"Phoenix." Evandor lifted his hand in warning.

For a moment, James was confused. "What do you mean, *take him back?*" James frowned at the constable. "Take him back where?"

The constable licked his lips, looking unsure for a moment.

"Don't be fools." He spoke quietly. "You've burned down an entire nest. They will punish you. They will punish us all. Just give me the boy."

James instinctively took a step away from the man, placing himself firmly between Phoenix and Evandor. He couldn't see whether the boy was awake, his head was nestled in Phoenix's shoulder, but he could hear a soft whimpering.

"You'd give the boy back to those creatures?" James spat at the man, and at this, the constable gave a nod.

"I didn't make the price." He put up both his hands. He saw the disgust on James's face and his eyes narrowed. "You think I'm the monster because I close my eyes to a few children who go missing in the middle of the night? What will you do when they start crawling into windows by the hundreds, stealing scores of children from their beds each night? Will you four be able to save them all?" he asked, his eyes growing wild. "This is the price we must pay, or they'll raise the levy. Give me the boy or there will be more blood, and this time it will be on your hands."

"Luckily I've never had a problem getting a little blood on my hands." Anna spoke, and then two things happened at once. Anna moved towards the constable, laying a hand on his chest, and a bright light flashed, nearly blinding them all. There was no grandstanding or flash in the movement, no creativity or flair. There was only heat and screaming and blood. And then they were all running.

*

By the time they had made their way back to Migdasha, James was tired and his body ached. He was weary in a way he had never been before, a mixture of fear, confusion and horror fogging his mind. He had travelled for more than an hour with the child held tightly to his chest before Anna took her from him. A warm relief spread through him that had less to do with ridding himself of her weight and more to do with the fact that she had started to grow cold, and it had unnerved James in a way that he hadn't felt possible since he had awoken to that creature in his bed.

They hadn't travelled long before Phoenix and Anna had broken off the group, with a plan to take both children, one breathing and one not, to Balhatchett. Evandor and James travelled the rest of the way in silence.

When they arrived at the large, stone castle, James was irritated at the warmth that seemed to radiate from its many windows. Soft candlelight glowed from his bedroom windows and he hoped there would be a warm bath waiting for him. He paid little attention to Evandor when they reached the heavy, wooden door, which swung open as soon as they arrived at the threshold. He walked straight up to his room, where he found soft, cotton bedclothes laid out on the bed and the bath filled with hot water. Humbert must have tidied the room because nothing was out of place.

It took him longer than he would have liked to scrub the smell of the smoke and blood from his skin and hair, and when he was done, he threw his clothing into the fire that blazed and brought warmth to even the stone floor of his bedroom. The water was pink with blood. He turned his attention from it, tired at the thought, and then he got into bed.

He blew his candle out and watched the ember glow red and then disappear altogether. Just then, someone knocked softly on the door.

"Yes?" James called, his voice low.

It was Evandor carrying a small candle. His expression was apologetic. "We are leaving for Balhatchett in the morning." He spoke softly, his face softly lit by the candle in his hand. His breath caused the flame to shake and gave the room an eerie, lonely feel. James could smell burning wax in the air. Evandor did not move away from the door. "I want you to come with us," he said. "Things often look different in the morning light."

"I don't want to go back there, Evan," James said simply.

"Please," Evandor said, "I know it is no small favour I ask you." With that he was gone and James was left to consider his decision in the dark.

*

The next morning, Evandor was standing in the entrance hall when James joined him, fully dressed, with his pack over his shoulder.

"You've made a decision." There was something in Evandor's voice, and it wasn't disappointment.

"Yes." It infuriated James how Evandor seemed to know what he was about to do before he did it. He tried to leak a hint of defiance into his acceptance. Evandor just nodded. They waited a few minutes before Anna and Phoenix joined them. Phoenix looked somewhat surprised to see James, as if he'd expected him to slip away in the night. He smiled when he walked by and slapped James jovially across the back. James wasn't sure what Anna might be thinking. She greeted him and walked out the door as if the last two days hadn't happened. He followed her lead, slipping his pack over his shoulder and leaving Migdasha once again for the home of the forgotten.

NINE

A KNIGHT'S INTRODUCTION

The sounds of children greeted them the moment they reached the tall hedges that marked the entrance to Balhatchett. Once again, Anna pricked a finger and James watched the vines come to life, unbarring the entrance to the village, allowing her, James, Phoenix and Evandor through. Cerberus was there to meet them as they entered, but this time he did not bar the way. James made sure to keep his distance from the large animal, with his human eyes and muscles that rippled just underneath his dark, brown coat. The ground beneath the large hound shifted beneath his feet, and James could feel his warm breath on his skin as he sidled past him, trying not to meet his eye, but also trying not to look afraid. He breathed easily again once he had passed the entryway.

Balhatchett was as busy as ever, but there was something different about it today. The sun was out and James felt it warm against the back of his neck. It was the type of sun that could bite if you fell asleep under it for an entire afternoon, but for a couple of hours, it was almost a sedative. A few children had the same idea and were lying out in the fields, while others carried large baskets of apples on their backs, following the winding lane down to a cottage that reminded him of the bakery he used to pass by on the way to work. Anna called over to a girl of about twelve who was carrying a bundle of laundry in one arm and holding the hand of a little girl of about seven in the other. The little girl was lazily twirling a small flower in her empty hand, her mind wondering off the way most people's minds often do when they are in the process of completing chores.

The moment the girl was in earshot, Anna spoke. "Where is Kale?" she asked.

"He's in the infirmary. He was worse than they thought, but they think he'll live." The girl smiled.

"Thank you, Adriana," Anna said, and started off again. James and the others followed her to a small building that was located on the outer edges of Balhatchett. It was a bright red hut that seemed to be purposefully separated from the rest of the village, but close enough that it still looked to be a part of it. Anna walked briskly to the entrance and knocked on the door. It took a couple of minutes before the door was opened by a young woman with bright red hair and rosy cheeks. She was wearing a white apron and her hands were raised up at her sides, as if she were trying not to touch anything.

"Anna." She smiled warmly at her, then saw all of them standing right behind her and her smile quickly faded. "Phoenix, Evandor, it's good to see you but I'm afraid I can't let all of you in here." Her eyes then shifted to James.

"It's alright, Lacey, this is James," Anna stepped aside so that the red-haired woman of about eighteen could see him. He waved awkwardly.

"Hello, James," she said, smiling kindly.

"How is he?" Anna asked.

"He was in pretty bad shape, but I've cleaned and stitched his wounds. The bleeding has stopped and I have given him something to sleep. Sometimes sleeping can heal a wound faster than medicine." She stepped aside, looking back pointedly. "The two fingers that he has left work just fine."

James wasn't sure if this was much to be happy about.

"We're going to the archery range." Phoenix spoke up quickly, and he and Evandor turned to leave. James took a step away from the door, intending to follow them, but Anna grabbed his arm.

"No, don't leave," Anna said. Lacey waved them in and Anna passed over the threshold. James took a breath and followed behind.

The room was warm, but it wasn't stuffy. The sun was warming the room and the drapes had been thrown aside to let in as much light as possible. Because of this, it didn't look like the flea-ridden sickrooms that were hidden in every corner of the city. People feared ending up in those places because you were more likely to die in one than heal. You could tell that you were within a mile of a sickroom because it smelled sour and the air was heavy. This was different. The room was light and smelled of lavender. Fresh air filtered in through the two windows that were located in such a way that at least one window got the sun coming up and another got it going down.

A half dozen beds were lined up across the room. They were spaced far apart enough so that Lacey could move swiftly between them without bumping into them, but they were close enough that the space between them didn't feel empty and cold. James immediately recognised the boy on the bed at the farthest end of the room. He lay on a bed only a few feet from the open window. His skin was pale and his eyes were closed, but James could see the rise and fall of his small chest and knew that he was alive.

A weight he hadn't known he was carrying lifted from his shoulders.

"He should wake in a few hours." Lacey spoke gently. He realised he must look worried. For a moment he felt the need to brush it off, but it was useless. It suddenly felt wrong to hide his worry, especially in this place.

Anna and Lacey spoke quietly amongst themselves for a few moments and then Anna was heading for the door. James followed her out into the sunshine and was glad to hear the voices of the children surround them again. He could hear someone calling out to someone else. There was giggling and then a little voice shouted in frustration – not fear or anger, just the ordinary frustration of a child that wasn't getting their way. He remembered the creatures that writhed and twisted like maggots among the bodies of those small children in the warehouse and the angry weariness returned.

"I have something else to show you," Anna said. She was headed into the hills, towards the east. James hurried to catch up with her. They walked for a while before coming to the top of the hill, and Anna looked down, towards the gravestones that lay in the distance.

"We missed the burial, but they say it was beautiful. The children sang a song for her and when they put her in the ground, the little ones cried." Anna pursed her lips, looking into the distance. She held out her hand and James saw a perfect lily lying in her palm. "We can't save them all, no matter how hard we try," she continued, "but we remember each and every one. That much we can do."

"Why didn't you take her body back to her parents?" James asked. "And what are you going to do with Kale?"

Anna was quiet for a moment. "Lacey sent scouts back to Beleage early this morning to find the children's homes. Kale's parents were dead when they arrived. He has no family and has asked to stay here with the others. We could not find the little's girl's home – if they are even still alive."

James nodded and took the flower from Anna's hand and started walking towards a small, white stone that had suddenly popped up among the others. It was tiny and innocent and everything the little girl had been in life. When he reached it, he kneeled down and put his hand against the cold stone. He stroked it gently and closed his eyes for a moment. The anger was replaced with an ache that he knew would rest with him for all his days to come. Something was different. There was a tear that couldn't be stitched somewhere deep inside of him. He placed the flower carefully in front of the grave and got to his feet, but somehow felt the weight more than before.

When he turned around, he saw that he and Anna were no longer alone. Children had begun to appear on the tip of the valley, curious. One of them pointed at James and another waved. Then they were running again, chasing one another down into the heart of Balhatchett.

"I will fight for you," James said finally, turning to Anna.

"Don't fight for me," she replied, and nodded towards the children scattered throughout the noisy village. "Fight for them."

He looked at her for a moment, took a deep breath and said, "Okay, tell me what I have to do."

*

The bonfire burned brightly, making it difficult for James to remember the chill of the autumn that was setting in quickly. A large circle had formed around the fire and the night was filled with young voices, some singing, some whispering conspiratorially, as most people are prone to do when they are gathered under the stars. A young man with a dark beard had a young girl sitting on his shoulders, and he was in the process of chasing a small boy. Both the girl and boy squealed in delight.

Three children were sitting a few feet from the fire, playing a game, using the sand and a stick as a makeshift board, and stones as some sort of counters. He recognised one of the boys as the speaker at Dima's funeral. The boy laughed as one of the younger children captured one of his counters – at least, that was what James thought was happening – and James smiled along with him, as if he were playing too.

Phoenix nudged James playfully in the ribs as he sat down next to him. "The show is going to start," Phoenix said.

"Show?" James asked, resting back against a log and setting an empty bowl down beside himself.

"Like all children, the residents of Balhatchett like to put on shows." Evandor joined them, speaking with a mouthful of bread, dipped in a dark, rich gravy. He motioned towards the children who were appearing into the firelight, all wearing elaborate headdresses and garlands of flowers around their necks. They were barefooted.

"This one is supposed to be good," Phoenix said.

A drum started beating and the children began to dance. It was a mix between a choreographed show and something entirely last minute. The moment the dance began, many children got up from their seats and began to join in, and suddenly it looked a lot like a summer festival, with children dancing in a great circle around the firelight, laughing, falling and giggling loudly at every misstep. Anna began to clap and James joined in, in time with the beat of the drum.

James caught Lacey's eye and she smiled broadly at him. A small boy was resting against her, tired but smiling gently at the festivities. He realised that it was Kale, the little boy from the factory. The little boy with the chewed hand. Lacey was holding him affectionately, swaying softly from side to side. Her long red hair was tied in a loose plait, and she was close enough for James to see that her eyes were different colours – one shone a deep green, while the other was a light blue. He didn't know how he could have missed that before. When she turned her eyes to him, he suddenly realised he was staring and he flushed. He looked away, but it was too late – he saw her brow furrow.

He turned back to the game being played by the three children in the sand and tried to make it seem as if he were intensely interested in the outcome for a few seconds before he turned back to the dancers. A few children were throwing what looked like flower petals into the air, and these were picked up by the soft wind and released the smell of sweet vanilla into the air. He allowed himself one more glance at Lacey and noticed that some of the white petals had settled in her hair.

The drums stopped suddenly and the children dropped to the floor. It seemed that all the children were in on this because it happened so quickly. The only thing he could hear was the wind, the sound of the children trying to catch their breath and a few hushed giggles.

It was in this silence that he heard something else – something that was picked up and carried by the wind. The sound of wolves. They were hidden deep in the woods and the sound was so faint that he might have mistaken it for something entirely different if it hadn't been so quiet, but it was, and he didn't.

No one looked concerned. The children began to get up from the ground, their cheeks red from exertion, broad smiles on their faces, looking around for approval. Anna started clapping loudly and soon everyone joined in.

"Did you hear that?" He leaned in towards Anna, who was still clapping.

"We are safe here," she said, still smiling.

James wanted to believe her, but he was feeling uneasy. There were so many small children here; how could they possibly feel safe?

Then he looked across the firelight and saw Cerberus, with his human eyes, lying just outside the circle of fire, watching him, watching the children. He was so large the bonfire paled in comparison. As he breathed, the fire moved, as if being shifted by a strong wind.

The sound of the children lifted, then fell, and he could hear the howling once again. The sounds were like dancers in a ballroom, rising and falling, as if in time with each other. This time, James looked to Cerberus and saw his ears shift slightly at the sound, but he didn't look disturbed. In fact, Cerberus gave a short snort and shifted somewhat, getting comfortable, before closing his eyes and falling into a light sleep. For the first time since arriving in Balhatchett, James was glad for his company.

*

The journey back home seemed to pass quickly, even though James was tired. He had shuffled home with his eyes half closed, and more than once, Anna had nudged him as he was about to wander into a stream or down an embankment.

Humbert met them at the door, and by the time James had set his cloak out to dry, gave his boots a good scrub and got upstairs, a hot bath was waiting for him in front of his bed. The creature had even lit some candles and sprinkled sprigs of lavender in the bath to sooth his aching body. He lay there for a long time, soaking in the warmth.

When he had scrubbed himself down, he got out and dried off with a large towel. As he slipped on his nightshirt, he noticed a light making its way down the path, towards the edge of the lake. Looking closer, he could see Anna's pale skin and long, dark hair lit by the lantern she held in her hand.

He decided that bedtime could wait for a little while longer and quickly got dressed, making sure to kill the candle's flame before leaving the room. He stopped by the door on his way out to slip on his boots, which had been drying by the kitchen fire, and set off after her.

All he could hear as he walked by the lake were the crickets and the sound of his own footsteps on the wet grass. The air smelled as it always did after it rained; it was clean, fresh and hopeful. The lake itself was still. Silent. He could see the hills off in the distance and he knew that the heart of Dasdaya lay nestled just beyond them.

Migdasha looked even bigger against the brightly lit sky. He could see the flickering of the fire from the study and thought about returning. It was getting cold. He pulled his cloak closer to his body and rubbed his hands, looking out towards the hills again.

That way lay Aventias, the land of the Canyons of the Dead. It was said that if you screamed loudly enough into those great canyons, the dead could hear you. James wondered if that were true.

Traders from the great city of Malyn often ventured into Dasdaya with stores of hand-crafted wooden horses. They weren't children's toys. Far from it, in fact, since only the wealthy were ever able to purchase them, displaying them as centrepieces in their homes.

He followed the sound of water to Anna, who was seated on the lip of a large fountain. She was trailing her fingers in the water and looking out over the hills. The tall statue of a man in a cape that came right down to his toes was displayed in the middle of the fountain and appeared to be leaning over her protectively. His eyes were still, staring in the same direction as his visitor.

Unlike her silent companion, Anna turned to him and smiled when he approached, and it reminded him of the night they had met. He put his hand to his cheek at the memory.

"Who's your friend?" he asked, motioning towards the statue.

She smiled fondly at it. "This is a knight." She gently traced the edges of the statue's robes. "His name is Oakin Fayne, and they say he was a Knight of Valore." James raised his eyebrows, impressed. "Some stories say that he is the one who chained the fool, after he escaped so long ago," she finished.

"Which stories say that?" asked James.

"They are children's stories," she admitted reluctantly, "but there may be some truth to it."

"Phoenix doesn't believe that," James said. He wasn't trying to goad her.

"He will," she replied.

"What makes you so certain?" he asked.

Anna said nothing.

"What is a statue of Oakin Fayne doing here?" James wondered aloud.

"Migdasha is very old. If the knights existed, this is where they were supposed to have lived." She motioned to the hills. "Oakin would have hunted in those hills. He would have bathed in that river."

"How do you know all of this?" James asked her.

"There are records in the library. Whether Oakin Fayne was a knight is still debated, but his existence is not. He was a good man and the locals had this statue commissioned for him after he died."

James could see something written just underneath the cloak of this stony, silent figure.

We journey for you.

"He wrote the knight's cry." She was silent for a moment, then she began to recite, "Into the field once more we go, ne'er to return, we heed Uriaha's call." She paused. "Take my place, brother, should I fall. Mors Vorcat, death calls to us all. Until we meet again." When she finished, she smiled, clearly fond of the words.

"What is Uriaha?" James asked.

"You mean, who is Uriaha?" she corrected. "In Fiachra, he was a warrior that was supposed to unite the counties: Aventias, Fiachra, Dasdaya, Morvoren and Ancasta. He became a great king, but the counties remained divided. The call is supposed to be a reminder about that which the knights were fighting for – they weren't just trying to chain the fool. They were trying to unite a kingdom." She suddenly seemed weary. "But that is a story for another day. It is getting cold," Anna said, standing to her feet. "Hot chocolate?" she suggested.

James looked back towards the warmth of Migdasha. A light was flickering in the library and he was sure that both Phoenix and Evandor were still awake.

"After you." He motioned.

TEN

THE KEEPERS OF THE DARK

The next morning breakfast was laid out on a light wooden bench outside, where it was already warm from the autumn sun. James saw Humbert scuttling back and forth from the house to the table that was decorated with yellow flowers and a bright red runner, and nearly toppling over with apples, baked tarts and pancakes, piled high and dripping with butter and syrup.

James noticed Phoenix was already at the table, biting into a bright orange peach, the juices dripping down his wrist and onto the yellow grass beneath his feet.

James took a seat down next to him and picked up a jug of orange juice, pouring himself a large glass. When he drank from it, the juice was sweet and tart, and made him realise just how hungry he was. He served himself a mound of scrambled eggs on deep brown toast and took a large bite.

"Sleep okay?" Phoenix asked, this time chewing on a crumpet that dripped with golden syrup.

James nodded, and for the first time since arriving in Migdasha, something occurred to him. "Who pays for all this?" he asked.

Anna and Evandor had arrived, taking a seat opposite them. Anna poured herself a cup of black coffee, while Evandor reached for the juice.

"I mean, who pays for all this?" James motioned at all the food. "And that?" He motioned towards the house.

Phoenix raised an eyebrow and looked pointedly at Anna.

"We do." It was Anna who replied. "The Keepers."

"The Keepers?" James echoed her. "The Keepers of what?"

"The Keepers of the Dark. That's what we do here." Anna began to explain as she buttered a piece of toast. "Do you remember the story I told you last night, of Oakin Fayne? Well, when he died, he left a large fortune that has allowed us to carry on his work. Much of his story might be legend, but his money is real." She took a bite of toast and there was silence while she chewed. When she was done, she took a slow sip of her coffee and continued.

"The Keepers of the Dark were formed by Oakin, but many think we go back much further than that. Some even believe it is where the original Uringi came from – that we were always warriors.

"The Keepers used to protect the counties from the dark – the sorts of creatures you saw the other night in Beleage and many more you still have to meet." This made James pause between his eggs and toast. "We are protectors of Gedeon – protectors of all five counties – and that comes with perks, at Migdasha, at least." She smiled again, raising her mug as if to toast James.

"Humbert is in charge of more than just housework," Anna said. "He is in control of everything in Migdasha. He's the only one that knows where the fortune is hidden."

James took a few moments to take all of this in. "How do you know all this?" He shovelled a large mouthful of creamy egg into his mouth and washed it down with the juice. He wiped his mouth on the back of his sleeve.

"Each member is brought in by someone who came before them." Evandor jumped in. "Phoenix and I came in together, and we initiated Anna."

Anna nodded at this as if to back up his story and then she added, "And I was the one who found you."

"Who found you two?" asked James, looking at Evandor and Phoenix. Phoenix gave a short shake of his head, and a dark look came over Evandor's face.

"The Keepers of the Dark used to have many members. They filled the rooms of this great house," he explained. "Those you don't see here fell to the dark."

"Fell to the dark?" James asked.

"Died," Anna said, too coldly. Phoenix gave her a reproachful look and she took a long sip from her mug, shrugging as she did.

James nodded his head, understanding. "So it's just us then?" he asked. He could hear a songbird in the distance, and it seemed out of place amidst their discussion. It pulled his attention to the sunshine that warmed his arms and the back of his neck, and he realised that autumn would not last forever, and the cold was on its way.

"You saw what happened the other night." Phoenix spoke. "We think something is targeting the children of Gedeon. We're seeing a lot more things crawling out of the dark lately – many of which we have never fought before, and some we've never even heard of. At first we tried to get the constables to help us, until we realised that whatever we are fighting is much bigger than a couple of opportunistic monsters."

"There have always been monsters in Gedeon," Evandor said, "but most people don't even know they exist."

"Which is a problem for us, because there is no one left to protect the children, except for us," finished Phoenix.

"That's why the children are fighting, isn't it?" asked James. "Because no one else will?"

"We will," said Anna, then her tone softened. "But you are right. Without us, they are alone. They have been abandoned."

"What about the law?" asked James. "Why aren't the constables doing anything?"

"We're not sure, but we know they aren't on our side," Anna said.

"Then who is on our side?" James asked.

"The Weavers," Anna said, and James heard Phoenix snort into his mug. "Oh, don't start again." Anna shot him a dark look and he put up both hands in apology. She continued, "The Weavers are known by many names, and their legacy is woven along with their purpose, drifting in and out of stories of the ages. There is said to be four of them and they weave the fabric of time."

"*Kings* have spoken of the Weavers in their last and final testaments. They have been brought up in prophecy. Legends of them fill our storybooks."

"Everyone's heard of the Weavers," James said. "They are supposed to weave the destinies of men, and all that."

"The Weavers have the power to alter the course of destiny – but this is not their sole purpose. They were created to weave stories: tales of the world and the heroes that have shaped it. They are the most powerful creatures ever to have existed."

"And they are chained to their looms," James said suddenly, remembering the book he'd read in the library.

"Yes…" said Anna, surprised.

"And you believe they will help us?" James asked, enjoying the look on Anna's face.

"I have no doubt." Her tone convinced him that she didn't, but James couldn't quite believe what he was hearing.

"What do you two believe?" He turned to the others.

"Their legend died out hundreds of years ago." Phoenix turned with a knowing look to Anna, as if she had left this part out on purpose. "Their stories may have filled the great library of Goreth, but no one has breathed mention of them for decades. We don't even have proof of their existence – we only hope."

James looked to Evandor, but he didn't speak. "If they exist, how do we find them?" he started. "And how do we know that they will help us?" A week ago, he might not have asked these questions, but after Beleage, he was more willing to accept the fact that creatures crawled out of storybooks and meddled in the affairs of men.

"We aren't sure." He could hear the frustration in Anna's voice.

"So that's it?" James asked. "An army of children, a king who's all but forgotten by his own people and an army of monsters that is growing by the day – and our only hope lies in a children's story—"

Evandor interrupted James at this. "If the Weavers are gone, we stand alone against an army. This is why we must believe."

James thought back to Balhatchett; he looked up to Anna once again, sighing with a weariness that had nothing to do with fatigue. He took a long minute to let everything sink in and thought back to his small room in Dasdaya.

Then he thought of a little girl, staring up at him from a dirty warehouse floor, and he let anger flood the space where fear stood only a moment ago.

"What do we need to do?" he asked.

Phoenix gave a deep, long laugh. It was then that James saw a small figure running across the lawn. When he got closer, James saw that he was a boy of around twelve years of age. When he got closer, James realised it was the same boy from the funeral – the young boy that James believed to be the brother of Dima, the boy they had placed in the ground.

The boy ran straight to Anna. "Penhallurick, what are you doing here?" Anna grabbed his arm, her eyes wide with fear, flitting to the blood that stained his small hands and the front of his tunic.

"Inkuanu have taken Balhatchett," he cried. "They are killing everyone."

ELEVEN

BALHATCHETT IS FALLING

Anna's body shook as she grabbed her sword and travel sack. Phoenix and Evandor were already moving for their own. James went to grab his cloak.

"How many?" she asked softly.

"I couldn't count them all. At… at least twelve," he stammered.

"How many are…" she struggled to finish the sentence.

"The smaller ones were ordered to run. Anyone strong enough to carry a sword remained. There were five fallen when I came for you."

James was ready with his belongings and his sword sheathed by his side. Phoenix and Evandor were standing ready too.

Anna looked down at the boy, and James saw that he barely reached her midriff. As she spoke, he saw a gentleness that seldom escaped her eyes. "Stay here. We will be back as soon as we can."

Penhallurick looked shocked, and James realised that he intended to return to his home.

To return to a slaughter, James thought in disgust.

"No," the boy said with a determination that almost made James laugh. In another life, this boy could have been a stubborn child, refusing to do his chores.

"Pen…" she started, but the boy was already out the door. "Phoenix—" Anna's eyes were wide, desperate, but Phoenix shook his head.

"There's nothing we can do, Anna. If he's going back, we can't stop him," Phoenix said.

Anna bit her lip, shaking her head, then she took a breath and nodded, resigned. She busied herself by preparing to leave.

"What is out there, Anna?" James asked. "What are Inkuanu?"

"They're mostly human." She spoke as she pulled on her coat and slipped her blade into her belt.

James grabbed for his sword. "*Mostly* human?"

"They are worse than ghouls," spat Phoenix.

"And more dangerous," finished Evandor.

James felt his first wave of real fear since entering the warehouse.

"We have to go now, Anna, or there will be no one left by the time we get there." Phoenix motioned towards the door. "And we need to move quickly."

Anna led them out of the house, and James felt the cold fingers of air tentatively reach for his skin as the door opened and they stepped out into the cold autumn sun. James knew that before the sun began to set, he would yet again be standing beside the graves of children that should not have been called to battle in the first place.

That is, if we do not find ourselves lying next to them before this day is over, he thought before they began to pick up the pace.

*

He could hear Ceberus howl and it made him feel cold. It was long and hungry, and the screams began soon after. He was sure that the hellhound was claiming his share of blood.

When they reached the entrance to Balhatchett, Anna pushed back the hedges and he could smell the smoke. It took a few moments for him to register what was happening. Many of the small cottages were burning, and the children were scattered like ants, throughout the village, right up to Uriaha's Hill.

"What did you say we are fighting?" James asked the others.

"Cannibals," replied Evandor and Anna together.

"If it bites, kill it." Phoenix smiled, before shouting, "Into the field once more we go," as he raised his sword and ran into the fray.

"Ne'er to return, we heed Uriaha's call." Evandor followed him.

"Take my place, brother, should I fall." Anna nodded towards James.

"Mors Vorcat, death calls to us all," he said. "Until we meet again."

Then they were both running.

*

The moment they passed through the hedges, it was chaos. There were children everywhere, some fighting, others helping friends to their feet. The older children showed a surprising level of skill with their swords, and the smaller ones were fighting in bands.

James took a few moments to take in the scene, but Phoenix was already pulling a bloody sword from the chest of what looked like a normal man – the only difference was that this man's hands and legs were covered in a red powder, much like the ochre that the children used during the Sepultura Bellator. A group of three children, who all looked to be around ten, had ambushed another of these red-soaked intruders and were stabbing at him with sharpened metal too rudimentary to be called swords. James felt a strange sense of pride. They stabbed furiously, giving the man little time to react, and in a few seconds he was on his knees, bleeding out.

"Be careful, James," Anna called to him, "I've heard they can bite through steel," and then she was gone.

James's mouth went dry.

A small child was running towards him, a deep cut across her face. She must have been no older than seven.

"They won't wait until you're dead to start eating you," she screamed as she ran past him. She looked scared. He turned to see her raising her dagger, aiming it at a man who was hunched over a small boy, tearing into his thigh. She brought it down and the dagger cut into his lung. He made a sharp hiss before he fell to the side. She used her whole body to pull her dagger from his, pushing her leg against his back for leverage. When it was drawn, she wiped the blood against his shirt and went to help the boy, who was whimpering softly and very white in the face.

"Let me help you." James motioned that he would carry the boy, but the young girl hissed at him.

"Help us by fighting for us. I'll get him to Lacey," she said fiercely, throwing the boy over her shoulder and bowing under his weight. For a moment, James was sure she was going to drop the boy, then she straightened herself and began to move towards the direction of Lacey's cottage.

James pulled his dagger from its hilt and his eyes darted across the field. There looked to be about ten of these red-stained men scattered across the field, and they were cutting down children like grass. He picked one and began running.

He was a few feet from the cannibal when he noticed him coming and bore his teeth like an animal. It was no longer powder that stained his hands but blood, and it squelched against the rusted blade he held in his hands.

James cleared his mind. If the children could fight through their fear, so could he. The cannibal came at him, sloppy and too confident, and James moved out of the way of his first thrust with ease. The second and third were more difficult to avoid.

James waited until the fourth thrust was dealt, and without moving his feet, he turned sideways, allowing the cut to flow past him. The Inkuanu's throat was exposed and James slid his dagger across the main artery. He jumped as blood began to spray from the wound, covering him. James fumbled and dropped his danger. He wiped at his face and watched the cannibal fall to the ground. Kneeling down, he picked up his dagger, trying to swallow the bile that rose at the sight of the blood spouting from a hole in the man's neck.

Not a man, James chanted to himself, *not a man*.

He turned around and looked for the others. Anna was beating an Inkuanu with a rock, and like him, blood masked her face. He couldn't see Phoenix, but he saw Evandor fighting alongside another of Balhatchett's keepers, the young man with the bearded face that he had seen by the fireside during the bonfire. The young man was ferocious and roared as he turned the head of the Inkuanu backwards with a snapping sound.

For a second, everything went black as something hit James, hard, against the side of his head. It was as if he slipped underwater; all sound was lost and then the noise of the battle hit him as he resurfaced facing two Inkuanu. They both lashed out at the same time; he was cut on the side of his face by a blade but managed to block the other. These two had bright orange hair and looked eerily similar.

"He has nimble fingers," one said to the other.

"I want his ears," said the other, "for my collection." Their voices were soft, unsettling.

He heard another man scream in the distance and the two stopped suddenly, turning their heads at the sound.

"Was that a friend of yours?" James spat, but they only smiled. James didn't care. Taunting them felt good. He didn't want them to know that he was afraid. If nothing else, it gave him a second to catch his breath.

"Flesh is flesh, whether it is torn from friend or foe," said one. James tried to shake off the words, but there was a thirst on their thick, red lips and it made James feel sick.

Then they were advancing again, their blades cutting the air in front of him. James attempted a thrust forward, but it was sloppy and mistimed, and he received another cut to his shoulder for his efforts. This time, his arm went numb and he dropped his weapon. He felt one of the men fall on him and a mouth closed against his thigh and bit down. It was then that he realised these creatures were really more animal than human.

James screamed, a shrill, high-pitched sound that couldn't come out long enough or loud enough. While his brother held James down with strong hands and began to chew loudly on his flesh, the other lay himself next to James, as if they were lovers in bed together. He ran his hands over James's face, gently.

"When your muscles are nice and warm, I will cut them, carefully, in nice, long slices. I will roast them with potatoes over a fire," he whispered in James's ear. He could smell blood on the creature's breath.

"I like my meat raw," the other interrupted.

With no dagger, James felt helpless. There was another sharp pain on his thigh, and then a tearing of flesh. He screamed again and the creature lying next to him bathed in it. His head was rocking from side to side and there was a soft smile on his lips. James couldn't move his body – they were too strong – but they had left his head free. James lunged forward, opened his mouth wide and bit down on the cannibal's cheek. As he pulled a chunk of flesh away, warm blood filled his mouth and nose, and he began to vomit. The creature screamed and threw himself away from James.

"Be careful, brother. We are not the only creatures here that bite." The Inkuanu without the hole in his cheek laughed, seeing his brother in pain. "Would you like to taste me?" he asked James.

"I'll rip his lungs from his back," the other man shouted, blood still pouring from his wound.

They won't wait until you're dead to start eating you.

He felt sharp teeth tear into his side, and he screamed, unashamed, savagely as if that would help him release his pain into the world. Flesh parted from his side and he screamed again. He felt a leg push down on his chest, making it difficult to breathe. He could hear his heartbeat in his ears, its drum pounding and pounding, over and over again.

He closed his eyes and the world began to fade, like a song that played in the distance. Teeth tore into him again and he opened his eyes to see one of the men chewing on his flesh, then swallowing. Then he fell to the dark.

*

"Wake up," a voice said to him. James woke to see a young man with dark hair staring down at him. James was lying on his side with blood pooling beneath him.

One of the cannibals lay keeled over, still on his knees, propped up against his cheek, his eyes open but empty.

"You are hurt," the stranger said, kneeling next to James.

James bit back a remark. He could not remember being in so much pain before.

"You didn't use your powers." It sounded like the man was chiding him, and this irritated him.

"I really wanted to know what it felt like to be eaten alive." James's voice was dull with pain.

The man gave him a dark look. "I can help you. Lie down and put this between your teeth."

James frowned as the man handed him what looked like a worn piece of leather from his belt. It was a knife sheath and it looked like it had bite marks running down its length. James hesitated.

"The Inkuanu are well known for their dirty mouths. If they don't kill you, an infection will. Besides," the man motioned to James's side, which was strangely numb, "you have lost a lot of blood."

This convinced him and he took the leather, hesitantly.

"You are hurting. This is going to hurt more." The stranger tapped James's hand as if to nudge the sheath into his mouth and James complied, taking a deep breath and lying down on the grass. He had been warned about what was to come, but he was still unprepared. He felt the man place his hands on his chest, palms downwards, and then James began to scream. It felt as if someone were stitching, inch by inch, hot, live muscle.

For a moment between the pain and the black, he wondered if that was all he'd be doing today – screaming. Somewhere in the dark, he smiled, and then for the second time that day, he fell into it.

And then there was silence.

"Wake up, it is done," he heard someone say, and the screams returned, except they were coming from all around him.

The young man was standing in front of him, reaching a hand out to help him up.

"You will be unsteady on your feet for a while, so take it slowly," he said, and James realised that the world moved beneath his feet as he stood, but there was no pain in his body. His shoulder, side and thigh were no longer bleeding, and there were shallow cuts where the wounds used to be. The only thing that still hurt was his pride, as he realised he had fainted not once but twice in front of this same stranger.

"How did you do that?" James touched each spot on his body slowly, sure there were gaping holes before. He noticed Anna standing a few feet away, staring at the man with a strange look on her face, but she was running back into the fray a moment later.

"I am Chadrick." The man held out his hand as if this explained it all.

James gave him a silent, loaded look, expecting more, but nothing came. The two men stared at each other.

"Chadrick – where did you learn to heal like that?"

"I am a skilled healer." Chadrick looked at James for a moment, and it was then that he noticed the man's light grey eyes. They were unsettling.

Chadrick continued. "I am Uringi, like you," he finished, then his eyes flitted past James, into the distance.

"Use your power," Chadrick chided him again. "You are useless with a weapon." Then he was running again.

James wondered whether he should follow the man, then Anna screamed and James began to run blindly towards the sound.

James could no longer see past the few feet in front of him, but when he turned his head towards the sky, he could see that they had cleared Uriaha's Hill and were now standing on the north-western side of the forest that encircled this place. He knew that this side of the forest ran towards a sheer cliff that overlooked the ocean, and so there was no need to guard this area as well. He could hear Anna shouting something at Phoenix, who was fast to give his reply, but he couldn't make out their words. He was about to turn back, trying to figure out which direction they were coming from, but he knew that the smoke would have dulled their sound, when he tripped over something lying across his path. He looked down to see Penhallurick lying on his side. Blood stained his shirt until it looked as though it were dyed red. His eyes were closed and his lips slack. He was pale and his chest was still.

James bent down, bitter anger swelling into his chest. He shook the boy, trying to wake him, but the boy didn't move. James heard Anna call out his name and his voice broke as he replied. She was much closer than he had thought because all of a sudden she was at his side, kneeling over the young boy. A keening sound escaped her lips as she touched his shoulder, pulling her hand back in shock as she realised that Penhallurick was not breathing.

Anna dove for the boy, her hands searching for a wound, but there was more than one. She began to tear at her clothes for cloth to soak the wounds, cloth to make a tourniquet to stop the blood.

Then Chadrick was there, leaning over the boy and feeling for a pulse. "His pulse is there, but it's faint. He has lost too much blood; he's in too much pain." Chadrick was trying to explain to Anna, but she only screamed in response.

"Save him!" she begged savagely, choking on her tears, unable to restrain herself.

Chadrick looked stricken, undecided. At first it looked as though he would deny her, and then he was on his knees.

At first, James thought that Chadrick was going to give the child the kiss of life, but his hands were still on the boy's chest and his eyes were closed.

"Save him, please!" Anna screamed again, her voice was thick and broken. James pulled her closer to him, trying to comfort her, but she pushed away from him, her eyes focused on the stranger as if she could will him into action.

Then James felt something stir. Something woke just underneath James's skin. He could feel power begin to rise from the ground, knitting itself into a different shape, being woven like a blanket.

Anna had stopped crying and he could see her lips moving. James had never seen her pray but he was sure this is what she was doing now.

Chadrick's eyes were still closed and James was not sure anything was happening until his breathing began to change. At first, the short breaths turned to long ones, then they began to take on a strained sound, as if he were running uphill.

Beads of sweat began to appear on his forehead and his lips turned blue – the same colour Penhallurick's were turning. Anna's eyes began to widen. Her lips stopped moving. James wasn't even sure she was breathing.

The power James could feel lulled, like a drop in music, and Chadrick fell, just an inch, as if he was finding it difficult to hold himself up, but when James moved to help him, Chadrick put up a hand, warding him off.

"Please," he said, "whatever happens, don't touch me."

James took a step back and Chadrick closed his eyes again, placing his hands back on Penhallurick. The power returned, skimming like a stone across James's skin, but the boy's chest had been still for too long and his lips were too dark a shade of blue. James wondered if Penhallurick was about to take Chadrick with him into the dark.

Anna's gasp brought him back like being dunked in a bucket of cold water. The power had overwhelmed him. It was almost deep enough that he might drown in it if left under for too long. He took a deep breath, trying to steady his heartbeat, and he saw what had made Anna draw her inhale so sharply; the boy's breath has returned.

He could see his small chest rising and falling; it was so faint at first that James thought he might have imagined it, but it started to rise more fully and drop with more vigour after a few seconds, and James noticed that his colour was slowly returning to his face. Chadrick's colour, on the other hand, left a lot to be desired.

For a moment James thought it might be the smoke that lay low against the ground, but when he looked carefully he noticed that the man was breathing more heavily and his body shook with the effort of kneeling.

Penhallurick opened his eyes and Anna immediately bounded onto the boy, careful not to touch his wounds that looked as though they were newly sewn. Anna was holding on to the boy's face, her tears cutting roads through the blood that stained her cheeks. James couldn't tell if she was laughing or crying – perhaps it was a bit of both.

When Anna had moved in, the man suddenly bounded back. He was kneeling when he pushed himself away from her, as if he didn't want her too close, and so he landed abruptly on his side as he moved, wincing with pain.

Penhallurick was now in Anna's arms, being rocked like a small child as she cradled him while sitting on the ground, and so James went to help the man who was catching his breath without going through the trouble of getting to his feet.

When James approached him, the man simply held out his hand, as if to ask James to stay away. He stopped, giving Chadrick some time to catch his breath. It was only a few more minutes before the man found the energy to move to a seated position, his legs crossed in front of him, staring at Anna holding the child.

Anna returned Chadrick's gaze. Her eyes were swollen and red, but she wasn't crying anymore.

"Thank you," she whispered as she cradled the child. She smiled, and dimples appeared on both cheeks. It was a wide smile that went to her eyes. Chadrick smiled weakly back at her.

Then her smile faded. "There he is!" she shouted, her eyes fixed on something in the distance. James turned his head and saw what she was looked at. One lone cannibal stood amongst the tombstones, crouched over a body, ripping into its flesh. James couldn't tell who it was from here, but he could tell that it wasn't a child. It was a young woman, one of the few adults of Balhatchett. Her body was being shaken like a ragdoll to part the flesh from the bones, and still they were limp. For the first time, here on the Uriaha's Hill, James could see that Balhatchett was winning the battle. The Inkuanu among the tombs did not realise it, but he was among the last of his kind surviving. The rest had either run away or they were lying among the dead and dying. He could see Lacey and a few others scrambling through the bodies, administering aid where they could.

"I saw him. He was the one that attacked Penhallurick." Anna started to get to her feet, but Chadrick raised his hand.

"He's mine," he said. It took a few moments for him to gather his strength, but he pushed himself off the ground and started running.

He was about ten paces from the creature when it looked up, saw him and bared its teeth. Chadrick did not miss a beat. He was within an arm's reach of the creature when it lunged at him. Chadrick moved like water, parrying the man's attack with one arm and then using the other to grab at its neck. James heard the creature hiss – in pain or anger, he didn't know. And then Chadrick had two hands on him and the creature screamed. This time, it was pain, sharp and fierce. The scream was cut short as blood began to pour from the creature's eyes, ears and mouth. It was as if he were imploding. His body began to bulge and he crumpled to the ground, but Chadrick wasn't done. He followed the creature down to his knees, keeping his hands on his chest and only removing one to get behind the creature's head and bring it close to his own, as if in an intimate embrace. The creature screamed again and then went silent. Chadrick got to his feet, shook his hands, allowing the blood to spatter onto the ground, and spat at the corpse at his feet.

"The Inkuanu have abandoned Balhatchett," Evandor cried as he joined the others. Like the rest, he had blood on his clothing and his face was black with smoke. "I'm going back to help Lacey with the survivors."

"I will go too." Anna held Penhallurick to her chest, but he was too large for her to lift.

"Give him to me." Phoenix held out his hands, and she shifted so that he could take the boy from her.

Phoenix and Anna made their way down Uriaha's Hill towards Lacey's cottage. James watched as Anna picked up a small, yellow-haired boy along the way. He gripped her neck tightly as they made their way through the crowds of children that were collecting around their fallen friends. There was no more screaming in Balhatchett, except for a few cries of pain. Instead, cries of celebration rang from the village and James could hear bells being rung in the distance. The smoke and ash was being carried away by the wind and the last of the fires were being put out by small bands of volunteers.

Once Phoenix had left, it was only James and Chadrick left standing on the hill.

"You fought bravely." Chadrick turned to James, tapping him on the shoulder. His hand shook with the effort, but James pretended that he did not notice.

"Can you teach me?" James asked him, staring silently over the ruin that was the home of the forgotten.

Chadrick turned his head, as if studying James. "I can," he finally said, shaking his head, "as long as you are talking about your powers." He shook his head again. "You are truly terrible with a sword, and I'm Uringi, not a god."

James nodded, grateful. The man made his way down the hill, chuckling quietly to himself.

TWELVE

A DAY OF LIGHT

By the next afternoon, Balhatchett was alive with noise, and James was surprised at how quickly he heard the children laughing again. They had congregated on Uriaha's Hill once more for the Sepultura, but this time, it had taken many more hands to dig the graves. Eight were dead – three of those were children – but once more, only the smaller children wept. James found it difficult to remain resolute, and he could have sworn he saw Anna wipe her nose with the end of her tunic while pretending to tuck a strand of hair behind her ear. The Inkuanu that had fallen in the battle were thrown onto a pyre carelessly, and burned.

During the Sepultura, each person's name was read aloud and red ochre was thrown onto their grave. There was a hint of rain in the air, and James brought his cloak to his body, protecting himself from a chilly wind. There was something about the promise of rain that always seemed to bring with it an earthen smell, and it was strangely comforting.

Chadrick attended the Sepultura after spending the night in Balhatchett. He had helped to dig many of the graves and by midmorning, his tunic stuck to his body and his black hair hung limp around his face. He had not said anything to James since the day before, but he had silently made his way to his side during the ceremony.

When the Sepultura had come to an end, everyone scattered, bustling away to do their part to set the village right again. It was amidst this chaos that Anna had come to find James. She held a mug of something warm in her hands.

"It is honeyed tea." She handed it to him and he took it gratefully.

"How is Penhallurick?" asked James, taking a long sip. It was sweet, and in the autumn air, it filled his stomach with warmth.

"He's alive." Anna nodded, taking a sip from her own mug.

They stood in silence for a while, watching the village. The smell of smoke still lingered in the air, but that same wind that brought the autumn chill was washing it away, slowly. There were children raking at the ground, gathering up the remains of cottages that had burned. Among these ashes were smatterings of their own belongings. James could see a small doll with red shoes peeking out of an ash pile. It was missing a head. Still, with the heaviness of yesterday still hanging over the village, there was a relief that comes with survival.

"The others are meeting in Lacey's cottage." Anna brought James back from his thoughts. "They want to discuss what we're going to do about all this."

James nodded. He took another long sip from his mug. "Lead the way."

Lacey was sitting outside of her cottage on a wooden crate, flanked by Phoenix and Chadrick, who had removed his shirt and was using a torn piece of white cloth to dab at a cut on his shoulder. Anna averted her eyes, taking a seat beside Phoenix. Crates had been arranged in a circle, with a small fire burning in the middle to keep them warm. Evandor joined them, and James took the last empty seat beside him.

"I am sorry for the poor accommodations, but as you probably suspect, my cottage is being used for more practical purposes." Lacey spoke, nodding to the door behind her. It had been left open, partially to let light in, and mostly so that Lacey could keep watch over those inside, he suspected. He could hear movement inside, and angling his head allowed him to peer inside. Lacey had cleared everything from her cottage and replaced them with mats that lined the floors from end to end. On each one lay a child, all of varying ages. She had enlisted some of the children to help her care for the wounded, so small hands and feet bustled from one mat to the other, tending to wounds, giving water and food where it was needed. A small girl with bright blonde hair who looked no more than four was busy gently stroking the face of another older girl with dirty brown hair.

"These are the worst of them," Lacey said to James, noticing his interest. "Those who were well enough to be cared for in their own quarters have been sent back."

James nodded.

"Right, so I suppose we should get started." Lacey pulled her bright red hair into a bun on the top of her head. She always wore a plain blue dress with a white overcoat, but today it was a dark brown. He didn't ask why.

"What happened? How did those monsters get in here?" she asked no one in particular.

"They were led here." James recognised the voice, and it didn't come from any in their circle. Cerberus.

The hound moved quickly, too quickly for his size. It was unsettling.

"I saw you yesterday." Chadrick motioned to Cerberus respectfully. "Many of the little ones owe their lives to you."

Cerberus snorted in acknowledgment, unsettling the dust beneath his large head.

Phoenix and Anna shifted their crates so that the hound could take a seat between them. He rested on his hind legs, watching them. He loomed over the group, his breath coming out in short, sharp bursts. His strangely human eyes scanned over the group, coming to a rest on James for a moment before moving over to Lacey.

"I could smell them. Something brought them here," Cerberus continued.

"Could you tell what it was?" Phoenix asked.

Cerberus shook his head and his jowls shook, flinging saliva to the ground.

"No. But they were headed for Baldur Forest," Cerberus replied.

"Then I was right." Chadrick squeezed red liquid from the cloth and then dipped his hands into a small bucket of water that had been placed next to him. He then put on his tunic. "I've been following them for months, but it's like walking on wet moss. Every time I get close, they slip out from under me." He winced as his tunic rubbed against his shoulder.

The others looked at him, questioning.

"Death Chasers." He grimaced. This time, it was not in pain.

"Death Chasers – in Balhatchett?" asked Anna, looking confused.

"What are Death Chasers?" asked James. Everyone else looked as though they had heard these two words before.

"They are rats." Phoenix laughed.

"They are ghouls," said Chadrick, spitting at the bucket next to him.

"They are *men*," corrected Anna, "and they bring death in their wake, just like the waves of an ocean."

"They hunt the dark, like us—" Evandor spoke, and Anna interrupted him.

"They are not like us, Evan." She turned to James. "They are just as dangerous as the creatures they *chase*," she explained. "Is that why you were in Balhatchett?" she asked Chadrick.

He nodded. "I've been following them through the Obsidian Desert, right down the Prior Coast. I believed they were heading for Morvoren, but I didn't think they would pass this far east to get there."

"Morvoren." Lacey spoke. "The dark lands?"

"Yes," replied Chadrick.

Everyone was quiet for a moment. They heard a child laugh in the distance.

"We have never been to the dark lands before," Evandor said. Anna and Phoenix shook their heads in agreement. James felt something heavy in the air.

"I've heard that Morvoren is a pretty scary place." James spoke. Anna looked up at him with wide eyes while Phoenix laughed out loud. It was a sharp sound, uncomfortable.

"It is," Chadrick said, nodding as he spoke. He picked up a small stick and stoked the fire.

"Why not leave the Death Chasers to whatever lurks in Baldur Forest?" asked Lacey. "They'll likely not make it out of Morvoren alive."

Chadrick lay the stick next to him and looked to be considering what she said. "This is a possibility," he said, "but Morvoren can be tamed by those familiar with its depths, and it's likely at least a few of them come from the dark lands." He looked around him.

"If the Death Chasers stand a small chance of surviving Baldur, how are we going to fare any better?" asked Anna.

Chadrick looked at her, his grey eyes narrowing, watching her closely, considering something. "I am of Morvoren. I will come with you. I will help you to hunt down these rats."

Anna considered this for a moment before turning to the others, leaving the invitation open to a vote with a tilt of her head.

"I'd be glad to have you on board," said Phoenix.

"You saved my life," said James, as if that were enough.

"You saved Penhallurick," said Anna, giving her approval.

Evandor studied Chadrick, his eyes narrowed. Silently weighing something, it took a few moments for him to come to a decision.

"So we leave for Morvoren?" asked Evandor.

"We do," Chadrick said.

THIRTEEN

SIGNS

This time, when they left Balhatchett, children lined the small stone walkway that led out of the village, standing silent as Anna, James, Chadrick, Phoenix and Evandor crossed the hedges that would lead them out of Balhatchett and onto the road to Baldur Forest. It would be no more than a couple of hours' walk to reach deep into the heart of Baldur; with Chadrick, Phoenix and Evandor being skilled hunters, they packed light.

"Baldur is a wild place, and though it is dangerous, it is also brimming with life," Chadrick had explained.

Lacey had said her goodbyes at the cottage. She had held James close when they said farewell, kissing him on his left cheek and leaving him flushed and just a little giddy. She thanked them all before heading back into her cottage to tend to the occupants.

Penhallurick stood at the entrance of Balhatchett. Bruises covered the right side of his face and he was hunched over, leaning heavily on one foot, looking every one of his twelve years.

He extended a hand to Chadrick and the man took it and shook it firmly. Penhallurick then pulled away and moved to be embraced by Anna. He was shorter than other boys his age, and at twelve, he just about reached her elbows. He buried his face in her arms and she leaned down and kissed him, gently, on the top of the head. She whispered something to him and he nodded, then let her go. He didn't look back as he left the companions standing at the edge of Balhatchett, making his way back towards the village.

Cerberus was the last to greet them on their way out, and he nodded to each in turn as they passed him. Once again, the moment the hedges closed behind them, all was silent.

*

Chadrick led the way, walking a few steps ahead of the group in silence, his eyes focused on the way forward. James was walking beside Anna, with Phoenix and Evandor taking up the rear. He could hear the two whispering softly as they forged ahead.

As they walked, it began to grow dark, and James realised that they had been in Balhatchett for the better part of the day. The wooded area they had entered when they first left Balhatchett had quickly turned into a forest, dense with tall, thick trees. It took more effort to navigate around the foliage, since there was no clear path into Baldur, but it wasn't so dense that it blocked out the light, making their way easier to see. Every now and then Chadrick stopped and listened to something James couldn't hear. Sometimes he would kneel to the ground, seeing something that James couldn't see. Then he would get to his feet and begin moving again. At times James wasn't sure that Chadrick was aware they were still following behind him.

The ground was relatively flat and this helped them to move more quickly. With the evening came a deep, warm smell that spoke of rain, and James wondered whether they had crossed the threshold into Baldur or whether they were still on the fringes of Balhatchett. He spoke his thought out loud to Anna.

"You will know when we've reached Baldur," she replied.

"How do you know?" asked James. "You said you've never been there?"

"Corpsewood," she said. "Baldur's borders are said to be lined with Corpsewood trees. You'll know them when you see them. Or better yet, you'll smell them."

They continued onwards and the rain began to fall, softening their footsteps as it dampened the dead leaves beneath their feet. James took a deep breath, taking in the clean smell of the rain.

He was almost beginning to enjoy the walk. It was very nearly pleasant until he noticed something sickly sweet lingering just beyond the fresh smell of rain. It was death. He stopped moving and Phoenix bumped into him from behind.

"Watch your step," Phoenix scolded him.

Anna looked back to see what happened, saw James's face and laughed. "Corpsewood," she said, still laughing. Phoenix chuckled before giving James a gentle nudge forward.

"We'd better keep up or Chadrick will leave us behind," Phoenix said. Chadrick wasn't paying them much attention, forging ahead on his own. Anna moved quickly to keep up and the rest followed.

Within about ten paces, their surroundings changed dramatically. The canopy of trees closed in and the forest became dark – too dark to see much more than a few paces ahead of them – and the sickly-sweet smell began to stir a dread in James.

The line of Corpsewood began to come into view, looming over them, beckoning and warning all at once. They were as magnificent as they were grotesque. The trees were enormous, towering over the oak that fought for light and water. They were gnarled and bent over, as if they were old men hobbled with pain, screaming silently in the darkened forest. The branches swept down to meet the ground, and the large, dark leaves swayed with a wind James could not feel. The warm smell stuck in his throat.

James covered his nose with the sleeve of his tunic.

The others came to stand beside him, except for Chadrick, who stood apart from the rest, staring off into the distance, beyond the line of these giants. He reminded James of the priests who stood before their altars at morning mass. There was a reverence in it that he couldn't quite understand.

James took a few steps to close the distance between himself and the young hunter. He put a hand on Chadrick's shoulder.

"We are here," Chadrick said in a hushed tone, before turning to face James. "Are you ready?" he asked. James wasn't sure whether Chadrick was speaking to the group or himself.

James turned towards the forest. The branches of the trees bobbed and swayed, beckoning, calling. He wanted to turn around and run back to Migdasha.

"No," James decided to answer, "but I'll go anyway."

Chadrick gave a wry smile and nodded his head, turning back to the wood.

James turned back to the others. "Well, what are we waiting for?" he called back.

*

Once they crossed the line of Corpsewood, they lit fires from branches, the tips of which were wrapped in twigs and other materials, before being covered in pieces of torn cloth and dipped in a dark liquid that Chadrick had gathered from a tree at the edge of a small lake. He claimed that it would keep the fires going for hours, and so far, they had.

James thought it would be darker, somehow, this deep in the forest, but even as the trees grew thick and interlocked above their heads, the moonlight found a way through. They needed little more than the light from their torches to be able to see the path ahead. It was so light, in fact, that James had wondered, out loud, why they were even bothering to use the torches, and that was when Chadrick had reminded him about the wolves.

"I've heard that they grow to the size of horses," Phoenix had said, looking over his shoulder as he spoke.

"They do not show fear like ordinary wolves. They are not scared of men," added Chadrick. "They only thing they fear is fire. Keep it close – they will be waiting for an opportunity…" He didn't finish the sentence, perhaps sensing the unease of the rest of the group.

James had definitely felt uneasy since entering Baldur Forest, and he wasn't sure if it was entirely because of the wolves. Stories from the dark lands were spread throughout Gedeon since he was a child, and he had always said he would never step foot in this part of the world, but here he was – and in Baldur Forest, no less. The warmth and the earthen smell of loam was not enough to comfort him.

He brushed past a plant that was covered in bright, purple flowers that moved gently from side to side, even though there was no sign of wind in the air. He leaned in close to smell them, but they didn't have a scent. As he brushed past the leaves, they felt like cobwebs breaking across his skin, and he shivered.

"Grave mourners," whispered Chadrick. "When they come into contact with a dead body, they begin to produce a light blue fluid, and it looks as though they are crying. In Morvoren, it is believed that this liquid can bring back the dead."

"Can it?" asked Phoenix, and Chadrick looked at him, surprised.

"No," he replied.

A wolf howled and it made James jump.

"It is time to settle for the night," Chadrick said, and stopped a few feet ahead before taking the packs off his back. He wasn't waiting for their response. It was then that James realised that Anna hadn't said anything for a while. He searched for her and found her cutting a bright purple flower from its stem before wandering over to the fire that Chadrick was attempting to build.

"Here, I'll do that," she said, passing him the flower so her hands were free to start the fire.

Chadrick jumped as if she'd burned him. He threw the flower into the fire and wiped his hands on his tunic. His eyes were wide, frightened, then his cheeks flushed.

"What do you think you are doing?" he asked her. "Have you forgotten where you are?"

Anna's eyes went wide, then darkened. Chadrick's face flushed. Anna's jaw clenched.

For a moment, Chadrick looked as though he wanted to apologise, then turned and walked off into the forest.

Anna stared at his retreating back and for a second, her lips pursed in a hard line. James thought she might call after him, but she didn't. Instead, she turned back to the kindling and brought it to life with a motion of her hand. Then she busied herself with preparing her own sleeping area, refusing to speak to anyone.

Chadrick returned not too long after he'd left with a brace of rabbits for their dinner. Anna was either uncomfortable or still angry, but either way she refused to meet his eye.

Huddled together, with the fire burning hot and the smell of rabbit causing James's stomach to growl, it almost felt cosy in the forest – that was, until James heard the wolves begin to howl again. They were far off, but Chadrick had mentioned that their presence would be enough to draw the wolves in. James tried to ignore the howls and focus on the warmth of the fire and the looming thought of dinner.

Finally the rabbit was cooked and each of the companions received a portion. The skin was crispy and the meat tender, and with that and some of the hard cheese Evandor had brought, James's hunger was entirely sated by the time he was done. He finished off his meal with some cool water from his skin.

Once he had eaten, Chadrick lay down with his pack under his head. Evandor was digging thirty-two small holes in the ground, dividing them into four rows of eight, while Phoenix collected small stones and split them between first two holes. Then Phoenix put his hands behind his back and brought them out in front of him in fists. Evandor tapped his left hand and Phoenix opened it to reveal a small, brown stone. Evandor smiled, clearly the winner.

"Me first," he said, and he began by dropping one of the stones into an inner row of the makeshift board. At first the game was slow, with both players taking time to fill their respective rows, but it began to speed up and James could see that stones could be captured, allowing the other player to take hold of more stones before advancing along the board. The stones ahead could act like lily pads on a pond, allowing the player to jump ahead as long as there was a platform of stones to use for support.

"Would you like us to teach you how to play?" asked Evandor.

James shook his head. "Maybe another night," he said, and Evandor went back to his game.

James turned to Anna. "I want to learn to create fire," James said to Anna, who sat with folded legs, repairing a hole in her cloak with a needle and thread. Her brow furrowed with concentration.

"It doesn't really work like that," she said, cutting the thread with her teeth.

"Then teach me how it works," he said.

She pulled out a small pouch and threaded the needle through its inner leather strap. She put the pouch back into her sack.

"Where do you come from, James?" she asked him, tightening the leather ties and shoving her travel sack out of the way.

"I'm from Dasdaya – you found me there, remember?" he answered, but she shook her head, obviously not placated.

"No, I mean, where is your family from?" she asked, as she began to form a pyre of small twigs and leaves between them. This question threw him.

"I believe my mother and father were from Dasdaya too – but I was raised by an uncle. They left when I was very young. I don't remember them." He rushed to add, "My uncle died a few years ago."

Anna listened, nodding, but her eyes were fixed on the pyre she was creating. When she was finished, she looked up to face him. Evandor and Phoenix had come over to watch what she was doing. Their game had come to an end and it was clear by Phoenix's irritated expression who had won the game.

"Our powers stem from the lands we come from," Anna began to explain. "Fiachra is the land of smoke and fire, and those are the powers I yield. You've heard this explanation before…" As she spoke, James nodded. She had explained how Evandor was from Aventias and had the power of water, while Phoenix was from Ancasta and so had the power of wind.

"But Dasdaya has always been something of a question mark when it comes to the Uringi. Traders moved freely through Dasdaya, whether they were from Fiachra or Ancasta. So many Uringi settled in Dasdaya that it became impossible to tell which powers someone yielded unless they could tell which land their ancestors came from," she continued. "It basically means that we have no way of knowing which powers you have — we're just going to have to try them all."

"All of them?" James said. "Where do I start?" he asked.

"We'll start with fire," she said, shifting from side to side, making herself comfortable. "We don't create fire from nothing. We are not magicians — not in that sense, at least. We focus the energy that is already there, all around us, and direct it to a source that can burn. You cannot create fire where there is no heat and you can't expect it to burn without kindling. With that being said," she smiled, "the most talented Uringi can always find heat somewhere. They can always find something to burn.

"So it's quite simple when it comes down to it," she continued. "You simply draw the heat from the air around you," she gestured to the air with her hands, "and direct it towards the pyre, and…" The pyre sparked to life, but before it could consume the kindling entirely, she put it out with the heel of her boot. It took a few minutes for her to build up the pyre again.

"Now it's your turn," she said to James.

James laughed. "It's that easy, huh?" he said, shaking his head. "I don't think I really understand, Anna."

"You're Uringi," she said, "you don't have to understand. Close your eyes." He closed his eyes and felt her place her hand on his chest. She leaned in close and he could smell something sweet in her hair. Her breath was warm and pleasant as she spoke to him. "Feel the warmth from the sun." She directed him.

"It's night-time," he stated the obvious, "and it's autumn." He felt the flat of her hand against the back of his head. "Ouch!" he cried, rubbing his head. He opened his eyes and saw Anna frowning at him.

"I know what time of day it is," she said. "Even though the sun is down, its heat is still all around us. Close your eyes," this time she gave him a look of warning and he closed them quickly, not wanting to risk another correction, "and feel it around you."

This time he closed his eyes, focused, trying to feel some heat – any heat – but all he felt was the unsettlingly warm breeze that tickled the hairs on the back of his neck.

"I feel nothing," he said.

"Nothing?" Anna asked. "Nothing at all?"

"I mean, I feel the wind. It's warm, I suppose. But I don't feel any sun," he said.

"The wind." Anna sounded pleased. "Yes, focus on the wind. It carries the warmth of the sun. Focus on its heat."

James tried to focus his mind again, concentrating on the warmth of the wind, but it was difficult because the wind wasn't always there – it ebbed and flowed, as wind does.

"What do I do now?" he asked, his eyes still closed.

"Now draw that heat into you," she said. It sounded so simple it made James laugh again.

"It's that easy, is it?" he asked, and he received another jolt to his head for his efforts. "Ouch, stop that will you!" he cried out again, rubbing his head, but his eyes remained closed.

"Sometimes it helps to practise your breathing. Imagine you are drawing the heat into you with each breath. See the bright red light move in through your nose, building up as it enters your stomach. When you breathe out, picture yourself stoking that fire with your breath." James tried to follow her instructions. "Once the fire is hot enough, use your hands to direct it to the pyre," she finished.

James continued to stoke his stomach fire and imagined it large and hot, but when he tried to make that flame appear on the pyre, nothing happened. Again and again he tried, but the pyre remained cold and bare.

"Nothing," he said, disappointed.

Anna nodded, as if this made sense. "You might need practise," she said, "or you might not have the power of fire."

"Should I try something else?" he asked, turning to Phoenix and Evandor in turn. "Could you help me learn how to work with wind, or water, like you two?"

But they shook their heads. "It is usually best to stick with one element until you're sure it isn't right for you," said Evandor. "It can take time for your abilities to show themselves, and if you're spreading yourself too thin, it can take longer for them to appear."

James nodded, but it was hard to hide his frustration. "How will I know if it's working?" he asked again, closing his eyes and trying his best to draw in fire from the air around him.

"You'll know it's working when the pyre's on fire," Anna said simply, laying herself down and closing her eyes.

*

James was still practising when he was brought out of his reverie by Phoenix's snoring. He looked up to see that Anna,

Evandor and Phoenix were fast asleep. Chadrick was on his back, but he looked as though he was carving a figure with a short, thick blade. James realised it must be getting late. He rubbed his eyes and lay down on his back with his travel sack behind his head for some support.

"Why did you tell the others you were from Dasdaya?" Chadrick's voice was loud enough to travel the few feet between himself and James, but not loud enough to wake the others. James turned his head to look in the other man's direction. Chadrick's face was dipped in shadows, lit only on one side by the firelight. He was looking up at the sky.

"What do you mean? I am from Dasdaya," James replied.

Chadrick turned to look at him. His eyes were dark and questioning. "I can feel the dark in you, James," he said. "This is my homeland, after all." He motioned towards the forest that surrounded them. "You are my countryman."

James frowned, half smiling. "I really don't know what you're talking about. My parents never said anything about being from Morvoren. What do you mean you can feel the dark in me?"

Chadrick was quiet for a while, as if choosing his words carefully. "Perhaps I was wrong," he said, turning away from James so that he could no longer see his face, "but I don't think that you'll be successful in calling the fire. Not if you are of Morvoren."

"If I'm from Morvoren, will my powers be like yours?" James asked.

He heard Chadrick laugh quietly to himself. It sounded bitter. "Perhaps," Chadrick said. "Morvoren is of the earth. You might be able to heal, but it is more likely that you'll be able to call the earth – to move it to your will." He was quiet for a few moments again, considering something. "I will help you, if that is what you want."

"Yes, please," James replied. "That's what I want."

"Tomorrow," Chadrick said, and then he was quiet.

*

The next day they were up early. It was a cold morning and dew covered the ground, soaking their boots as they walked. Chadrick stamped out the fire, but they were all given their torches and told to keep them close.

They travelled for most of the morning before they stopped again to eat and rest, and then they were on the move again. The forest continued to thicken and grow darker, even though James could see the sun shining high up between the leaves of the tallest trees.

"Stay close," Chadrick had warned them. "We move as one, to appear as one." The others nodded, closing the gaps between them.

They did not take a path, as there was none carved into Baldur, and if there had been one once upon a time, it had long since been reclaimed by the forest.

It's probably one of the reasons so many never returned from Baldur, thought James. Without Chadrick, he was sure they would never have been able to find their way through.

By late afternoon James could feel blisters forming on his feet and he was struggling to keep up with the rest of the group. He was concentrating hard on putting one foot in front of the other when he tripped, falling into Anna who was walking in front of him. Anna grabbed him just before he hit the floor and Chadrick, who was leading them, looked back for the first time in hours.

"We will rest here," he said, throwing down his pack and immediately lighting some of the torches that he carried with him, setting them in a circle around their makeshift camp. "Nc one leaves this circle," he said, motioning to the line of torches that surrounded them. The others nodded.

Once they were settled and they had a fire going, Chadrick went off to hunt. Phoenix had insisted on going with him and when the two returned, they carried a large, plump bird with a fiery red beak between them.

While Evandor and Anna plucked it, Chadrick came to sit in front of James. "Are you ready?" he asked.

"For what?" asked James.

Chadrick turned his head to the side. "For our first lesson?"

"Yes!" James remembered their talk from the night before. He wondered if this lesson would go any better than Anna's.

"What are you doing?" Anna overheard them.

"Chadrick believes I'm from Morvoren. He's going to try to teach me to…" He suddenly wasn't sure what he was going to be taught. He looked at Chadrick.

"We will start with something simple." Chadrick was digging his fingers into the soil, gathering a small pile of earth between them. When he was done, he rubbed his hands together, dusting off the earth. "Move the earth." He motioned to the pile he had formed.

Just like the night before, James had no idea where he was supposed to start. "Am I drawing the earth into me, like last night, or…" He drifted off, seeing the horrified look on Chadrick's face.

"No," the man said, "I am sorry, I forgot you are like a child."

"I'm not a child!" James spat back.

"I apologise." Chadrick spoke again. "What I mean is that even small children are taught the fundamentals when they are very young. As they grow older, they simply need to build on those skills before they can start using their power. You don't know these fundamentals," he finished.

James was placated, barely.

Chadrick continued, "Close your eyes and place your hands on the earth." James followed his direction. "Now visualise yourself reaching deep into the earth. Feel its warmth. Feel it crumble beneath your fingers as you squeeze your hands closed. Connect with it."

This time, it was easier for James to visualise himself reaching into the earth, maybe because he could smell it so strongly within Baldur. The earth was warm beneath his hands, and it had a rich smell. He pictured the earth parting as he reached into it, but his hands were still. As he reached deep into the ground, the smell of loam filled his nostrils. He thought he heard something scuttling through the ground, maybe a beetle, stopping briefly, then moving on again. James drew back, surprised by how easy it was. He could feel a larger creature, perhaps a mole, push against him with the earth. He looked up and saw Chadrick smile.

"You can taste the power," Chadrick said. "Now you must breathe life into that power, like stoking a fire."

James dipped back into the earth.

"Now direct yourself to the mound before you," Chadrick said.

James followed his directions. He pictured himself navigating his way to the mound, coming up beneath it, pushing against the weight of it.

"Did that move?" he heard Phoenix ask.

James opened his eyes, pulling his hands from the earth. "Really? It moved?" James asked, excited.

Chadrick began to laugh. "Your friend is playing a trick on you, I think."

Phoenix burst out laughing and James saw Evandor break into a smile. James gave them both a dark look.

"Ignore them." Chadrick put a hand on James's shoulder. "Keep practising. You are going to need to get a lot better and you don't have a lot of time." Chadrick motioned to the dagger that lay beside James. "And that is not going to help you."

James continued to practise until it was time for dinner. They ate together, and for a long time there was nothing but the sounds of meat being pulled from the bone and mouthfuls being washed down with water. When they were done, Chadrick had them bury the scraps of food deep in the earth. He went on to inspect each of the torches and, once he was satisfied, he returned to take a seat next to Anna. James went back to his practise while Chadrick and Anna talked softly about something that James could not hear. There was a familiarity in the way that they spoke to one another that James had not noticed before. At one point, Chadrick brushed a hair from Anna's face as she spoke. She wasn't expecting it and jumped before smiling widely, embarrassed. James felt bad for them. In Baldur they had no privacy. He turned away to give them as much privacy as he could offer and continued practising.

James had lost count of the times he'd placed his hands on the ground and began his searching, sifting through the ground. He'd placed a stone on top of the mound of ground before him. He thought that if he managed to move the earth, the stone would roll off and alert him, but so far, the stone might as well have been glued to the mound for all it was moving.

James rubbed at his temples, trying to rid himself of the sharp pain that had lodged itself between his eyes when Chadrick hissed and held his hand up, motioning for them to be quiet. He was listening to something James couldn't hear. And then he could. Footsteps and low voices were headed for their campfire.

Phoenix was on his feet, his sword unsheathed, the fingers of his other hand worrying at his side. James realised that he was reaching for his power. Evandor was kneeled low, watching, his weapon ready. Anna and Chadrick took to their feet.

It didn't take long for the intruders to come into view. They were a group of about ten men with dark skin and sharp facial features. All but one had long, black hair that reached down to their waists. One alone had red hair, shaved short. He was shorter than the rest, who were all tall and slim.

"Good evening, friends." One of the men stepped forward. He looked older than the others, probably in his forties. He was handsome, with fine features and golden skin. He looked like he could pass for one of Anna's siblings, if she had any. His voice was deep – it reminded James of oak.

James didn't return the greeting, but Phoenix and Evandor did. Chadrick faced the man who was clearly the leader of the group. He offered them his hand and the man took it.

"I am Chadrick, of Morvoren and the Ash Isles," he said.

"I am Oren," the man returned, "of Fiachra-Rádha and the Silken Valley." As he spoke, he turned his head to the others as if announcing himself to the entire group. Then his eyes rested on Anna.

"Anna," the man said, his voice low with surprise.

James turned to Anna, frowning, and saw that the others were looking as confused.

"This is where we set up camp." He spoke loudly and they quickly began to unload the packs from their backs.

"What do you think you are doing?" Anna asked quietly.

Oren looked surprised.

"Will you not share a fire with an old friend?" he asked.

"We are not friends," Anna replied. There was something dangerous in her voice.

The man studied Anna for a moment. Anna stared him down. "I was high protector of Kianaya, and right hand to your father until he lost his seat. Now it seems we are both foreigners in a strange land. If you turn us away from your fire, I will take that as a sign that we are enemies," Oren said.

Anna spat in his direction. Chadrick put a hand on her shoulder. She shrugged him off and gave him a biting look.

Oren gave her a look that even James felt was patronising, putting up his hands. "I know what's the problem. I should have addressed that first. You once believed yourself to be without a price, is that right?" he asked. "They asked a fair price for you, Anna, and we would have accepted. It was your father. He asked for half of what you were worth, and accepted half of what was asked."

Chadrick closed his eyes and when they opened, they were a darker shade of black.

"I know my price," Anna hissed, touching her hand to the back of her neck. James had noticed her doing this before – she did it when she was anxious, sometimes when she was tired.

"You should. It must still be burned into the back of your neck," the man said simply. James glanced at her neck and realised that what he had previously thought of as a tattoo must be a price. Her price.

"You are slavers?" Chadrick said. It sounded like a question, but James knew it wasn't. He could feel the air begin to whisper, as if it stirred from sleep. He now recognised Chadrick's power when he felt it. Oren noticed something, too.

"In Fiachra, I am noble," he said, as if that granted him some measure of protection.

"You are no longer in Fiachra," replied Chadrick. It was a warning.

"I mean what I say, Anna, if you turn me and my men away, we walk away enemies." Oren turned to Anna.

"You can stay." Evandor spoke up.

"The hell he can." Anna didn't look at him.

Phoenix drew his sword but stood rooted to the ground, as if unsure what to do.

"If Anna says you are unwelcome, I would advise you to leave." Chadrick spoke, his hands tapping at the sides of his thighs.

Oren laughed, but there was something sharp in the sound, something cutting. He rubbed at his face and the men beside him began to grow restless.

Evandor held his hand out to them, as if to placate them, and then turned to Anna. "Anna, you forget where we are, but I haven't. We don't need another enemy in Baldur, we won't survive the night," he explained. "I have heard stories of what happens to traders who are turned away from a fire. We cannot die tonight," Evandor added.

Anna's face flushed for a moment, and for a second, James thought she would refuse him again, but she just turned on her heel and walked away. The traders took this as a sign and began to unpack once more, settling in for the night. Anna moved over to her sleeping quarters. James felt her silence like a heavy rock in his gut.

"I see you boys are enjoying the hospitality of our country. Our Anna here always did have the bite of a scorpion. I must admit, I used to wonder what it was like between her thighs myself, but I was afraid to stung." An older man placed a hand on Oren's shoulder as Chadrick got back to his feet, his jaw clenched with anger. Oren threw both hands up, as if in apology, and took a skin of wine from one his companions.

The older man settled himself next to the light of the fire. "What are you men doing in Baldur?" he asked when he got no reaction from them.

"Do not mistake my acquiescence for hospitality," Evandor said. "I am no friend of you or your leader." He motioned to a man who had quietly seated himself on the edges of the firelight.

The older man shrugged. "The question still stands."

"You first." Phoenix spoke protectively.

The man smiled and pulled out a pipe. He reached into a dark sack that was tied around his waist and pulled out a smaller bag, filled with strong-smelling tobacco. He began to tap the pipe against a log, allowing the dark contents to spill out onto the ground, before he began to fill it again.

"We are traders. Every year we pass through Baldur on our way through to Ancasta to ensure we make it on time for the autumn festival."

"You don't look like you have a whole lot to trade," James said.

The man laughed again, but this time it was laced with something darker. He was annoyed. "This is Baldur Forest," he said simply. "We are scouts. Our caravans will follow, once we are sure the way is clear."

"It is true." Chadrick stoked the fire, making sure it was big enough to warm them all.

"If Baldur Forest is so dangerous, why travel through it?" asked James. "Why not go around?"

This time, when the older man laughed, it was a deep, hearty sound, like warm soup.

"I was raised in the Obsidian Desert, as was Anna." He motioned to her, but she didn't look up. He seemed to think this explained something, but James looked confused. Oren noticed.

"Once you have spent a night in the Obsidian Desert, you will pray for the warmth and comfort of Baldur Forest." The man wrapped his arms around himself, as if he were embracing a lover. "Baldur is like a moody woman – she may test you, but as long as you don't fuel her temper, you have a good chance of walking away alive. The Obsidian is like a scorned lover. She will smile and invite you into her bed, feed you sweet grapes and pleasure you in every way you can imagine. You won't even know she is angry until you walk into the point of her blade."

Some of the men around the fire laughed, including Phoenix. Anna looked up and gave Phoenix a dark look before settling back against a tree stump, bringing her cape up to her chin for warmth. Phoenix didn't seem to notice.

"I spent a summer venturing across the Obsidian Desert," Chadrick said, and a handful of the traders looked surprised. The older man raised an eyebrow.

"I was hunting red elk," Chadrick said. "They migrate to the foothills of the Chantese Mountains during the late summer."

"We know them well. We will be trading their pelts at the festival in Ancasta this autumn," Oren said, impressed.

"So you are a hunter?" The man Evandor had motioned to earlier now spoke.

"I am," Chadrick replied.

"You know, in Fiachra, we consider hunters to be warriors in their own right." The man spoke again, getting to his feet. He looked much bigger standing up, not only in stature, but he was more muscular than most tradesmen had any right to be. When he walked towards the group, Oren got up and offered him his seat. This unsettled James.

"Who are you?" James spoke, looking from the younger man to the older, Oren. Chadrick nudged him, hard, but he ignored him.

"I am Kian, this is my tribe," he replied, gesturing towards the group. Evandor's words, calling Kian Oren's "leader" finally made sense. A thick, woollen shawl was wrapped around Kian's shoulders. The wool was dyed a bright red.

"Aren't you too young to be leading a tribe?" James said.

"You don't believe me?" Kian chuckled. "Ask Anna." He turned his head to face her, and James saw Anna's eyes go wide. "You remember me, don't you?"

"Who are you?" James asked again, turning from Kian to Anna.

"I'm the one who sold her father," Kian replied casually, as if he were remarking on the weather.

For a moment, no one spoke and then Evandor got to his feet, walked up to Kian and slapped him hard across the face. A fist would have been more effective, but James knew that Evandor was looking to hurt Kian as much as humiliate him and it worked. Kian's head whipped back and he nearly lost his footing, but he righted himself just in time and as he did, he swung at Evandor, hitting him squarely in the jaw. Phoenix jumped to his feet, but Chadrick stepped in between them, his hands outstretched, shaking his head at James who got to his feet, drawing his dagger.

No one noticed when Anna got to her feet, so they nearly missed her as she lunged forward, her cape falling to the ground, not bothering to draw her sword. Chadrick grabbed her just in time and lifted her from the ground to stop her from reaching the other side of the fire, where the traders were now drawing their own weapons. She was tearing at him with her hands, her nails, trying to break through, but he held her back, too easily, as if she were a small child.

James heard Kian laugh. "You are woefully outnumbered. Do you really want a fight?" he asked, but she wasn't listening.

Even as Anna was beating at Chadrick, James noticed the fire that had earlier been used to cook their meal begin to blaze hotter and grow more frantic. "Anna, no!" he shouted, but it was no use. She wasn't looking at anyone but Kian, and when the fire exploded, the young man took the brunt of it. It took a few moments for the dark, woollen wrap he wore to explode into flames. They heard him yelp in pain and then he collapsed to the ground, limp and heavy.

The rest of them were not untouched by the flames and James watched the hem of his tunic catch fire. He put it out quickly, seeing a few of the others do the same.

The fire was out in a matter of seconds, but the smell of burning hair and flesh lingered.

Anna gave a final push and Chadrick let her go. She was staring down at Kian, her face twisted with rage, until the seven men left standing lifted their swords.

"What are you?" Oren asked, his face white. The others looked afraid.

"I am death made flesh!" she screamed savagely, spitting at his feet. She looked too angry to be scared, but James felt it for the both of them.

Kian was breathing heavily at their feet, but he looked like he was in a lot of pain. His skin was raw and bloody. James couldn't tell what was bloody skin and what was muscle peeking through.

"Kill them." Oren seemed to find his voice, but before they could advance Anna spoke. "Take one more step and I'll burn this entire forest to the ground," she said, but there was uncertainty in her voice, and if James could hear it, so could they. He wondered if she was capable of that.

"Kill them." Oren had obviously decided she wasn't, and the men began to advance.

James's fingers squeezed the hilt of his dagger and his mouth went dry. Eight men advanced, all warriors with thick arms and hands that were large and hard with experience. He was sure he might be able to kill one, and perhaps Phoenix and Chadrick could kill two each, if they were very fast, but even then they'd still be outnumbered.

He saw the fire grow again, but the men did not shy from it. One of them raised his sword.

"Wait." Chadrick threw his arms up and they stopped, watching him. "I will save him."

The men looked from Chadrick to Oren and back again. Oren turned his head, as if considering for a moment.

"We have healers in Fiachra. You might just kill him anyway," he said.

"You know he will never make it to Fiachra," replied Chadrick. "I will save him. Here. Now."

"How is that possible?" the man asked, furrowing his brow.

"That is not part of the bargain," Chadrick said.

"We are striking a bargain?" the man asked.

"Yes," Chadrick said, "I will save him, and you will let us go."

The man thought for a moment. "Save him and we will ask him," Oren said.

"No," Chadrick replied, "I am striking this deal with you, not him."

The man snorted, but it was clear that Kian was dying. His breathing was growing shallow and there was a sick gargling sound coming from his chest that might be blood filling his lungs.

Oren's eyes were flitting over Kian, as if he were calculating some macabre sum in his head. Then he spoke. "Do it," he said.

Chadrick wasted no time. He kneeled down next to Kian and placed two hands on his chest, gently, but the young man moaned deeply.

Nothing happened for a few moments, and then James felt something shift in the air. The same feeling that might wash over a person when they step into a dark room, only to hear something breathing, softly, in the abyss. It raised the hairs on his arms.

He heard cries from the men standing across from them, and one stumbled as he took a step back in surprise. Evandor had an odd look on his face, as if he were trying to see something hidden in a shadow.

"It's working," James heard Phoenix say, and when he

looked down at Kian, his skin was a healthy pink and he was breathing deeply, sound asleep.

A few moments later, Chadrick lifted his hands from the man. James noticed Chadrick's hands were shaking.

"He will sleep for a couple of days. Make sure that you give him water. And when he wakes, he will remember little of what happened," Chadrick said.

The old man motioned to another to come forward and lift their leader, albeit hesitantly. They kept their eyes on Chadrick the entire time.

When Kian was safely among their ranks, Chadrick spoke again. "There is something else I want."

Oren looked up, angrily, but he was tired and James could see the years on his face. "I will give you your lives, and that is all," he replied.

"You will give me what I ask." Chadrick's voice was soft, dangerous. The men were afraid and Chadrick knew it. "We are searching for the ones that lead the Inkuanu to Dasdaya. They destroyed a village," he said.

Oren was quiet for a long time. He seemed to be considering his options. When he spoke, there was irritation in his voice, as if he didn't want to give up the information but didn't feel he had a choice. "They are here," he said. "We met them on this road about two days ago."

"What are they doing here?" asked Chadrick, but the old man quickly shook his head.

"I am surprised you do not know," Oren said, disgust leaking into his voice. "You could be brothers. They follow death like flies on a rotting corpse."

Chadrick's expression didn't change. "That is less than helpful," he said.

"They are searching…" Oren explained, "…searching out the monster lovers."

Chadrick looked confused.

"The Effluvium." Anna spoke. She was sitting on the ground, with her knees crossed in front of her. She didn't look at them.

"They had two girls with them." The man spoke again, this time his eyes moved over to Anna.

"Why were they…" Chadrick stopped midsentence and then his hands went stiff at his sides as he realised who they were speaking about.

"So the Death Chasers are recruiting girls to become effluvium now?" Phoenix said, shaking his head in disgust.

"It would seem that way," Chadrick replied before turning back to Oren. "Where were they headed?"

"Grove Hill," the old man responded. "Now if it pleases you…" he paused for a moment, making it clear the last thing he wanted to do was please Chadrick, "we will be on our way."

As he spoke, he motioned to the travellers to begin packing their things. One of the younger men with broad, dark shoulders lifted Kian as if he were carrying a bride, in both arms, close to his body. Kian stirred, making a small sound, but he didn't wake. Within minutes, the men were heading off into the trees. Anna watched them leave, her anger shimmering on the surface of her face.

"We'll never get to those girls in time," said Anna.

"We can try," Chadrick replied.

"I need someone to tell me what is going on," James said, looking between Chadrick and Anna.

"A group of young men and women calling themselves Death Chasers are seemingly selling young girls to the ghouls of Morvoren." Chadrick explained simply.

"Yes, that I know – but what are the Death Chasers?" James asked.

"They chase monsters – for thrills." explained Phoenix.

"So they are like us?" asked James. Anna looked disgusted. "I mean…" James tried to explain and but then fell silent.

Phoenix shook his head, "they are not like us at all."

"They are little more than monsters themselves." Spat Anna.

The five fell quiet for a moment. There was a light wind that caused the fire to flicker, and James felt the hairs on his arms rise. It was difficult to see beyond the firelight, but the moment their voices fell, he could hear the rustling in the treeline beyond their camp. Things moved and breathed that they would not be able to see. Things that hid just beyond the light.

"If we leave tonight, we might be able to catch up to them," said Anna, but her words were directed at Chadrick.

He shook his head. "We do not move beyond this fire tonight," he said as he threw more wood into the flames and stoked the embers with a large stick. James noticed that when he moved, it was slow, lumbering.

Anna pursed her lips at this but stayed quiet. Eventually, she lay down and closed her eyes. Chadrick did not waste time with pleasantries. He rolled out his sleeping bag, put his hands beneath his head and fell asleep. James noticed Evandor watching him. James decided to do the same, and it wasn't long before he heard the rest of them make for their own sleeping spaces. Before long, the only noise he could hear was Phoenix snoring in his sleep.

*

James heard the voice calling to him before his eyes opened. It was Anna.

"James, come quick, I want to show you something," she said.

James heard a desperation in her voice that quickened his heart. He sat up, reached out to grab his sword and head for the treeline, in the direction of her voice, when he saw Chadrick motion to him, his finger on his lips. His eyes were wide and urgent. James searched their campsite and his eyes fell on Anna. She was still nestled in her cloak, lying between Evandor and Phoenix, fast asleep.

"James, come quick, please." Her voice broke through the treeline again, even though Anna was silent. Then she giggled.

"What is that?" mouthed James silently.

Something moved out in the forest. Then he heard it laugh.

"It is a skin walker. It taunts you," said Chadrick. "Go back to sleep, but stay close to the fire." Chadrick settled back into his own sleeping quarters, but he didn't lie down. He was carving something out of a small piece of wood. His hunting knife whittled the wood quickly and his fingers moved with a familiarity that came with practise.

James lay back down and tried to get some sleep, but the voice did not rest. It called to James until the sun rose, laughing when it didn't get a response and then growing more urgent. The others did not wake, and James could not tell if they couldn't hear it or if it wasn't loud enough to wake them. When the sun filtered down through the trees, the calling stopped and James fell into a deep, though brief, sleep.

*

"If this was not Baldur, I would not have stopped you from taking your revenge, Anna." James woke to the sound of Chadrick's voice, low and sincere. "But there were too many of them, and too few of us. You are mine to protect in this forest and I could not be certain that I would not lose you."

Anna said something that James could not hear, but her voice was not as angry as he expected it to be this morning.

"One day, if it pleases you, I'll help you track Kian and I will help you kill him." James opened his eyes and saw Anna nod at Chadrick, but she said nothing. He yawned, loudly, to ensure that they knew he was waking. Anna moved over to the fire, throwing sand onto the remaining embers while Chadrick went to wake Phoenix and Evandor. After they had eaten, they set off once more. This time, the trees began to thin. James knew this meant they were finally leaving Baldur Forest.

FOURTEEN

THREE WITCHES AND A KING

A young woman was sitting outside of a cottage as they broke through the treeline and appeared at the edge of a valley. She was stitching something that could be a sock or a scarf, James couldn't tell which. Her hands worked quickly, but her eyes were focused on the five companions that emerged from the forest. Her face was black with smoke and dirt, and her light brown hair was shiny with oil. She smiled at them as they approached and the first thing James noticed were her eyes – one bright blue, the other a deep green. *Just like Lacey's*, he thought.

"They said that you would come," she said, barely looking up.

"We are looking for two women – they were being taken here by others… we're not sure how many. Have you seen them?" Anna called to her, ignoring the woman's strange welcome.

The young woman with the strange eyes tilted her head, as if listening for something. "They say you are searching in the wrong place." She spoke again, but she wasn't looking at any of the five companions. Instead, she was looking upwards, once again trying to listen to something. "They are afraid of him." She brought her hand up to her lips, as if contemplating something. "Now, why would they be afraid of him?"

"Who are *they?*" asked James, seeing Anna roll her eyes. He could tell what she was thinking. She was thinking that this young woman was mad.

"The witches," she said matter-of-factly, tapping at her own head, "in here."

"I'm sorry… did you say witches?" asked Anna.

"Let's move on," he heard Phoenix say. "I think I see smoke up ahead – there's bound to be someone living nearby that can help us."

"They won't be able to tell you where those young girls went." The young women spoke, and this time, her eyes were clear. James was having trouble taking his eyes off the green one. It was the same colour of an old emerald brooch his uncle used to own. He shook his head, bringing himself back to the moment. The girl was speaking quickly now. It was as if the madness had left her. "I am not crazy," she protested, tapping her head again. "Not all the time, at least. I just listen to what they tell me."

"You know who has taken the young girls?" asked Chadrick. "Where are they?"

"Sometimes they make an awful lot of noise," the young woman said without answering him, tilting her head again, listening.

"Did you say witches, earlier on?" asked James, still trying to catch up.

She smiled at him. "*Three* witches," she replied in a conspiratorial tone.

"And they speak to you?" James asked again, intrigued.

She shook her head. "They don't speak to me – they speak to each other," she replied. "I just listen to what they say."

"What are they saying now?" asked Evandor. His voice was gentle. He was smiling kindly at the young woman.

When she returned his smile, her soot-laden cheeks glowed a bright red. "They are speaking very fast. The *always* speak so fast." She rolled her eyes then tilted her head, listening. "I usually don't catch all of it, but they know where your girls have gone. They were taken up that road, about three days ago," she pointed to the east, "to a manor house on Grove Hill. It appears after the hedges become briar and bramble. They say they were taken through a red door, down into the darkness. They say the girls won't be coming back."

"These girls were sold to become Effluvium by a group of men – do they know how many there were?" asked Chadrick, as if she were speaking to someone beside her, not listening to voices inside of her head.

The girl stopped listening to the voices in her head and looked at Chadrick, taking him in for a moment. "They aren't really sure what to make of you." She frowned, confused. "They say you have a shadow around you. It's keeping you hidden."

A dark look came over Chadrick's face.

"There were seven of them. The ones with the tattoos on their ankles. Five men, two women. That's not counting the two *other* women they had with them. You know, the ones they were selling to the…" She didn't finish her sentence, but she made a biting motion and growled at the same time.

"These witches, they don't talk to you?" asked James, intrigued.

The young woman laughed. Anna gave James a dark look and Chadrick cleared his throat, as if indicating that James shouldn't pull at that particular thread. James wondered how much pulling it would take before the girl came undone.

"No, I told you, they only talk to each other," she replied, sounding frustrated.

"Do they live inside your head?" he asked, ignoring Anna's huffing.

"I don't think so," she said.

"Do they know you're listening? Can they hear you? Can they see us?" asked James, stopping himself as he realised he was interrogating her.

"I'm not sure. I've never thought about it." She stopped to think for a moment. "I don't think so."

James nodded, giving up, unsure he would ever really understand.

The young woman giggled. "They say you're a king." She shook her head. "I don't see a crown. Are you really?"

"They think I'm a king?" James asked, turning to the others, but they all looked as confused as he was.

"Sometimes they lie," she said, looking deflated.

"We don't have a lot of time." Anna spoke up, and she started to move towards the road that would lead to Grove Hill.

"Thank you for your help," said James, and he began to follow the others.

"You'll come back, won't you? When you've found him?" she called after them.

James stopped, turning back. "When we've found who?"

"The fool, silly." She laughed again. "He's been looking for you, but they think you will find him first." James froze and saw the others do the same. "He's hiding with the Upipita. They aren't sleeping anymore." Something about that name, *Upipita*, lingered with James, like a dark echo. When he looked back at the young girl, her face had gone white and her eyes were wide with fear.

"What do you know about the fool?" asked Anna immediately, taking a step towards the girl, but this only frightened her more. She got to her feet quickly, dropping her sock and needle into the dust.

"They sound angry. I'm not sure I should have told you that." She started to move towards her cottage.

"Wait—"

"No, no, no, I shouldn't have said that," she shouted back.

"I thought you said they couldn't hear you," James called back.

Just before the girl slipped through her doorway and slammed the door shut, she shouted, "Maybe I've never said anything worth listening to before!"

*

"She mentioned the fool. She knew we are looking for him," Anna said as they wound their way through the village.

"That doesn't prove he's on the loose, Anna," Phoenix argued back.

The dirt road quickly became a stone road, paved long ago and then forgotten. The sun was high in the sky and James could feel the back of his neck grow hot. Only Chadrick and Anna, with their olive skin, did not look as though they were burning in the August sun.

"It proves something, I just can't figure out what that is," she said.

They walked, two by two, until stone walls began to spring up around them, forming a maze that led them into the heart of the village. The walls were washed in lime and the sunlight reflected on their bright white surfaces, making James squint.

It was only when the walls began to grow dark with dirt and neglect that he realised they must be approaching Grove Hill. The deep, green hedges had indeed become overgrown with weeds and thorns – the girl had called it briar and bramble

– and then suddenly, the house was in front of them and it didn't look the same as James had pictured it. James had been picturing a dark, abandoned building of some description, but Grove Hill was not an abandoned building, at least not in the traditional sense, nor was it dark. Grove Hill was a manor house with large, stone pillars welcoming them, inviting them in.

Chadrick approached the front door, slowly, then he reached for the large brass knocker and beat it against the dark wood. They waited, but nothing happened. It was quiet. When no one answered, he pushed hard against it and found it open. It swung inwards, groaning, before permitting them entry.

The foyer was brightly lit, with white stone floors and high ceilings. The walls were lined with pictures in heavy wooden frames. On each one was painted a scene of uncensored revelry. In some, naked, nubile young women were wrapped around the limbs of lovers who were painted with shadow, disguising the expressions on their faces. Others were portraits of far-off places.

Down the stairs, through the red door, the young women had said. The five companions turned towards an ornate staircase that appeared to lure them away from the upper well-lit parts of the manor and down into the secretive heart of the building. There was no need to light a torch to find their way down – it was lit by something that shed light below. Something they could not yet see.

Chadrick led the way this time, followed by James, then Anna, Evandor and Phoenix. Phoenix could not stop looking over his shoulder, as if he expected someone to appear behind them. The staircase wound in such a way that it was difficult for them to see directly below. It arched so that only small sections of the floor below was revealed to them as they made their way down. It was as if the staircase was presenting the room to them, like a host.

As they descended, James could see that the room below was large enough to accommodate a ballroom, and it appeared elegant enough to carry the name. Heavy crystal chandeliers hung from the wooden beams that supported the roof, or the floor above, and they glinted with light from below. This gave them the appearance of stars, sparkling against a black night.

"Ready your weapons," he heard Chadrick say, and those words drew James out of his reverie. That was when he realised that something was wrong. Something didn't smell quite right. As if all at once, his eyes adjusted to the light and he looked down, taking in the room below him, all of which he could now see.

FIFTEEN

THE GHOULS OF DASDAYA

It was as though someone had left a bag of meat cuts in the sun. James knew that feeling well. Years ago, he had left a package from the butchers outside on the steps of their cottage. He had found it hours later and, realising the meat had spoiled, he had hidden it beneath his bed. It had taken a few days for the smell to begin wafting through the house and James had received a lashing for it after it had bene found by his uncle. He could still remember watching his uncle open the package to reveal hundreds of maggots bursting from inside. The scene before below them was very similar.

The dark, dank room looked like it had long been forgotten, allowing everything within it to rot. The bodies on the floor wriggled and undulated, careless of what was beneath them, pushing, scratching and biting through living and dead flesh combined.

James could see women moving within what he knew was a tight ball of rotting corpses.

"These are the Effluvium?" he asked, not taking his eyes off the mass, but he didn't have to ask. Not really.

"Yes," answered Anna in a low voice, almost a whisper.

All five of them had come to stand at the bottom of the staircase, unable to take their eyes off the ghouls until Chadrick spoke. "We are Uringi. Is anyone here able to speak for herself?" he asked.

A woman cried out, but it was a moan of pleasure, not pain. James winced at the sound. He saw a ghoul tear at the flesh of a young woman who looked a lot like Anna, but instead of screaming, the woman threw herself on the creature, the sleeve of her dress coming down to expose her breast. A few seconds later, she was lost in the gory heap.

A flicker of light drew James's eyes to the left corner of the room where there was a makeshift sleeping area laid out, with large pillows scattered about to protect against the cold, hard stone that made up the room. On the pillows lay a woman the same age as James. She was wearing a light summer dress and her hair was still pinned up. The light came from the diamond necklace she wore that sparkled beneath a glint of sunlight.

The others had seen the light shimmer too because they all turned to watch the women, who was completely unaware that they were there.

"She looks well bred," said Phoenix.

"Probably a runaway." Anna spoke. There was no pity in her voice. "Didn't want to marry a rich lord and went looking for love in all the wrong places."

James frowned at Anna.

A few feet from the women lay a ghoul. In life it must have been a tall, handsome man. It had long hair that fell over its face and sharp, well-defined cheekbones. In life these features would have given the man an irresistible charm. In death, he was gaunt and sorrowful, his skin stretched too thinly over his bony face.

"I can't sleep." The creature shifted uncomfortably, raising its head with visible effort. James could see the white of its spine peek through the skin at the base of its head as it tried to sniff her out.

"I know, my love." Her voice was tired, strained. The creature's hand was sweeping across the filthy, overstuffed pillows, searching for her. It found the white of her leg and dug its claws into her, drawing a sound that was both pain and pleasure from her. It started wriggling towards her again, like a maggot searching out a piece of rotting meat. James resisted the urge to cover the last few feet between them and throw it off her.

He heard a cooing sound to his left and turned to see one of the creatures wriggling towards Anna. Bloody gums were visible through its rotting face. It reached her, its hand sweeping up her thigh. Anna removed her sword from its hilt, placed it at the base of the creature's neck and pushed downwards, severing its head from its body. The ghoul went limp and those surrounding it began to wriggle away, like maggots from the heel of a boot.

James turned his attention back to the woman and her dead lover. It had crawled into her lap and was chewing at her breast, drawing blood, like a macabre infant. She stroked its head, hair and scalp coming away in her hand.

"How do we know which of these are the girls the traders were talking about?" asked Phoenix. "None of them look as if they were just sold."

"Look at their eyes," said Evandor. "The newer ones will have clear eyes. They only begin to cloud over after a few months in the den."

They five searched the room, but it was difficult to see with the bodies constantly moving.

"There." Chadrick pointed. "The red dress."

They followed his hand and found the girl that he had spotted.

"You're right. Her eyes – they are bright green," said Anna.

"So who is going to wade in and get her?" asked Phoenix, his lips a tight, white line. James thought he looked as though he were about to be sick.

"I will," said Evandor, and he began to move forward, but Anna stopped him.

"These are creatures of death, Evan. They'll fear fire more than water," she said.

Evandor looked unsure for a moment and then nodded in agreement, taking a step back.

"I'm coming with you," Chadrick insisted, but he did not draw his sword. Instead, he placed both hands on the ground, the way he did when he had moved the earth for James, and this time, it was not the earth that moved but the creatures. They began to writhe and undulate like the ocean in a storm.

James hissed as something touched him. It wasn't human hands, or even the hands of a ghoul. It was Chadrick's power, and it felt as though it pulled at a thread inside James's gut. As if a tendon he didn't have was waking, flexing. Then it was gone.

"That is a strange power to have," Evandor whispered, "even for someone from Morvoren."

No one had noticed James's reaction and Chadrick did not respond to Evandor's comment. He offered Anna his hand and they began to wade in. As they made their way into the throng of pulsating bodies, the ghouls parted for them. Those that were too slow felt the touch of Anna's fire, but it was not enough to set them alight or the entire manor would quickly burn to the ground.

Even with Chadrick and Anna's powers combined, it took them a while to reach the girl in the red dress, but they made it without being bitten. When they got to her, she was wrapped within the limbs of a short, petite female cadaver with dark hair and amber lips. The amber lips would have beautiful once, when the girl was alive and the lips were not coloured with blood. As they approached, the woman in the red dress smiled at them.

"Put your weapon away," she said, closing her eyes as her lover bit down against her inner thigh. "There are no victims here." She looked to be around twenty years old, with light, curly hair that would have reached down to her hips, had she been standing. Now, that hair was spread beneath her like a silken blanket.

"It does not look that way from up here," said Chadrick.

The women laughed, and it was a light sound, like bells in the wind. "Then come and join us down here."

Chadrick recoiled at this.

"Something eats at all of us," she spoke again, "but not everyone derives pleasure from their parasites."

"You are intelligent." Chadrick sounded surprised.

The girl laughed again. "You were expecting a dimwit?" she asked, closing her eyes and stroking her lover's hair.

"Yes," replied Anna.

The girl looked up sharply, studying Anna. "There is anger in your voice?" she questioned.

"I think you're confusing anger with disgust," replied Anna.

The girl nodded her head, as if in understanding. "You don't approve," she said, smiling again, but this time in pleasure at her lover's sharp touch.

"We're looking for the men who sold you to these creatures." Chadrick broke in, watching Anna's anger grow.

This time, when the girl laughed, it was cold. "Sold?" she asked. "I was not sold. I came here willingly, just like all the others."

This time it was Anna who laughed. "If this is the life you chose, I feel sorry for you."

"There is no need to feel sorry for me," the girl said sharply. "I will experience more pleasure in a week than you do in your entire life, even if mine is cut short."

"So you admit that this is killing you?" asked Anna, disgusted.

"We are all dying," she retorted, "or are you going to live forever?"

"I—" Anna wanted to say something, but Chadrick stopped her.

"I think we are getting side-tracked, Anna. We came for the Death Chasers, not to redeem these women," he said.

When Anna didn't protest, he continued, "We were told there were two of you."

"There were," she replied, and pointed to her left. James turned and saw who she was pointing at – a young woman with dark hair and olive skin. She was wearing a light blue dress, or at least it used to be light. She was moaning, throwing her head back as three creatures bit down on her. The young woman in front of Anna giggled, like a schoolgirl seeing someone's first kiss. "She's not going to last long, but god, what a way to go. It warms the blood just thinking about it." She ran a finger over a nipple that had stiffened under her dress. Anna turned her head, looking away. The woman smiled, sensing her discomfort.

"We are looking for the men who brought you here." Chadrick held her gaze. "Did they mention where they were headed when you were with their party?"

"They did," the girl said, turning over to face him. The petite ghoul screeched at her movement, like a baby whose milk is being taken away. It nestled into the women, biting down on her buttocks, and then it was quiet.

"Are you going to tell us?" asked Anna, irritated.

"I'll tell you," she replied languidly, "if you do something for me."

"What do you want?" asked Anna.

The laughter came again, tiny bells in the wind. "You can let my lover taste you," she said.

This time, James could feel the heat prickle around him, like thousands of fingers brushing lightly against his skin. He saw Evandor reach for the nape of his neck and realised they must have felt it too.

Anna's cheeks reddened. "No," she said. There was a warning there.

"Then you can leave here and try to find them on your own. But remember, they are like the wind. They hide from Death himself. What makes you think you will be able to catch them?" the girl responded, and she turned over, away from them, to focus on her lover.

A few moments passed and Chadrick put his hand on Anna's shoulder. "Let's leave here," he said. He made to turn back, but Anna did not move with him. She didn't move at all.

"I'll do it," Anna said. Hers hands were tight balls at her sides.

The girl looked back, surprised. She smiled.

"Don't do this," Chadrick said, but Anna pulled away from him, keeping her eyes on the young woman.

"If I do it, you'll tell us where to find them? The Death Chasers?" she asked. The young woman nodded her head, suddenly intrigued. "If you're lying," said Anna, "I'll come back and burn this whole house to the ground."

"I believe you," came the reply. The young woman reached out to Anna, inviting her to take her hand. Anna took it and was led to the pillows, where she lay down.

"Anna, please," Chadrick pleaded, "you don't have to do this."

"Yes, I do," she said. "They are the reason Balhatchett was nearly destroyed. They are the reason those children died. If I do this, we can stop them." As she spoke, the young woman began to unlace her tunic.

Anna slapped at her hand. "I get to choose where," Anna said, staring at the ghoul who had stopped chewing on the young woman and was now watching them both, as if it knew something new and exciting was happening. James looked at the ghoul more closely now. It wasn't as rotted away as many of the others, but it was decomposing nonetheless. It had dark hair that was only starting to become patchy, and its face drooped with the lack of life. Its eyes were a milky white, just like many of the willing participants within this manor.

Anna offered it an arm, turning her head to look at Chadrick. He had taken a step closer and offered her his hand. She took it.

"There's no need for such dramatics," said the young woman, who moved to caress Anna's hair while she beckoned her dead lover closer. "You might even find that you like it." The woman's dress fell from one shoulder, exposing her breast. She ran a finger down the side of her breast, closing her eyes, enjoying the caress of her own touch.

Anna did not respond. The ghoul moved in closer, cradling her.

"It smells of death." Anna's face wrinkled in disgust. The ghoul began nuzzling at Anna, looking for purchase. When it found Anna's arm, it bit down and Anna screamed.

"Stop!" shouted Chadrick.

"No!" Anna shouted back at him. "Let it finish."

Chadrick's face looked pained as he watched Anna writhe under the creature that drew blood as it bit down. His fists were clenched at his sides and the same electric prickling ran down James skin, like a whisper in the dark. The ghouls felt it too and began to stir. The floor came alive with their writhing, wriggling. *A bag of meat in the sun,* thought James.

"Enough." Anna's voice was strained. The creature's jaw kept moving, taking in her blood and flesh. "Stop," Anna said again. Still it bit down.

"Enough!" Chadrick commanded, stepping forward and pulling the creature off her in one swift movement. It hissed at Chadrick as it landed on its knees, and like a dog, it bore its yellowed teeth, or what was left of them, before once again searching out its lover.

The young woman reached out and brought the creature to her lips, and it bit down, taking in her flesh and her moan.

Chadrick helped Anna to her feet, gently. "I will take care of the wound as soon as we are free of this place." He drew her close in an embrace.

When he released her, Anna turned to the young woman. "Tell us where they are."

The young woman drew back from her lover, her lips bloodied and raw.

"A promise is a promise," she said. "They have returned to Dasdaya. To the heart of the great city. They have been tracking their prey, and they believe that is where he is hiding."

"Their prey?" asked Anna.

The woman smiled, but this time it was laced with fear. "They track a demon, and where would a demon hide but in the heart of Dasdaya itself?" she replied.

"Where in Dasdaya have they gone?" asked Anna.

"Underground," the woman replied, sighing into her lover's hair.

"The catacombs?" asked James, and the companions turned to him.

"You know of them?" asked Evandor.

James nodded. "I have, but the catacombs run throughout most of the city. We'll never find them in there. We'll get lost trying."

"Then we'll have to find someone to guide us," said Chadrick.

"You said they are tracking a demon – did they say what kind?" asked Evandor.

This time, there was something else in the woman's eyes – a hint of fear. "Adaïr," she said. "A demon of the dead."

The five companions were silent for a moment and James waited for an explanation, but she said nothing.

Then Anna whispered, "It's the fool."

"Anna, please—" Phoenix started.

"What else could it be, Phoenix?" asked Anna.

"A thousand other things," replied Phoenix. "The fool doesn't exist. He can't exist."

"He exists," said Chadrick.

They turned to look at him.

"What do you mean, he exists?" asked James.

"I have seen him," replied Chadrick, turning to James, "and so have you."

Memories of cold hands burning into his flesh flashed like picture cards in James's head.

"How could you—" James started.

"You liked it, didn't you?" the young woman interrupted, watching Anna as she threaded her lover's hair between her fingers. All thoughts of the Adaïr were gone. The five companions turned to her.

Anna's face went pale. She was standing close to Chadrick, closer than she usually would. It looked as though he were shielding her.

"I can tell," she said again, "by the way you screamed. I've heard those screams. You can hear them now – they aren't screams of pain. You want more, I can see it. *She can smell it.*" It was clear she was referring to her dead lover. "Come here," she was patting the space next to her, "and give her another taste."

"You heard wrong." Anna was angry, but there was uncertainty in her voice. It worried James.

"You are lying," the young woman said. "She can make you moan. She can please you in ways that he can't." She raised her eyebrows at Chadrick. Chadrick frowned.

"That's enough," warned Anna again, but the young woman did not listen.

"Once they taste you, you always come back. Why do you think I'm here? Why do you think we are all here? One taste is never enough. One day, you'll come crawling back, begging them to take your flesh. And what divine flesh it is."

James did not even see Anna pull her sword, but a moment later, it pierced the neck of the young woman's dead lover, and its head fell from its body like a lump of meat.

The young woman screamed, first tearing herself away from the creature and then, after realising what had happened, throwing herself onto its limp body.

"What have you done?!" she screamed, pulling at her hair. "How could you?" She was sobbing into her lover's chest, pulling at its tattered clothing, shaking it, as if to wake it up. But it did not wake. It did not move. It was finally dead to the world. Really dead.

"We need to leave," Chadrick said, pulling at Anna, who was staring down at the body, her face resolute.

Anna finally turned to go, all the while hearing the woman cry for her dead lover like she would have her first love.

"That wasn't necessary, Anna." Evandor spoke softly, chiding her.

They continued to hear the woman's cries until they stepped foot outside and closed the door to the manor. It was then that Anna turned to Chadrick and began to weep softly into his chest. Chadrick held her against him, his eyes closed, his hand wrapped around her wound. When he moved his hand again, her arm was healed.

When Anna's sobs finally quietened, they gave her a few minutes to collect herself before they moved off again, down the stone road, over the threshold, and past the briar and bramble. They passed the young girl's cottage, but she was nowhere to be seen. It was quiet and her shutters were drawn. James wondered if she was inside, watching them pass by her cottage.

"This will be our last night in Baldur," said Chadrick, "but don't let that comfort you. We'll take turns keeping watch, just as always, and we must keep the fire burning all night."

The others nodded in agreement, each setting up their own sleeping quarters. Once they were settled, James focused his attention on practising delving into the earth. James had been thinking of what had happened in the den since they left. His thoughts weren't drawn to the ghouls but to the power it had awoken and the way it felt when it had reached out to James. It had inspired him to keep practising, and he felt on the cusp of… *something*. Of what, he wasn't sure. As soon as he began to focus his thoughts, it felt as if his powers began to pool, but just like water in a cupped hand, it drained so quickly that he couldn't actually do anything more than watch it drain away. It was becoming easier and easier to enter the ground, to explore its depths, but he couldn't find a way to move the earth.

"It will take time, James. Be patient." Chadrick had seen him grow more and more frustrated, but James didn't feel he had time.

"I felt something…" James began to explain, and Chadrick raised his head, "in the den. I think I felt your power." This time, James looked at Chadrick, and the hunter nodded.

"That is a good sign," Chadrick said, confirming what James had been thinking.

"I can't seem to get any further than that," James explained, frustration building around the edges of his voice. "It's like I'm trying to see in the dark. It's difficult to explain."

James noticed Evandor frowning at him but he didn't say anything.

"Keep practising," Chadrick encouraged him. "You'll find your way."

For some reason, James didn't feel inspired, but he continued to practise, at least until dinner was ready. It was Phoenix and Evandor who went hunting for their meal, and they came back with two bright blue eggs and a small duck-like creature that hung limp over Phoenix's shoulder.

Unbeknownst to James, Phoenix turned out to be an avid cook, and he prepared them a meal of fowl with the eggs roasted inside of the creature. When he carved the bird with his hunting knife, the bright yellow yoke crumbled from down the red meat. It was the best thing James had tasted since leaving Migdasha.

After dinner, James pulled out his water pouch and washed his hands and mouth, then settled back on down to practise again while Phoenix and Evandor distracted themselves with a game.

Anna had not said anything since they had left Grove Hill manor. She was sitting beside the fire, warming her hands.

Chadrick sat beside her. "How has your wound healed?" he asked. "May I have a look at it?"

Anna lifted her arm and pulled back her sleeve. "The wound has healed and the mark has faded completely, thanks to you," she said.

Chadrick ran a finger down her arm before gently pulling her sleeve back down into place. "We have not spoken of the mark you carry on the back of your neck, Anna." His voice was gentle. Her hand went to the back of her neck, as if reminding herself of the feel of the mark.

"I can remove it for you, if you'd like," Chadrick said.

A few moments passed before Anna turned to him. James was surprised by what she said next. "I am not ashamed of my price, Chadrick. I am not ashamed of who I am. Are you?" she asked.

Chadrick recoiled in surprise. "Of course not, Anna. I would never..." he started to say, but Anna held up her hand.

"Don't." she said.

He looked as if he was going to protest, but then fell silent.

That night, they ate in silence, each turning the memories of the day's events over in their minds.

Anna was the first to go to sleep, wrapped up in her cloak. Chadrick stayed close to her.

James took a seat next to Evandor and Phoenix, and Chadrick came to join them.

The fire was burning bright, lighting their circle and a few feet beyond, but after that, it became too dark to see. No light filtered down through the trees, and it gave the night a weight that sat against James's chest.

They sat in silence for a few moments before Evandor turned to Chadrick. "You brought up Anna's price. That wasn't wise." His voice was brushed with sympathy, but it also had a hint of rebuke.

"I did not want her to be constantly reminded of that evil man," Chadrick replied, referring to Anna's father.

"Kian?" asked Evandor.

"Her father," replied Chadrick.

"Anna doesn't believe him to be evil." Evandor said.

Chadrick looked up at him with a confused frown on his face. James knew his own face must have had a similar expression reflected on it.

"Anna doesn't believe in evil," Evandor continued.

"What do you mean, she doesn't believe in evil? If she doesn't believe in evil, what does she think we are doing here?" asked James. "Isn't that what we're fighting?"

Evandor shrugged. "I believe that she once thought him to be evil, but that was before she was taken by the traders."

"She believed her father to be evil *before he sold her to the traders?*" asked James, even more confused.

"Yes," replied Evandor. "Anna got her revenge swiftly after she was sold. Civil war had been brewing within her village for some time, and shortly after she was sold, her father was overthrown. A young warrior took his place and her father was sold to eastern traders. That warrior was Kian, the man we met in Baldur."

"Bastard got what he deserved then," James spat.

Evandor looked around, making sure that Anna was still asleep, then shook his head. "It was years before she saw him again, and when she did, she no longer recognised him. When they met again, they were both slaves. He'd been sold by Kian, just as he'd sold Anna. He was thin and sickly, and he smelled of disease. He cried when he saw her, but it was for his lost youth, not his daughter. The tribes had gathered for the autumn trading festival. It takes place every year. Anna knew that he wouldn't last the summer trek across the Obsidian Desert. His feet were swollen and festering with blisters that never had time to heal. He had dark circles under his eyes and he cried often, and openly."

"Serves him right," Phoenix interjected with a disgusted look on his face.

Evandor continued as if he hadn't heard him. "Traders had come from miles around to the city of Lortooth, where Anna was living, to sell their wares. It is one of the largest summer gatherings in Fiachra and just about every sort of trader spends at least a couple of weeks there, making connections and discussing possible new trade routes through the county. It is here where Anna found her father, although how she found him among the thousands of slaves is still an incredible feat. She believes something in him had called to her.

"The first night, she slipped out of her camp. She had seen him from a distance, but she wanted to see him up close. If she had been caught outside the borders of her camp, she might have been killed, but vengeance made her brave. She wanted to see him suffer.

"When she arrived at his camp, she saw that he didn't sleep among the other slaves. He slept with the animals, on a cold, damp piece of earth. The Verlani traders are savages, but even they know the price of a slave, so she was shocked to see him lying in the dirt.

"The first night, she just watched him. That night, like every night after until his death, he cried himself to sleep. She had never seen him cry before, and she took no joy in it. The next night, she went back, but this time, she let him see her and he wept like a child. He begged her for something to eat, anything, but she shook her head, telling her she had nothing. He sat back into the dirt, defeated, and fell silent.

"On the third night, she returned with bread and a clean cloth. She wiped down his wounds and watched him tear into his food. She saw that his skin had become raw because his clothes were constantly wet. She told him to take them off and she lay them beside a fire. She knew that they would only get wet again once he lay down to sleep, but she wanted him to be comfortable, even if it was only for a little while."

"On the fourth night, he told her that he was sorry for what he had done. He had fresh bruises on his face. His once-proud blue eyes were bloodshot and weary. Anna wasn't sure whether he felt sorry for her or for himself, but she placed her hand on his chest as it shook with sobs. That night, he put his head in her lap and fell asleep. When his breathing deepened, she placed a thin blanket over him and she left.

"On the fifth night, she found him lying in the dirt, dead. His camp was empty – they had left and they hadn't even bothered to bury his body. They had beaten him; she could tell by the blood around his mouth and the way his eyes had swollen shut. She could see animal shit smeared across his lips and face, and this was when she cried."

They were all silent now.

"If you have seen her weep on the anniversary of his death, it is difficult to believe that anyone is evil. Her price is not just a reminder that she was sold. Her price is a reminder. It's the only thing she has left of him." Evandor shook his head. "It is a heavy burden she carries. It is not one that will be forgotten by removing a mark on her skin."

Chadrick was staring at his own feet, his hands wrapped around his knees. "I am ashamed that I offered to remove it," he said.

"You did not know," said Evandor.

They listened to the sound of Anna breathing, her chest rising and falling in her sleep.

"We should probably get to sleep. Tomorrow is going to be a long day," Phoenix reminded them. "I'll take the first watch."

SIXTEEN

THE CATACOMBS OF DASDAYA

The early morning brought a chill that forced James to walk with his cloak pulled in tightly against his body for warmth. They were on the outskirts of Dasdaya and it was here that many of the wealthier citizens of the city had built their homes. The closer they got to the heart of the city, the more tightly packed the homes would be. On the outskirts, there was space to build large homes with windows that reached the ceilings and beautiful, sprawling gardens.

It didn't take them long to enter into Dasdaya's heart. James had heard about one of the entrances to the catacombs. It was one of the good things about working in the tavern — you heard about people and places you might not hear about otherwise. It was to this destination that they moved, quickly, without saying much to each other. James felt that so much had passed between them in the past couple of days that they needed time to process everything. Chadrick had been keeping his distance from Anna after learning about her father, and Anna was more sullen than usual.

They had to navigate an embankment in order to reach the catacombs and the moment it was in sight, they saw a young boy of about twelve leaning against a low wall that presumably marked the entrance to the catacombs. The boy was throwing a stone up into the air and catching it again.

It was Chadrick who spoke to the boy first. "We're looking for some bad people," he said to the boy. "It is said they have their home in these tunnels."

The boy thought for a moment. You'll need to give me a bit more than that," the boy said, "The place is home to all sorts." He gestured to the entrance.

"They are Death Chasers," said Evandor, "it is likely that they have…" he paused for a moment, "*things* following them, *hunting* them. It would be difficult for them to keep their location secret."

James saw something like recognition flicker in the boy's eyes. "The ones with the tattoos?" the boy asked.

James frowned, but the others did not look surprised.

"Yes," said Chadrick, "they'll each have a tattoo on their left leg."

"I know who you're speaking about," said the boy. "They're in the big cavern. They burn fires day and night, even though fires are forbidden in the tunnels."

"They are trying to keep the dark away," said Phoenix, scoffing. "That won't last long."

"I can show you the way," said the boy, "but it'll cost you two copper Kilns."

Chadrick put his hand into his pockets, pulled out three gold coins and placed them into the boy's palm.

The boy's eyes went wide and he reached out quickly to grab hold of them. He shoved them into his pocket and scrambled down the stone steps, turning back just as he was about to duck under and into the tunnel.

"Watch your head," he said as he slipped through into the darkness.

Chadrick took the lead, with Phoenix, Anna, James and then Evandor following after.

The moment James passed over the threshold, he was blind. It was not only dark in the tunnel, but the walls were narrow and the ceiling low, which meant that it was stuffy and smelled of damp. It took a few minutes for his eyes to adjust, but even then he could barely see Anna, who was no more than two feet in front of him.

"Stay close," he heard the boy say. "It is very easy to get lost. If you do, you won't find your way out again."

"How are you able to find your way through these tunnels?" asked James. "It's so dark."

"I know how to read the walls." James could hear the boy's smile in his reply. "They are carved with instructions, directions and warnings. We learn to read them with our fingertips. It's really hard, but I'm the youngest ever to do it." He smiled, clearly proud of himself.

James extended his hand until he reached the wall and ran his fingers across it as he moved through the tunnel. He quickly realised that the boy was right – the walls were covered in what felt like carvings, but he couldn't tell where the carvings ended and the stone began.

"That is quite a talent," James said, his voice falling dull against the dirt floor. The boy did not respond. James was hunched over as he made his way through the dark. It was an awkward feeling, trusting that someone else would guide the way when he wasn't able to see anything in front of him.

"Grab the hand of the one in front of you. The tunnel is going to start winding now, so it's going to get trickier to navigate," the boy said.

James reached out and found Anna's hand waiting for him.

He extended his hand to the back so that Evandor could grab hold, which he did. Evandor's hand was damp, but he wasn't sure if that was because the air in the tunnel was growing increasingly warm or because the air had become thick as the walls closed in around them.

He felt Anna moved towards the right, so he followed, guided by her hand.

They moved slowly, but in the dark, their pace still felt reckless and hurried. He could hear Evandor's breathing become laboured.

"Are you alright?" James turned his head back in the direction of his companion.

"I don't…" Evandor hesitated. "I don't like small spaces." Evandor's clammy hands suddenly made sense. "The dark makes it worse."

It was then that something sparked in front of James and landed at his feet. It wasn't a bright spark – more like the sudden appearance of a firefly being dropped at their feet, except it wasn't alive and quickly lost its shine the moment they passed over it. And then there was more – hundreds – of tiny *fireflies* being dropped, like breadcrumbs, at their feet, providing just enough light for James and Evandor to see in front of, and around them.

"Thank you, Anna." Evandor spoke, and James saw Anna turn back and smile.

"You are welcome, Evan," she said.

The light also allowed James to look around, and he noticed that they were not just travelling down a narrow tunnel. They moved through a maze of tunnels, with the boy picking quickly every time they came up to a split in the "road" ahead. James also noticed that the tunnel opened up to deep caverns on either side of them, and more than once he saw eyes shining back at him from deep within them.

Since James could now see better, his senses didn't feel so overwhelmed and his ears picked up on something– a scuttling that seemed to follow them through every twist and turn of the passageways. He wondered if it had been there in the dark. Sometimes it seemed very far from them, and at other times, it was as if it was next to him, staring over his shoulder. He could see nothing when he looked around him and Anna's light only allowed him to see a couple of feet either side of him. James's tunic began to grow wet with the heat.

"Evan," James whispered, turning his head, "do you hear that?"

"You mean, do I hear *it*?" asked Evandor. "And the answer is yes. We seem to have added a seventh member to our group."

"What is it?" asked James softly, not wanting whatever it was to overhear him.

"I don't know," replied Evandor. "but it's not a friend."

"What are you two whispering about?" asked Anna, loud enough that her voice echoed off the walls.

"Something is following us." James leaned in close to whisper in her ear. Anna stiffened.

"Hey!" called out Phoenix, looking back at them. "How come you guys get light and we have to stumble through the dark?"

Anna stopped quickly to avoid bumping into Phoenix. For a moment, a brighter flare let James see to the front of their group where the young boy was looking back at them with a mixture of horror and anger on his face.

"What have you done?" he shouted at them. "How could you have..." His eyes were flitting to each member of the group, confusion brimming to the surface. "You brought no torches, no kindling. How could you possibly have made a fire?" he asked.

"It was me," said Anna, holding up her hands. "Please don't be concerned, I left only enough light for my companions to see by – not enough pose a danger."

The last of the fireflies died out, but just before it went completely dark, James saw the boy shaking his head. "No, you don't understand. It is not fire that we fear in these tunnels. You have led her to us, with your fire." The boy's voice was cold and frightened.

"Who is she?" asked James, wanting to look over his shoulder but realising it was no use.

"Black Annie," the boy whispered. "The hag of the Dasdaya catacombs."

Evandor's hand was suddenly wrenched from James, nearly pulling him over.

"Anna – we need light!" shouted James, and with that, two flames appeared in Anna's hands, lighting the circle around them. James saw a figure crouched over Evandor, who was flat on his back. It looked up at James and he flinched, jumping back, frightened.

It was an old woman with long silver hair and dark eyes, but she was anything but frail. Her mouth was wide and blackened, and her white gown was stained in blood. She hissed at the others and then plunged her teeth into Evandor's chest. He screamed but placed both hands on her shoulders, throwing her back. She hissed, baring sharpened teeth.

Phoenix ran to Evandor while Chadrick drew his sword. James felt something in the air begin to stir. The hag hissed again and then, climbing one of the walls like a spider, she scuttled away into the darkness.

Everything went quiet.

Then Anna spoke, looking around. "Where is our guide?" The rest looked around, trying to see past Anna's light, but they were alone. The young boy who had been guiding them was gone.

"How are we going to find our way out of here?" asked James, suddenly aware of how narrow the tunnels were.

James heard something hiss to his left and before he had time to draw his weapon, two blackened hands were grabbing at him, tearing into his skin. It pulled him into the dark, wrapping itself around him.

"James!" he heard Anna scream as he fell into a cavern, hitting his head against a stone wall. A sheet of pain and light wrapped itself around him, and he felt his mouth go dry.

"Where are you?" he heard Anna shout again, and his thoughts shifted into focus. He felt two hands wrapped around his neck and a pair of lips on his own, drawing his breath. He could taste something foul in his mouth.

His hands reached out to push back at the hag, but it was as if she were made of stone. He realised he did not have much strength left, and he could not call for help.

"Anna, we need more light!" he heard Phoenix shout.

"I can't risk a bigger fire!" she shouted back. "If it spreads, we will all die in these tunnels."

"James – where are you?" he heard Chadrick call out.

He could hear the sounds of their footsteps. They passed near him, but he was struggling to move. The hag was too heavy and his head ached with every breath.

He felt himself begin to slip into a dream. It felt like dipping his head in and out of a pool of water. For a few seconds, he would go under, and then he would wake and it was as if a crowd were shouting in his ears. He realised it was his heartbeat. It was slowing.

"He is not here," he heard Anna say as he emerged from the water. "She must have taken him somewhere."

James felt the hands tighten around his neck. It was then that he realised the creature had been limiting his air supply – but not enough to kill him, just enough to cause him to lose consciousness. But as her fingers tightened, he knew that had changed. It was done playing with him. He was standing next to a pool of water, about to dive in, and this time, he would not resurface. Desperate, he tried to draw on his powers, trying to ignore his heartbeat as it began to thump loudly in his chest, slower and slower, desperate for oxygen. He felt a trickle of power delve into the ground, as Chadrick had taught him, but then it was gone. He tried again, frantically trying to gather up his power, but it was like stoking a dying flame.

He could feel the heat of her hands against his neck. It was so warm in these tunnels.

He tried one more time and this time, when his power sank into the ground, like water pooling in loamy soil, he began to feel vibrations of something else.

Just before his feet left the ground – just before he dived into the icy cool water – he felt something enter into the cavern. Even as he teetered on the edge of death, he could feel it, and somewhere inside him, something that had been sleeping long and deep, woke and looked up into the creature's face, but all he could see was a bright, golden light. And then there was screaming and he could breathe again.

The blood rushed back to his face and he heard a drum, beating itself in the dark. And then he fell into it.

*

James woke to Anna's face staring down at him.

"He's awake," she said, waving the others over. He saw Phoenix's face appear, then Evandor's and then Chadrick's.

"It's about time." He saw Phoenix smiling broadly, offering him a hand up.

With a heavy head, James looked around him, trying to piece together where he was and what had happened. He remembered the tunnels and then the hag, but little else. The confusion on his face must have shown.

"She was suffocating you. We could see by the finger marks on your neck," Anna explained, "but you fought her off."

"How?" asked James, sitting up, taking stock of how he felt. It hurt when he spoke. His fingers went to his neck and his winced. He could feel welts against his skin, but other than a few cuts, he felt he was alright.

"That is the interesting part," said Evandor, coming closer. They had surrounded James, but Anna had built a pyre of twigs and what looked like peat to allow enough light for them all to see clearly.

James looked to Evandor, waiting for an answer. "It looked as you had set fire to her robes," Evandor said.

"Really? Are you sure?" asked James, confused.

"It would seem that way," said Chadrick. He was the only one who would meet James's eye.

"What is wrong?" asked James. "I thought that was a good thing."

"It isn't really…" Phoenix started, trailing off.

"It isn't a good thing?" asked James.

Anna took a deep breath. "We're not sure what it is."

There was silence for a moment and then Chadrick chuckled. It seemed to ease the tension. "It seems you're more powerful than we thought," he said.

"I'm… powerful? Really?" James took a mental stock of his body. He ached with every movement. He didn't feel powerful.

"Perhaps," answered Evandor, looking unsure.

James got up slowly, looking around, trying to ignore that voice in his throbbing head that was whispering of something that had visited him the dark. They were still in the cavern that Black Annie dragged him to. It was a small space, but large enough for the five of them to gather.

"Where's the body?" he asked, looking around.

"What body?" asked Anna.

"Black Annie – isn't that what the boy called her? I thought I set her on fire," James answered.

This time, Chadrick laughed mockingly. "You did not kill the hag. I felt her power. She is older than these caves," he answered. "She ran off."

"So she's still here somewhere?" asked James, suddenly aware that just beyond Anna's firelight, they were surrounded by darkness.

"She won't be coming back until her wounds heal," replied Chadrick. "You injured her – but it would take a lot more to kill her."

James nodded, glad to be rid of the creature for the moment.

"One danger is behind us. Now, how do we get out of here?" asked Phoenix. "Our guide is long gone by now."

Anna looked worried, but Chadrick stood up, contemplating. "We're going to have to learn to read the writing on the walls," he said.

SEVENTEEN

THE INTRODUCTION OF A DEATH CHASER

With Anna's help, they were able to get a better look at the walls, and at first, James didn't think they were going to be able to decipher them in time. They had little water in their packs and James could feel his tongue sticking to the roof of his mouth. His mouth watered at the thought of drinking something cool and refreshing, but he realised that he was only tormenting himself and he tried to pry his thoughts away from that.

With the light, they could see the walls were etched with symbols that looked to be a mess of lines and circles that were not only incomprehensible but downright confusing. In some cases, the symbols were lined up, one on top of the other, while at other times, two, three or more symbols were etched right next to each other.

"How are we ever going to figure this mess out?" asked Phoenix, echoing James's thoughts.

"It is possible," said Chadrick, running his fingers over the symbols, as if that would help him better understand them.

James took a step closer to the walls, inspecting the symbols. They were a mixture of lines, brackets and circles, some with lines running through their centres and some without. He ran his hands over the symbols, just as Chadrick was doing, and followed the one set of symbols to the other, which looked to be about four feet away. He then moved onwards to the set of symbols further down the passageway before returning.

"These are paces," he said suddenly, making his way to the first set of symbols and running his hands along two faint lines that had been carved on to the surface of the wall.

"How do you know?" asked Anna.

"Look here." He pointed to the carvings. "These lines are the only constant throughout the passageway, so they must indicate distance. There are two lines here and the next set of lines is four paces away. There are three lines etched into the next carving, which is set six paces from the symbols after that."

"That makes sense," said Chadrick, "and if those indicate distance, the others must be either directions or features within the tunnels. We just have to figure out which is which."

Phoenix looked somewhat confused and Anna was silent, listening.

"We need to see what is ahead if we're going to figure out the rest," James said.

Chadrick nodded and they moved on to the next set of symbols, but not before Anna stamped out the fire. When they reached the next set of symbols, she made a new fire with some kindling she had been gathering as they made their way through the tunnels. There was no wood down in the catacombs, but she had been gathering up any materials she could find that they could burn, including old droppings from animals that lived in the tunnels.

The next set of symbols were made up of a bracket with its mouth facing left, a wavy line and three straight lines, which they had already figured out indicated paces.

"This one is pretty simple," said James. "If the straight lines indicate paces, that means that the other two symbols must indicate features, or possibly direction. There is a large cavern to the left, so I am guessing that the bracket indicates left or right, depending on which way it is facing."

"That means this wavy line is the symbol for a cavern," Chadrick finished.

"Do you see the way these symbols are lined up next to each other?" asked James. "The others are lined up differently – they are placed one in front of the other."

"Why would they be placed differently?" asked Anna.

"What if they are directions?" asked Evandor.

Chadrick and James went to get a closer look at the symbols that were lined up in front of each other. This time, the symbol at the end of the sequence showed what looked like a pool of some kind.

"Could it be a lake?" asked James.

Chadrick shook his head. "There is no way to know for sure."

"Anna, James – you need to see this." It was Evandor, calling them over to a piece of the tunnel situated at the opposite end. It was then that James realised that there was writing on both sides of the tunnels.

"Look here…" Evandor pointed to a group of symbols, lined one after the other, indicating directions rather than showing them what was directly ahead. The last symbol, indicating a destination, was a sun. "It's the exit." Evandor was smiling widely. "This is how we are going to find our way out."

James could feel relief echo throughout the group.

"Since we're not going to die in here, do you think these markings can lead us to the Chasers?" asked Phoenix.

"I'm not sure. Is there even a marking for a group of bastards?" asked Anna, rolling her eyes.

James and Phoenix chuckled.

"The Chasers can't be the only ones in these tunnels," Evandor said. "If we find someone else, maybe they can lead us to them."

The rest nodded in agreement. "I'll feel better exploring more of the tunnels knowing that we know how to get out again," said James.

For the next twenty minutes, they moved deeper and deeper into the catacombs. Anna illuminated the way by lighting small pieces of twine and letting them drop to the ground, dying as they passed over them. No one could read the markings on the walls with only their fingertips and so whenever the markings were more complicated than a couple of lines etched into the walls, they would have to stop, make a larger fire and read the next set of directions. This caused them to move very slowly, but they learned to read many more markings as they moved. A circle indicated a slope, while a circle with a line running through its centre indicated a very steep slope. They learned more than once that a circle with an x marked through it meant they were coming up to a dead end. It was Phoenix who learned the hard way that an overhang was forewarned with what appeared to be the letter "V".

James was starting to get worried that the catacombs were indeed empty when they began to hear voices. It was a group of people talking softly and it appeared as if there was a light ahead.

Someone had built a fire, but it was hidden behind an alcove of some kind. The markings on the wall indicated that there was a cavern to the right, and after they had traversed the promised six paces, they came across it. It wasn't large, but it had an overhang at the lip of the cavern that would cause injury if they hadn't seen it.

When they came to the entrance, there was enough light that Anna no longer needed to help them, and it was by this light that James noticed the white line of salt that had been drawn across the floor, right at the entrance to the holding.

The talking stopped and as his eyes adjusted to the brighter light, James saw six people surrounding a fire – two men and four women.

"These aren't the Chasers," said Anna. "At least not the ones that we're tracking."

One of the women had long, pin-straight blonde hair. "Who are you?" she asked them. There was no fear in her voice and there was something about that that unsettled James.

The two men had long dark hair that fall across their back and face. They both had weapons at their side, but they didn't move for them.

The last of the six were two women, one with curly, red hair and another who was short and squat. They looked up from their fire for a moment but quickly became disinterested and began talking amongst themselves.

"We are looking for someone," said Chadrick, taking a step forward to cross into the cavern. It was then that the men reached for their weapons, but the blonde put up her hand and they stopped moving.

"You are new to the catacombs, and you don't have a guide?" The blonde spoke, but it came out as a question.

"We came into some trouble and our guide ran off," replied Chadrick.

The woman turned her head to one side, as if studying him.

"How did you find your way in the dark?" she asked.

"Who said we travelled in the dark?" asked Chadrick.

"Everyone travels in the dark in the catacombs, or else *she* comes for you," came the reply. The redhead and her companion had stopped whispering to each other and seemed suddenly interested in them.

"If you're talking about Black Annie, she came," said James. "She attacked us not too far from here. But we managed to fight her off."

"You mean that you managed to fight her off," said Evandor.

The woman raised her eyebrows. "That is impressive," she said. "That alone is deserving of a warm drink and a hot meal. Come and sit with us." This time, she smiled broadly at them.

"We don't have time for that," said Anna. "We are looking for a group of men who have made their home in these tunnels. They call themselves Death Chasers."

The blonde didn't react when she heard the name. "Whoever they are, they will still be here when you have shared our fire and drink, and perhaps told us a bit more about where you are from and how you managed to fend off old Annie," she said.

Anna made a sound that showed her frustration, but she did not argue. They could now understand some of the basic directions on the tunnel walls, enough to feel confident in exploring more of the caves with the knowledge that they would find the way out, but there were no directions to the Death Chasers that they knew of. James knew they would need some help if they were going to find the Death Chasers, and he was sure that the others knew it too.

The five companions passed over the threshold of the cavern and each took a place by the fire. The two men with the long dark hair didn't say much, and this made James uneasy. Of the two women, the one with the red hair looked to be in her early twenties and her short companion was no older than sixteen. They smiled at Phoenix as he sat down, giving them a broad grin in return.

"I'm Satria," said the blonde woman, "and these two are Abt and Sienna." She pointed to the redhead first, then the shorter one second. "The gloomy twins you see there are Jason and Hivan." James nodded to each in turn. Satria beckoned James to take a seat next to her, which he did.

"These tunnels can take a lot out of a man," she said, handing him a mug filled with something warm and sharp. It ran hot into his stomach, soothing his aching neck and shoulders. "It is much too late to be wandering through the catacombs. Even in the dark, the night is always more deadly than the day. It's as if these creatures can smell the dark outside."

"I didn't realise the time," said James. "You are right – it is hard to keep track of time in the tunnels."

The woman smiled, stretching her legs out in front of her, pointing her toes as she turned her neck from side to side. She wore leggings that reached down to her ankles, and this was a good thing, since it was cold in the tunnels. There was something comfortable, and comforting, about her.

"What are you doing in these tunnels?" James asked her, taking another sip from his mug. "And why do you have salt across the entrance of your cavern?"

"It is the price we pay for this." She motioned to the fire. "Old Annie doesn't just hunt in the tunnels. She smells the warmth from the fire. But she can't cross the salt. So the line must remain unbroken," she explained.

James nodded, understanding.

"You still haven't told us who you are," said Anna.

"I could say the same for you…" Satria replied.

Anna was about to say something but swallowed her remark.

"We are Uringi," said Phoenix, prying his eyes from the redhead, Abt. "The Death Chasers led Inkuanu to a village under our protection. They must answer for it." Phoenix let a touch more bravado into his voice than was usual.

Satria wrinkled her nose. "I have heard of these Death Chasers, but the Inkuanu are news to me. What makes you think it was the Chasers who led them to the village?"

"We have it on good authority," said Chadrick, not mentioning the traders they had met in Baldur.

Satria frowned, mulling this over. "What if your authority isn't as good as you think it is?" she asked. "I have heard troubling things about these Death Chasers. You have risked a great deal to find them already. I am sure that Black Annie was not easy to put down," she winked at James when she said this, "but what if it is not them you are looking for?"

"What do you mean?" asked James.

"Who is it that you think we should be looking for?" asked Anna, her voice edged with something sharp and inviting.

Satria did not take the bait. She put both her hands in the air. "I am not sure who you should be searching for. All I know is that the catacombs can be deceptive. They are large enough to get lost in – to starve to death within their depths – but they are not so large that stories of the Death Chasers and the things they hunt go unheard."

"And you?" asked Anna. "Why are you in these tunnels?"

Satria gave her a long look. "We're hiding," she said, motioning to Abt and Sienna. "Those two are runaways," she nodded at Jason and Hivan, "and those two we picked up in Arborn, a few miles from here. They were once in the King's service, I believe, and deserted a few years back. There are people looking for us. The catacombs keep them out."

Anna frowned at Satria's words but didn't say anything.

"What about you?" asked James.

Satria laughed, and it was a light, gentle sound. "My story is much of the same. A runaway. Wasn't in the mood to go entertaining the undead. So here I am." Her head shook from side to side as she giggled somewhat uncomfortably. James smiled kindly at her. "We're really not all bad." She spoke to Anna this time, who was still watching her carefully. "Please, share our food." This time she motioned to a small woven basket that was filled with large leaves and covered to preserve heat.

Phoenix moved over to the basket and opened it; a smell of onions and stewed meat wafted out of it. James's mouth watered. Abt fetched another basket that was filled with bread and placed it next to the first. She then went to find ten wooden bowls and handed one to each of the company.

The meat was soft and tender, and the gravy was sharp with salt and rosemary. The bread was freshly baked. James didn't see an oven but suspected that the baskets had something to do with their ability to be so versatile with their cooking so far underground, with no access to ovens and other conventional cooking methods. The poor in Dasdaya – the ones without easy access to ovens – often cooked with straw baskets that they buried in the ground, along with heated stones. It took a great deal of skill, but done right, they could produce food that was mouth-wateringly good.

Satria must have had the skill because the food was delicious. Once he had had his fill, it didn't seem so cold in the cavern and Satria's cheeks took on a sweet flush.

It was Sienna that brought out the wine once the plates were cleared away and Satria sat down next to James with a full mug. He could see flecks of green in her wide, blue eyes as she motioned to Anna to take a seat next to her. It was the first time in what felt like days that James saw Anna smile as she sat down.

"You still haven't told me how you managed to scare off ol' Annie?" Satria drank deeply from her mug, her eyes widening with playful mockery.

James laughed.

"He was very brave," said Anna, surprising James. Chadrick took a seat next to her and took a sip from Anna's mug. It was nearly half empty and James realised it might have something to do with Anna's sudden warmth. He pretended not to notice when Anna laid her head against Chadrick's shoulder.

"She's afraid of fire," he said, and then laughed at how ridiculous that must sound considering how she used fire to hunt her victims in the dark. "I mean, she's afraid of being burned by fire." He realised that was no better and fell silent.

"James is Uringi," explained Chadrick, handing Anna her cup, which she took and drank from, deeply. "He set her alight."

Something about the way Chadrick described James gave him a sense of pride that he had never had before.

Satria's eyes widened again, but this time with respect. "So I take it if you're Uringi, then you all are?" Satria said.

"What makes you say that?" asked Anna, her tongue not quite able to catch up with her words.

"Uringi rarely admit to being Uringi unless they are travelling in groups," Satria explained. "Not to mention the fact that you all carry the mark," she continued.

Anna nodded in agreement, but this time, she closed her eyes against Chadrick's chest. He whispered something in her ear and they moved off to a darker corner of the caverns to fall asleep together.

James was alone with Satria. "Except for you, of course," she said. "Where is your mark?"

James rubbed his wrist where his mark would have been, had he been raised an Uringi, but there was nothing there.

When he didn't say anything, Satria continued. "What was your life like before all this, James?" she asked, filling her cup and offering some to James. He declined, still holding a full cup, but he smiled at the memory. His old life seemed like it had happened to someone else, many years ago. "It was different," he said. He didn't know why, but a part of him wanted to say *lonely*.

"Tell me about it," she said, turning over and lying on her side, resting her head on her hands.

"I lived with my uncle since my parents died," he started, thinking back to their small cottage that always smelled of wood shavings and smoked meats. "My uncle loved preparing meals," he added. "He loved the simplicity of it, I think, of bringing together ingredients. He was a hard worker, a carpenter. I used to think I'd follow him into that profession, but it didn't work out that way."

Satria nodded, gently, and it was as if the movement offered some form of sympathy.

"If he had any special abilities, as Uringi, he never used them, so neither did I," James finished.

Satria was watching him with eyes that reflected the firelight. She made him want to keep talking.

"What about you?" he offered.

Satria smiled, but it had no warmth to it. "For some reason, I find it difficult to be honest with you, James," she said. "You are so innocent, in your way. I don't want to ruin the world for you."

James's cheeks flushed when she said this. "I'm not innocent," was all he could find to say.

Satria giggled, then her face was serious. "There is something warm in you, James. Like a warm bath in winter. You smell like home," she said, then she laughed again. "That was a very strange thing to say."

"You smell like lavender," James said. He could smell her hair when she moved.

"Are you going to kiss me, James?" she asked him, and he choked on his drink. He looked up at her, trying to figure out if she was joking. He couldn't tell.

A silence fell between them as she took a long drink from her mug before wrapping a blanket around her shoulders.

"Will you sleep next to me tonight?" she asked him.

James expected to hear her giggle again, but when he looked at her, her bright blue eyes were hopeful. "Yes, Satria, I will," he said.

She nodded, grateful, took a long deep sip from her cup and then motioned him to lay next to her. By then, the cavern was quiet. Everyone was asleep except for them. He lay down and she moved herself into him, placing her head against his chest. In moments, she was asleep, and it wasn't long before he joined her, soothed by the smell of her.

*

James woke to the sounds of people talking softly on the other side of the cavern. He lifted his head and saw that Phoenix and Evandor were helping Chadrick to set a grate over the small pit fire, while Anna was pulling a loaf of bread from a basket in the ground. Jason and Hivan were giving them directions while they sat and sipped at their mugs.

It was difficult to tell the time in the caves because it was always dark, but James imagined it must be morning. His movements woke Satria, and she turned her head and smiled. James couldn't help but smile back.

"How did you sleep?" he asked her.

"Like the dead," she said back. "And you?"

"I slept really well," he said. "How do you tell the time down here?"

As he said the words, he heard a bell began to toll from somewhere far off. It was as if he could hear each *bong* from underwater – it was faint, but it was there. He counted seven.

"That's the old clock in Dasdaya Tower," she explained.

James nodded, understanding.

"Breakfast?" Satria asked, getting up and running her fingers through her hair.

James was ravenous. "What are we having?" he called over to Anna.

"Fresh bread," she shouted back, "but you'd better get here quick. Phoenix is eating like he's in some sort of competition."

"I am not!" said Phoenix, sounding insulted, but then he laughed. "But I'm not making any promises."

James got up and ran his fingers through his hair. It was starting to get long enough to fall into his eyes. He held out a hand, helping Satria to her feet. She took it and they made their way to the fire.

They served themselves thick chunks of the bread and James smeared a thick layer of butter on his. The bread was warm, not only from being freshly baked but from being placed on the grate over the fire so that it could be toasted.

The crust crumbled as he bit into it. He watched Satria do the same. The fire began to dance, as if a wind had swept through the tunnels.

"How many larger caverns are there in these catacombs?" asked Anna, getting straight to business.

"I'm assuming you're talking about the Death Chasers again," said Satria, "and there are a few, but they haven't been filled in many years. Trust me, Anna, if the Death Chasers you are searching for were in these tunnels, we'd know about it."

"I think we're the ones who will need to make that decision, Satria," Anna replied.

"Be nice," Phoenix said, taking a big swig from his cup.

Anna rolled her eyes.

"The Chasers are notoriously difficult to find – trust me," Satria said again, "let them come to you."

"It's not wise to let your prey chase you," said Chadrick.

"How do you know that's not exactly what's been happening?" asked Satria.

"You seem to know a lot about them," Anna challenged again.

"If you don't want my help, I won't give it," Satria said, "but remember, this is still my home and you are still my guest. I don't appreciate having to defend myself so insistently."

Anna turned away, not saying anything.

Satria turned back to James. "I know you are going to have to leave, but before you do, I'd like to show you something," she said.

He nodded. "What is it?"

"A surprise," she replied.

After they had finished their morning meal and cleared everything away, Phoenix offered to wash the dishes, but Abt and Sienna shook their heads.

"You won't find the way to the river," Sienna said. "Just let us do it." Phoenix didn't disagree. They packed everything into a basket and disappeared into the darkness of the tunnels.

"Are you ready?" asked Satria.

James nodded.

She took his hand. "Do you trust me, James?" she asked as they neared the cavern entrance where the line of salt protected them from whatever was outside.

"Maybe," he said back, smiling. He took the hand she was extending and stepped out into the darkness with her. She began to move forward as if she knew exactly where he was going. They had no light with them. He could only judge the direction they were headed by the movement of her body.

As they moved through the tunnels, he heard her whisper, "Are you okay?"

"Yes," he whispered back.

"It isn't far," she said, and they turned a sharp corner. James felt the ground beneath him change form. It turned from stone and ground to something softer. Sometimes that shifted under his feet. Then he began to hear water.

"You need to lower your head," she whispered, as people do in the dark. "The ceiling is going to be low for the next few steps."

He ducked his head, crouching awkwardly, not quite sure how low he needed to be moving. But he wasn't hitting his head on anything, so he thought he must be ducking low enough.

"You can stand up again," Satria said as soon as they'd gone about five or six steps.

Once he'd righted himself, he thought he saw a shape in the darkness. He couldn't make out if it was in his head or if there was something there. Then more shapes began to come into focus. A blue light was filtering into the tunnels.

"It smells like fresh air," he whispered.

"Yes," said Satria. "Look up."

James looked up and saw the sky. It was the sunlight, blue with early-morning light that filtered down into the caverns and lit up the way in front of them. James could see where they were now, winding their way through a narrow corridor. They made another sharp turn and suddenly they were standing in front of a large underground lake. Mist was rising from its surface.

Satria stopped and let go of James's hand. Her hand went to the top button of her dress, stepping out of her shoes as she did so. She removed her tights then followed the line down her middle, undoing each button until her dress dropped to the floor, exposing a shift beneath it. She pulled that over her head and she was naked before him. James's eyes went wide.

Satria took a few steps towards the edges of the pool and then jumped.

The water splashed, spilling out onto the banks.

"What are you standing there for, James?" She laughed.

He pulled his tunic over his head, then unlaced his trousers. Next he pulled off his shoes, standing naked as the day he was born. She smiled more widely still.

He took a step to the banks of the lake and dipped a toe in. It was warm.

He took a breath and jumped. In seconds, he was enveloped by warm water. He rose again and when he did, Satria was waiting for him. Her hair was wet and sticking to her face. Her green eyes were wide with excitement.

"What do you think?" she asked, moving towards him, motioning to the lake with her eyes.

"I like it," he replied, smiling. "I think it's my favourite spot in this whole place."

Satria laughed. It sounded like bells ringing. She moved into his arms and kissed him. She smelled of lavender.

*

The journey back to the cavern felt much shorter, and when they reached it, Anna's eyes went wide, seeing both James's and Satria's hair still soaking wet from the lake. Phoenix just laughed.

"We went swimming." James shrugged, and this time Chadrick laughed out loud. Anna looked at him as if she wasn't in on the joke they were making.

Satria went to warm her toes by the fire, stretching out before it. She motioned for James to take a seat next to her, and he did.

"I am glad you've enjoyed your swim," Chadrick said to James, "but we need to get moving soon."

"I know," James said, but he didn't move.

Satria held out her hand and he took it. "I told you – the Chasers aren't here," she said again.

"Then we need to find them," Chadrick said.

"What if I told you where they are?" said Satria.

"What?" Anna turned to her.

Satria bit her lip.

"You've certainly made yourselves at home," James heard someone say. James felt Satria's warmth leave him, and he opened his eyes to find her staring, wide-eyed, at the cavern entrance.

"...sharing secrets that aren't yours to share?" The voice came from just outside the cavern, beyond the firelight, and James bristled at it. James had heard accents like that in the past, but only from the wealthy who were usually educated miles from Dasdaya. It was steeped in disdain, and arrogance dripped from every word like honey off warm toast. A young man stepped over the salt barrier and into the cavern, flanked by three more. All were carrying weapons, but it was the speaker's bronze-hilted sword that impressed James. The leather sheath was stitched with what looked like gold and a sliver of dark metal peeked out from the sheath's edge. James had heard of ash blades, but he had never seen one. He was sure that was what the man carried with him.

Satria's cheeks flushed when the men appeared.

"You know him?" Anna accused her. "You lied!"

James looked at Satria. She didn't meet his eye.

"Triador," she said, "we didn't expect you back for a few more days."

Phoenix had already got to his feet and James saw that Evandor had drawn his sword.

Triador swept his dirty blond hair from his eyes and smiled, his dark grey eyes passing over the newcomers. "I hear you have been searching for us?" he said.

James looked from Triador to Satria, confused at first, and then he saw the tattoo on Triador's ankle. *Memento Mori.* Triador caught him staring. "You like it?" he asked, turning his ankle so that James could get a better view. "*Memento mori.* Remember you will die. A little reminder to us that we can run – we can run, run, run – but eventually death is going to catch us." He smiled.

Chadrick's fists went to the earth, and the ground beneath Triador shifted. It would have swept him off his feet, but he was no longer there.

"Woah," he shouted, hands in the air. "Someone woke up on the wrong side of the *slave girl*." He looked at Anna and she lunged for him, but once again he was too quick.

James didn't have time to wonder how Triador knew about Anna. Chadrick moved in next and this time, his fist connected with Triador's jaw. James saw specks of blood spatter across the ground.

"Enough," said Triador, and two more men entered the cavern. Jason and Hivan moved to join them. They were as quick as Triador, and in seconds, one had a sword at Chadrick's neck and the other at Anna's.

"Risk her life, if you want," said Triador. "We chase *death*. If we don't move quickly, we have the breath snatched from our bodies. And we'll kill her before we kill you."

Chadrick sneered and then lifted both hands, offering peace. "Many have died because of you."

"We all take risks," said Triador. "It is just the stakes that differ."

"Children are not stakes," said Anna, growing angry. "Balhatchett was not yours to wager."

Triador's eyes darkened. "I did not kill those children," he said. "My men did not kill those children."

"That's not how we see it," said Phoenix.

"I could give a damn about how you see it," Triador spat back.

Phoenix bristled, his knuckles white holding on to the hilt of his blade.

Something hissed out beyond the firelight, beyond the entrance to the caves. James could feel the faintest beat of footprints against the ground. His powers dipped into the ground. Quickly, easily. He felt it move, like a hand sweeping over soft sand. Something moved towards them, towards the cavern. He reminded himself that they were safe from Black Annie behind the line of salt that protected the cavern, but he wondered what else it might protect them from, or not.

"Something is coming," he said, to everyone and no one in particular. He looked to Satria, whose eyebrows went up. She wasn't smiling anymore. She looked tense.

Anna looked at him, questioning, but after a few moments, she felt it too. Then he saw Triador smile and something clicked into place. He looked to the cavern entrance and saw that the line of salt was no longer a line but a scattering of salt across the entrance.

"You broke the line," James heard himself accuse Triador, but his mind was still trying to fight the logic of it all. It was trying to convince him that it was only coincidence that the Death Chasers had passed so close to Balhatchett on their way into Baldur. It was screaming that the woman they'd found in the Effluvium den hadn't been chosen, hadn't been waiting for them to arrive so she could tell them what they needed to hear, tell them just enough to lead them, step by step, to these caves.

They had two girls with them, the traders in Baldur had said. *Where were Abt and Sienna?* James thought. *They were here last night.* He remembered them helping to serve dinner, but this morning, he hadn't even noticed they weren't there.

How could I not have noticed? he thought.

He could still smell Satria on his skin. The ground moved beneath him. Something big was making its way through the tunnels, getting closer with every moment.

Triador watched James carefully, as if waiting for him to come to a conclusion on his own. Then he smiled. "Yes." Triador nodded once. "We are the ones you have been searching for. Or, to put it more accurately, we're the ones who've been luring you here." He motioned to Satria.

"That's a lie," said Satria.

"Is it?" Triador asked.

Satria opened her mouth, then closed it again. "I'm sorry," she whispered.

Chadrick went for his sword and two of the men beside Chadrick drew their own. Phoenix put out a hand to halt Chadrick but kept his other on his own weapon.

"Please," said Triador. "We're not here to fight. Not you, at least. I'm afraid we've been using you to reel in something much bigger."

Whatever was coming through the tunnels was very nearly at the entrance. James could feel the caves echo with its weight. James was surprised that whatever it was could fit in these tunnels. The line of salt remained broken. *Then again,* James thought, *would it stop whatever is coming?*

"It's too big," said James, shaking his head. "You can't possibly stand a chance against whatever it is."

"You can feel it?" asked Chadrick.

James realised that Chadrick must be feeling the movement too. He nodded.

"It is powerful. I've never felt anything like it," Chadrick said.

"Yes, you have," said Triador, then he turned to look at James. "You both have." He looked from James to Chadrick. Chadrick went pale. James frowned, confused.

"The fool is coming," said Triador, smiling broadly. "He's coming for us all."

EIGHTEEN

THE FOOL

"I'm sorry, James," Satria whispered. "I swear, I didn't know."

"You're a liar," said James.

The vibrations stopped and James felt the air go cold.

"He's here." Triador's voice was low, excited. "Memento mori."

"Memento mori," the men beside him whispered back.

He didn't have to see past the firelight to know that something was waiting for them just beyond the cavern entrance. He could hear the heavy silence weighing against the darkness. Something inside James was screaming, begging him to find a place to run and hide. A part of him wanted to close his eyes so that he didn't have to see whatever it was that stepped past the broken line of salt into the light.

And then something began to move. James expected a figure so large that it dwarfed them all – something so big that it filled the cavern. He could feel power emanating from the creature, like blood pulsing through a vein in the neck.

What emerged from the shadow was small – smaller than he was. At first, James thought it was a ghoul. Its skin was pale, almost white. Its limbs were long, too long, with fingers that stretched outwards, feeling the air. Its face was covered in shadow, making it difficult to tell if the creature had eyes at all. But it must have, because it seemed to be looking at James as it got closer, moving like it was floating above the ground, rather than walking. James felt his skin crawl as it closed in on him, soundlessly. No one in the room moved.

The creature stopped just a foot in front of James and he could feel the creatures breath in his face. It smelled of earth. He could see its face very clearly now – the eyes in its head were white, like those of a blind man. James remembered the blind man he'd helped across the street. It felt like so long ago. The creature smiled, as if he knew what James was thinking. It nodded, a tiny motion that only James would notice.

It was me, the creature seemed to say.

"Now," shouted Triador, and he and two of his companions attacked. They brandished swords and moved like water, but James could have told them it was no use. James could not see a weapon in the creature's hands, but the first of Triador's companions fell, a bloody smile forming at his neck. The moment he went down, the third of Triador's companions fell into formation and the attack continued. At one point, Triador stepped over the body of his friend to parry a blow from the creature, who didn't look like he was even straining himself as he danced just out of their reach.

"Why are you just standing there?" Triador shouted over his shoulder, and whether he was speaking to Satria and the two men beside her or whether he was calling to James and his companions, James wasn't sure, but his voice brought them out of their reverie. Phoenix and Evandor joined the attack first. Three quick blasts of air hit the creature in the middle of his chest, and he hissed in pain or anger. He lunged at Phoenix just as Evandor aimed a blow with his sword. The blow missed, but it forced the creature to turn from Phoenix and face Chadrick, who was standing behind it. Triador was still pushing forward with the sword, but in the small cavern, the other two of his companions had to step back to allow the Uringi space to fight. As the creature turned to face Chadrick, the hunter slammed his fists into the ground and something shifted from beneath the fool. For a moment, it looked like he had slipped and might be falling. Anna clapped both hands together and when they parted, something that looked like a small bird, in full flame, shot at the fool and set him alight.

It only took a few moments for the creature to be engulfed in the flames. The creature thrashed for a few moments and then went still, and James could hear Triador and his companions cheer. James couldn't believe it, but it was almost over.

Satria moved in with a knife. "It's not over until we cut out its heart," she said. As she said that, James saw something else enter the cavern. He knew instantly what it was.

"Black Annie!" he shouted, but the hag was already on the last of Triador's companions, tearing into him. He screamed and went limp, and she screeched, a high-pitched grating sound. Her long grey hair reached down to the small of her back and it covered most of her face. She lunged at Jason, who grabbed a fistful of her hair and pulled her head back. He plunged his knife into her, but it missed its mark and she fought back, rabid and angry.

James turned back to the fool.

"Anna, kill the flames!" Satria called out. "I want his heart."

She must be going for the fool, James thought.

"I'll do it," shouted Phoenix, and for a moment, James felt short of breath. He felt the air shift as Phoenix smothered the flames.

When the flames died down, James could see the blackened form of the fool, still on his feet, appear from among them. James saw his eyes move. His mouth was wide. Too wide.

"He's still alive!" James tried to warn Satria, but she couldn't move fast enough.

"Enough!" the fool hissed, reaching out a hand with long, sharp fingers. In one swift move he tore out Satria's throat.

James wanted to reach Satria before she hit the ground, but he couldn't move fast enough. He saw her head bounce off the stone floor, her blonde hair splaying out in all directions. Blood began to pool beneath her as he reached her, pulling her towards him. Her blood was thick and warm against his skin.

"No!" he screamed at the creature, rocking Satria to his body. Triador's two remaining companions attacked, viciously, but their efforts were in vain. The fool was stronger than any of them had imagined, and it was seconds before both of them were on their knees, bright, red smiles on their throats. The bodies collapsed and Triador took a visible step backwards.

"Out," the creature hissed, and James saw Black Annie move, like ink dropped into water, through the cavern. She hissed, her dark eyes fixed on James as she moved, catlike, slipping out into the darkness.

And then there was only the fool, but he seemed to fill the entire cavern.

Bodies littered the ground. Only Triador and Hivan remained of all the Death Chasers.

"What are you?" James heard Anna ask.

"I am death made flesh," it whispered back, turning its head once more with a mouth too big to be human. James remembered Anna's words in Baldur forest.

I am death made flesh, she had screamed at the traders.

James saw Hivan collapse, his knees buckling underneath him. His eyes were open but empty.

It hadn't even touched him, thought James as he rocked Satria to him, swallowing something that tasted of fear and revulsion.

"Chadrick, save her," James commanded weakly, but Chadrick shook his head.

"That is beyond me, my friend," Chadrick replied, pained.

The fool moved towards James, and the young man pulled Satria's body protectively against his own. Something tore inside him and the pain beat against his chest like a heartbeat.

"I told you I would take your heart with me," it hissed, and James could feel his skin begin to tingle. The fool shifted one foot in front of the other, moving ever closer to James. James could not tell if the creature was harmed by the fire. It didn't look like it was in pain, but it was definitely moving slower than before.

"But I am not done." It was looming over James now, its eyes boring into him. They were light – so light that they were almost glass, reflecting back at James. He could see his own reflection in those eyes. He was afraid. The creature reached out to touch James, rubbing a finger against the side of James's face. It burned where it touched him and suddenly, his power came alive, like thousands of snakes writhing inside him. James nearly collapsed into it, his face falling into Satria's hair. She was still warm. It was too warm. Too warm in the cavern. His skin was burning, but not just where the creature had touched him. It leaned in closer to him now. James could feel its breath on his face.

"I'm going to take them all, James," it hissed. Whatever was beating out a rhythm in his chest skipped a beat and James filled that space with rage. James was desperately trying to call the fire to his fingertips. He tried to remember what Anna had told him about feeling the warmth in the air around him, but it wasn't working. His power was alive, he could feel it, and it was like gaining another sense. Through it, he could sense the power around him, but he couldn't do anything with it. He tried to think back to his fight with Black Annie, trying to remember what he had done then, but still, he couldn't turn his power into fire. Then he remembered the dagger resting on his hilt.

"No," James looked up at the creature, "you won't."

James laid Satria down onto the ground. He kissed her forehead gently, then he got to his feet, slipping his blade from its hilt.

"James, wait!" he heard Anna shout, and fire began to fill the crevices of the stone floor. James turned to see Anna kneeling, guiding the flames that then became snakes, filling every gap around the fool, crossing the cavern floor and returning on itself, this time filling crevices in the cavern's roof and meeting in the middle. Chadrick, Phoenix, Evandor and Triador needed to take only one step back to ensure they were out of the flame's reach. The fool was surrounded.

James screamed again in frustration, this time at not being able to reach the fool before the fire did.

"You can't keep me here," he heard the fool call, but it was locked in the furnace.

James turned to Anna, his voice strained from screaming. "Run!" he shouted.

As they made their way towards the entrance, James stopped to lift Satria into his arms. She hung limp and heavy in his arms.

"I am coming for them, James," the creature called again, and for the first time, James could see the cage falter. The flames flickered for a moment, as if they were about to die, and even though they burned hot again, James knew they would not hold for much longer. He ran for the cavern entrance, turned the corner and moved quickly to join the others.

NINETEEN

THE LAST STAND

The tunnels twisted and turned at a much faster pace than before, but Triador seemed to know them well and Anna made sure they could see where they were going by lighting the way in front of them. Since escaping the cavern, James had felt a weariness come over him that made it difficult to keep up with the others, and when he fell behind, they slowed for him.

Eventually Chadrick offered to carry Satria, giving James a chance to recover his strength when they came to a fork in the tunnels that James had not noticed on their way in.

"This is where we part," said Triador. "You will take the left, carrying on until you get to another fork, then choose the left again. You will begin to hear the sounds of the town above you, and you might even see natural light filtering into the tunnels. The tunnels narrow then, so be sure to watch your step."

"Where are you going?" asked James, wondering if Triador would lie to them and abandon them to death in the tunnels.

"You forget who I am," he said, turning his head to one side. "I am a Death Chaser. You're not the only ones who are hunting us." Triador went to take Satria from Chadrick, but Chadrick pulled away.

Triador frowned. "She is a Chaser. She's mine to bury."

James's clenched his jaw. "You would have abandoned her in that cavern," James said, "and she isn't *yours*."

Triador laughed. "Don't be ridiculous. We don't have time for this." He attempted to take Satria from Chadrick, but the moment he touched the hunter's skin, Triador pulled back, hissing.

Triador's eyes went wide. "Adaïr!" he spat, his face turning pale with rage and something that tasted like fear.

"Leave." Chadrick spoke softly, but James could tell it was more than a command – it was a warning.

Triador was shaking his head, as if in disbelief, and then his eyes fell to James. "You cannot know what he is," he took a step back, away from the two men, "or you would not fight beside him." Triador cast one more glance at Satria before he turned and ran.

James watched him disappear into the tunnels before turning to Chadrick. "What did he call you?" asked James, suddenly feeling the need to take Satria from the hunter's arms. Her blonde hair fell in a shower from the crook of his arm as he held her gently to his chest. "What is Adaïr?"

"It's the same thing that girl called this thing we're fighting now – the fool?" Phoenix sounded confused.

Anna and Evandor did not say anything and James felt a heaviness in their silence.

The hunter shook his head but did not meet James's eye. "We need to move quickly – we don't know how long Anna's cage will hold that creature," Chadrick warned.

James turned his words over in his head and found he agreed with them, but he held his arms out for Satria. "I'll take her from here," James said. Chadrick nodded his head, handing her over, but his mouth was a hard line as he did. Phoenix was not placated either, but it was clear that they didn't have time to work this out in the tunnels.

The weight of Satria reminded James of that drum of pain that beat in his chest, a pain that was already bruising, making each pulse hurt all the more.

And then James heard a beating from somewhere outside of himself. Footsteps in the dark of the tunnels. Chadrick looked up, listening.

"Something is coming," Evandor said, echoing the thoughts of the four around him.

*

The five wound their way through the tunnels, but this time, they did not waste any time working out the finer intricacies of the patterns on the walls. They followed signs for the exit and moved as quickly as they could, with Anna lighting their way. Anna was first, followed by Evandor, James, Chadrick and then Phoenix, who kept a lookout behind them in case whatever was chasing them caught up. At first, James had thought that it was Black Annie chasing them, but he realised that he was wrong – or at least, partly mistaken. Whatever was coming, was coming *en masse*. James couldn't tell how many of them there were, but the ground moved beneath his feet and the echoes of their hurried footsteps echoed against the stone walls.

Satria had grown heavy and James was feeling the strain of holding her in his arms, but he would let no one else take her, even though both Phoenix and Evandor had offered. Chadrick had known better than to follow their lead.

"They are getting closer." The hunter's voice carried over

the group. "We might be able to make it out of the tunnels, but if they follow us out, we won't be able to outrun them."

"We don't know what *they* are," Anna called back.

Then James remembered the young girl they'd met outside Baldur – the one who'd spoken of witches, chattering endlessly in her head. She had spoken of the fool, surrounded by Upipita. *They're not sleeping anymore*, she had said.

"Upipita," said James, turning to the others, and suddenly, the others stopped running.

Phoenix was shaking his head. "It can't be," he said. "It can't be possible."

"You mean you hope it's not possible," retorted Anna, but James could see that she too was afraid.

James felt the weight of Satria begin to slow him down. He moved, slower and slower, until his legs buckled beneath him.

"James!" Phoenix shouted. Chadrick grabbed his shoulders to stop him from toppling over with Satria still in his arms. Phoenix took her from his arms and James collapsed to the floor.

"Black Annie – the fight took too much from you," said Chadrick.

James could taste something sour in the back of his throat and he was struggling to catch his breath. Anna and Evandor had heard Phoenix shout and had turned back.

"It won't be long before they catch up to us, James. We need to keep moving." Anna's voice was gentle but urgent. He could tell that she was scared.

"I don't even know what we are running from," James said. The nausea was passing, ebbing away. The bright lights that were making it difficult to see ahead of him were dimming.

"If the girl was right," said Anna, "we are being chased by the dead. They are different to ghouls – more violent."

"They are supposed to be victims of living burials," said Evandor, speaking quickly. "They woke from death, rabid and hungry. They move quickly – too quickly. We need to go. Now."

James nodded as he got up, but as soon as he lifted himself from the ground, he began to vomit and his knees buckled. He began to hear sounds in the dark of the tunnels. Screams, high-pitched and vicious. James knew he could not make it out of the tunnels. If he could not stand, he could not run.

"Leave me," James whispered, low enough so that his voice would not carry into the tunnels. He could feel the ground beneath his feet begin to shake. He could see nothing in the tunnel that stretched out behind them – the tunnel the creatures would use to find them, but he knew that any moment these monsters, these *Upipita*, would emerge and it would end.

Phoenix's body stiffened at his words. "We will not run, James." Phoenix's voice seemed to speak within him, as if the wind itself carried them ever so gently, masking them from their enemies.

"If you cannot run, we will carry you," said Chadrick, taking him by the arm, but James pulled away, knowing it would just slow them down.

"I will only slow you down. Run or you will die here." James's voice was more urgent now.

"No," Anna said. "If you stay here, this is where we will fight."

"She will die, Chadrick." If Evandor could not be convinced, Chadrick might, but he didn't move. Instead, Chadrick reached out and took Anna's hand protectively, stubbornly. Anna blushed but did not pull her hand away.

"Why?" James spoke through clenched teeth.

"Into the field once more we go," Anna said.

"Ne'er to return, we heed Uriaha's call," said Evandor, drawing his sword.

"Mors Vorcat, my friend," said Phoenix, smiling, "death calls to us all."

James had caught his breath again, but his muscles screamed when he moved. He wondered how long they would be able to survive the onslaught in these tunnels. He believed they could keep whatever was coming at bay for at least a little while. The tunnels were narrow and that would work to their advantage.

Still, he thought to himself, he did not relish the thought of dying underground. He wanted to feel the sun on his skin again. The smell of the earth was suffocating. The creatures were nearly upon them. The beat of their feet shook the earth, causing the bugs to scuttle down into the roots of large trees for safely. James was surprised that the roots could reach this far down into the earth. They dipped through layers of rock and loam, reaching into crevices and extending far below even the caves.

"Come back," he heard Chadrick call to him, and it was as if he was coming up for air. He wasn't even truly sure where he had gone, but he had touched a pool of it, and the excess dripped from his fingers.

"They are nearly here," warned Evandor. "We have maybe a minute."

"Anna – could you fend them off with your fire?" asked James, but she shook her head.

"I don't have enough kindling, James." She shook her head, biting her lip. "There's nothing here to burn."

James searched frantically, using his eyes and his powers, exploring, probing. As they were deep in the caves, between the earth and rock ceiling, they could reach nothing more than tree roots. Then he remembered something.

He smiled at Anna. "A good Uringi can always find something to burn."

He was still on his knees, but his breath was coming easier now, more slowly. "Chadrick, I need your help."

Chadrick nodded, stepping forward. "What do you need?" he asked.

"I don't even know if this is going to work. I don't know if it's possible, but it's the only way I can think of that might save us," James said.

"I'm listening," said Chadrick.

"I need you to follow me." James spoke, grabbing Chadrick's arm and at the same time plunging his mind's eye deep into the earth. His powers curled out beneath him and it was easier than he would have imagined. He reached into the earth and began seeking out the roots. He found them. They were like spiderwebs, woven beneath the floor of these caves. James could tell that they stretched out beyond that, but he pulled back. He felt a familiar power beside him, fuelling his own powers.

"Anna — we are going to guide your fire," called James. He guessed that they had about forty seconds left. "Give me your hand." Anna placed her hand in his and he felt her power reach out and touch his. She released her warmth, slowly at first, unsure where it was supposed to go, until it met with his and Chadrick's, who pulled it down, deep into the earth. The fire bit into the roots of an old willow, and then it began to spread, quickly, too easily.

"Evan, I need you to carry her. Get ready to run," James shouted. Evandor nodded and took Satria from Phoenix, who still looked confused.

James focused on feeding the fire, both with his own powers and with Anna's. Chadrick continued to guide it so that the fire began to smoulder, hot and fast, just a few feet beneath them. James could feel the ground beneath his feet begin to grow hot.

"Let's get going," shouted James, pulling himself away from the ground and back to the caves, where the sound of the creatures was now loud enough to drown him out. For a moment he was afraid he had waited too long. They had twenty seconds left.

Chadrick had released Anna's hand and went to help James to his feet. It was in that moment that something came out of the darkness. It moved so quickly, James saw only fangs and limbs. For a second, he thought it was a wolf, but once his mind caught up with his eyes, he saw the grey skin, long, lank hair and pale lips that belonged to a human. Or something that used to be human.

It slammed into Phoenix and they both fell to the floor, rolling. Phoenix's fist made a dull, smacking sound as he hit the creature in the face and it yelped, falling off him, but seconds later it attacked again, hissing before it lunged at Phoenix.

"This bastard thing smells," shouted Phoenix as he grappled with the creature that was clawing at his face.

"Anna, we don't have any time – I need your help to create a wall. The others are seconds behind this one. We need to give ourselves some more time," James said, focusing on the heat within the caverns, trying to draw out his power. He was trying to ignore the voice that whispered that maybe this time, it wouldn't come. But it did. Moss grew along the cave walls and it made for easy kindling. It wouldn't burn long, but it would give them enough time to get out of the caves.

"Evan, I need you," shouted James, and in moments, Evandor was at his side.

"What do you mean *you* need him. Can someone help to get this thing off me?" shouted Phoenix in between blows. Chadrick moved towards him, but James didn't have time to watch what happened. He realised that one of these creatures might be a nuisance, but they were just as vicious as Evandor had said, and fighting off a pack of them wasn't going to be easy. And he could tell that many more of them were coming. Many, many more.

"Evan, can you draw the water from the moss? We need kindling," James said, and Evandor didn't hesitate. James watched as water began to leak from the walls. The moss shrivelled, looking like a living thing. The walls went from a dark green to a dark brown in a matter of seconds.

Then they ran out of time. The first wave of creatures leaped into the circle of light, just feet from them.

James reacted on instinct, believing that Anna would follow his lead, and he was right. He watched as her power followed his own and for a moment, a bright light blinded them all. One of the creatures passed through a wall of fire that sprang to life and it burst into flame, screeching as it lunged at Chadrick. Before it could get to the hunter, Evandor reached out both arms and a cloak of water wrapped itself around the creature, killing the flame. Chadrick drew his sword and put it through the creature's heart. It went still.

James could hear the calls beyond the fire. They were somewhere between howls and screams, but James knew they were human voices making those sounds, and that was unsettling.

"The moss won't burn for long," shouted Anna. "We need to go."

"You're right," replied James, but he felt unsteady on his feet. He was feeling colder in the caves than he thought he should be. He was half expecting mist to come from his breath.

Satria was lying where Evandor had placed her. James knew he would not be able to carry her out.

"Let me." Chadrick had been watching James. James just nodded, saying nothing. Chadrick held Satria close to his body and began to make his way to the cave's entrance – and their exit.

They made their way through the winding tunnels, quickly but carefully. James was breathing hard now, trying to catch his breath, but it was no use. He knew the others would be able to hear him struggle, but he was past caring. All he could think of was reaching the cave's entrance. His only comfort was the knowledge that deep within the earth, the tree roots were smouldering, spreading but contained. Or at least it would be.

"Put your arm around my neck," Evandor offered, but James shook his head. If he could have spoken without retching at Evandor's feet, he would have.

James focused on putting one foot in front of the other. Every now and again, Chadrick would turn back from his position behind Anna to watch him for a few seconds before turning back. James attempted to give him a dark look, but he was sure it had come out more pained than anything else.

When he finally saw light – real sunlight – pouring into the tunnels, James nearly ran for the entrance. Instead, he followed the others as they spilled out into the daylight. From the position of the sun, James could tell that it was midday.

"What now?" asked Phoenix. Chadrick went to lay Satria down on a small patch of grass. He had slipped his pack under her head, as if she needed a pillow. James winced, trying to shake off the grief like a wet dog. *Not yet*, he thought, turning back to the caves. He could tell the fire had burned out. His powers only needed to dip into the earth for a moment to feel it shake. An army was headed out of the caves, and if they got past the five companions, they would have their share of Dasdaya.

"We are going to set the catacombs alight," said James, pouring his power into the earth, seeking out the perimeter he had calculated before he and Anna had set the roots smouldering.

"How are we going to do that?" asked Phoenix in disbelief. "That's not possible, is it, Anna?" Phoenix turned to Anna, but she didn't answer. She turned to James instead.

"Even if that's possible, what about the others living in the catacombs? The Chasers weren't the only ones in there?" Phoenix asked again.

"If there was anyone else, the Upipita have taken them," said Evandor, looking at James curiously.

"Okay, so how are you and Anna going to set these caves alight? That would take a lot more power than you have between you, wouldn't it?" asked Phoenix.

James could feel the earth begin to shake beneath their feet.

"You're right, we don't have that type of power." James was shaking his head at Phoenix, then he smiled, a weary, somewhat broken smile with a mischievous glint. "Luckily, we're not going to – you are," replied James.

TWENTY

THE KEEPERS AND THEIR KING

Phoenix laughed, long and hard, but stopped short when he saw the look on James's face.

"If that's your plan," Phoenix shook his head, "we're all lost."

"No, we're not," said James. "Listen to me – have you ever heard of root burn?"

Phoenix shook his head.

"I have," said Evandor. "Many years ago, fires ravaged Dasdaya. There were fears it would raze the city to the ground, the fires burned so hot. They had built great pyres to stop the plague, but when they put them out, they only put out the fires they could see."

James continued, "The tree roots continued to smoulder for days, weeks after the fire. No one realised that a fire was raging just beneath the earth. Until the wind came."

Phoenix's eyes went wide then fell to the ground, perhaps wondering what was hidden beneath his feet.

"Bring the wind, Phoenix," said James.

Phoenix nodded, wasting no time, and James felt something brush against his skin, like the fingertips of a lover in the dark. Seconds before the wind rose up, James saw the horde that was coming for them. It was a mass of limbs, hair and teeth that forced their way through the last few feet of the tunnel, hissing as they moved together as one. An army against James and his four companions. Anna drew her sword, as did Evandor and Chadrick. Phoenix had his at his side and James realised that he had just traded his last real chance to fight off the hordes for a plan that might not work. For a plan based on a story James was not even sure if had understood.

Two Upipita exploded from the caves, and Anna and Chadrick stepped forward, cutting them down. Three more followed after and Evandor joined in the fight. Seconds later he heard Evandor scream and he turned back to see one of the creatures burying its jaws into Evandor's shoulder. James ran to help, but Chadrick reached him more quickly, after slaying his own opponent. James turned back to Phoenix and saw him, eyes closed, fingers tapping at his thighs. He was calling the wind and James could only hope it would come in time. Two more Upipita threw themselves from the entrance of the cave and one slammed itself into Phoenix, who toppled over. James threw himself at the creature, pulling him off Phoenix. James landed, hard, and the creature's elbow hit him squarely in his gut, knocking the wind out of him. He lay there for a moment, stunned, and then it came for him, teeth bared and nails cutting at his skin. It was strong, much stronger than James had anticipated.

The creature shifted his hold, grabbing James by the neck as it tried to tear into his skin with its teeth.

"There's more of them getting through!" shouted Anna. "We can't fight this many!"

Someone screamed. James couldn't tell who it was, but it bit into him, and then so did the creature. James screamed and then did the only thing he could think to do. He thrust a hand out, blade in hand, into the creatures chest. He was surprised at how easily he was able to do it, but the moment he did, he realised it was a mistake. After a few seconds of struggling, the creature was still, but James was seeing spots again and this time, he could barely make it onto his knees.

Phoenix's face was pale and his hair was wet with sweat, but his eyes were still closed, focusing.

This was a mistake, thought James. *He's not strong enough.*

One of the creatures had Chadrick on his stomach, a fistful of his hair in its hands. It screamed in his face and was about to lunge when Anna put her sword through its ribs. James didn't know how long Chadrick had been struggling with the creature, but the moment he was free, he jumped to his feet and stumbled over to Phoenix. Chadrick reached out, grabbing at Phoenix's arm, and suddenly, the wind came. It rose up from the ground and hit the cave entrance like a wave of water, passing through into its depths. It took seconds before the heat rose up with it, and once it did, it was like a sickness, passing through the tunnels in a red fury, taking everything in its path with it. The creatures within the tunnels screeched and bawled, but nothing would stop the fire. It burned through everything it touched like something savage and alive.

And then there was silence.

The quiet that followed was unsettling, but James felt relieved. Anna and Evandor had managed to kill the last remaining creatures who had made it out of the tunnels, and they were still catching their breaths when Phoenix collapsed.

"Phoenix!" Evandor shouted, running to his side. Phoenix lay on the floor, barely breathing, his eyes closed. "Chadrick –

what's wrong with him?" asked Evandor, slapping Phoenix in the face to try to get him to wake up.

Chadrick stopped him and motioned for them to step aside to give him some space. Chadrick placed his fingers at Phoenix's neck and was still for a few moments. Then relief showed plainly on his face.

"He's okay. He's spent. He will be okay," Chadrick said to the others.

"But… how did…" Evandor was looking between Chadrick and Phoenix, and then his face went dark. James had never seen Evandor angry. Not truly. Not until this moment.

"Adaïr," said Evandor, his eyes narrowing darkly, realisation came over his face like a raincloud covering the sun. "What did you do?"

Something like fear passed over Chadrick's face when Evandor said that word. *Adaïr.*

"Evan, what are you talking about?" asked Anna defensively. "He's helping him."

Evandor shook his head. "No," he said, "I saw him grab Phoenix. Just before the wind came, I saw him grab his wrist."

James had seen the same thing but still couldn't understand Evandor's anger.

"They speak of such things in Aventias," said Evandor, pulling his sword and putting it to Chadrick's throat. Anna took a step forward, angry, but Chadrick put his hand up, wincing, his face pleading with her not to.

"I swear to you, I did not mean to harm your friend," Chadrick said. "I did not have another choice."

"Chadrick… what?" Anna's voice was soft, broken with disbelief.

"You did not mean to and yet you did," Evandor said, touching the tip of his blade to Chadrick's neck. James could see a spot of blood appear and roll down Chadrick's neck, disappearing into his open tunic.

"Evan, don't," Anna shouted.

"What did you do?" James asked Chadrick, still kneeling.

Chadrick closed his eyes, shaking his head.

"It might be best to ask him *what* he is, rather than what he did," said Evandor.

Chadrick's jaw hardened.

"What is he speaking about, Chadrick?" James spoke, then remembered Triador had called Chadrick the same word. "What is an Adaïr?"

This time, there was no army chasing them to save Chadrick from the question. Smoke poured from the tunnels, but nothing followed it. Whatever was in the tunnels died in the tunnels. James thought he'd feel more relieved at the thought, but he didn't.

"He is right, I am Adaïr," said Chadrick, his eyes flitting from Evandor to James. James wondered if he was purposely avoiding Anna's eyes. "Please, take the blade from my neck and I'll tell you my story."

Evandor shook his head, giving Chadrick no choice but to continue. "Adaïr has come to mean many things, in many places throughout Dasdaya and the surrounding counties. It is always associated with death, and that's not entirely wrong. In truth, it means *muse*. That is what I am. A descendent of Leanan-Sidhe."

Anna gasped. James tried to remember where he'd heard that name before.

"The witch?" asked Anna, but it came out more like an accusation.

Chadrick frowned, as if he did not expect that reaction from her, then his shoulders slumped.

Then James remembered the book he'd read in the library at Migdasha. The one about the plague. "She brought the plague to Gedeon," he said.

"They say she brought death to Dasdaya, Chadrick." Anna spoke softly. "Hundreds died because of her. How can you be descended from such a monster?"

"How can you?" Chadrick spat back, and then he winced. "I'm sorry…" He tried to apologise, but Anna's face darkened. He turned back to Evandor. "I didn't mean to hurt Phoenix," said Chadrick. "I gave him the power to do what he needed to do. It's just that… this power, it… comes with certain drawbacks…"

"You take his life in exchange for that power?" asked Evandor, his eyes narrowing.

There was a silence that hung between them. James had expected Chadrick to deny this. For a second, James wanted to defend Chadrick. James wanted to explain that Chadrick would never do that. That he wasn't capable of that. Then Chadrick began to nod, slowly, his eyes closed.

"But Phoenix is still alive!" shouted James. "How could you have taken his life?"

When Chadrick looked up at him, James could see a sorrow that turned his eyes a dark grey. "I did not take all of it, only some. It is the trade you make with a muse. Your power burns bright, but at a cost. The cost of life," said Chadrick.

James could still not accept it. He remembered how many times Chadrick had saved them. He had saved Penhallurick on the battlefield, and he'd saved James in the caverns, after Black Annie attacked.

"You can't be…" James stopped short, suddenly realising something. He had remembered what Chadrick had looked like after saving Penhallurick. His pale face, the shortness of breath. He looked as Phoenix did now. "You spent your own life saving me, saving Penhallurick, didn't you?" James asked. This time, he saw Anna look up, curious.

"I did." Chadrick's mouth was hard.

"Why?" asked Evandor, unrelenting.

"Because he was just a boy," said Chadrick, and then he looked at James, "and you are my friend."

"He's right, Evan, we needed him," Anna said. "We would have all died if Phoenix hadn't had the strength. He gave that to him." She motioned to Chadrick but didn't meet his eye.

Evandor had softened his grip on the hilt of his sword but didn't lower it. "You should have told us. It would have been a fair trade – if it was a trade. You had no right to steal his life from him without his permission," Evandor said.

"You are right," said Chadrick. "Forgive me – for hurting your brother."

Evandor hesitated, looking back at Phoenix, then at Chadrick. "Will he be okay?"

"I give you my word," said Chadrick, "he will wake in a few hours. His life will be shortened by some days, but he has come to no other harm."

This took Evandor a few seconds to swallow. James knew he was still struggling to swallow some of his anger, but he did it with the grace that James had come to know was unique to Evandor. The sword was lowered and Evandor took a step back. Chadrick nodded his gratitude and put a hand to his neck. He did not wince when he ran his fingers over the small cut that Evandor had made.

*

They waited at the entrance of the catacombs until Phoenix awoke. When he did, he chided them all, jokingly, for sitting back and watching *him* save the world. No one disagreed with him and they averted their eyes when he retched up the water that he was given.

James could see the sun was beginning to set and it was beginning to get cold. He wrapped Satria in his cloak, knowing that she would not feel the cold, but somehow it comforted him knowing that she was protected from the wind. Once this was done, he turned to the others. When Phoenix seemed to have recovered somewhat from the experience, it was Chadrick who told him what happened. For whatever reason, Phoenix wasn't bothered by the fact that Chadrick had traded a part of his life to strengthen his powers. Once Chadrick was finished explaining, Phoenix took his shoulder and nodded, as if to tell the hunter that all was well. Once he was recovered enough to get to his feet, he began demanding they make their way home for dinner and a warm bath. Anna seemed to have relented and was now offering Chadrick a drink of water from her water pouch. Bodies of the Upipita were scattered everywhere and James felt it was best that they leave before the constables arrived. Picturing what might happen if they had to explain themselves was the only thing giving James the strength to move. His muscles ached and a dull headache throbbed, beating at his temples. Then he remembered something.

"I almost forgot…" he started, and the others turned to him, expectantly. "I don't think it was me who fought off Black Annie when I was trapped in the cavern."

Anna looked confused. "What do you mean?" she asked.

James remembered the presence that he'd felt entering into the cavern. He remembered how large it felt, how powerful.

"It was something else… something else was there…" James felt silly as he said the words, but he couldn't keep it to himself.

"What was it, James?" asked Evandor softly.

"I… I'm not sure…" James trailed off. He didn't want to say it because he didn't think the others would believe him. *Besides*, he told himself, *it couldn't have been the fool.*

The others nodded, not pushing him further.

"I still don't understand how you knew…" James said, turning to Chadrick. "How you and Triador knew that I'd seen the fool before."

"I do not know how the rat knew," replied Chadrick, "but I knew because of that." He pressed a finger to James's wrist. He could see the faint mark the fool's hand had left behind the night it had visited him. The night it had burned him.

James nodded his head, touching the scar. "What now?" asked James, at a loss as to where to start.

He saw Anna take a deep, purposeful breath as she looked at the mess surrounding the mouth of the catacombs. "Let's go home," she said.

Those who had taken the opportunity to rest got to their feet. Evandor offered to carry Satria for part of the way and James agreed, thankful. That left Phoenix, who was strong enough to make it to his feet, but he needed some support. Anna took his arm over her shoulders so he could lean on her for support. They made their way up a short embankment that led to the road that would take them away from Dasdaya, back to Migdasha. As they reached it, James looked back to find Chadrick still among the dead Upipita, watching them leave.

"What are you doing?" asked Anna, calling back to Chadrick, and he frowned in return, confused.

"We fought the fool today, and we're alive," shouted Phoenix.

"I *told* you," said Anna, nudging him in the ribs.

He winced in pain, smiling reluctantly. "We've pissed off a legend," Phoenix called to Chadrick again. "Don't think you can get off that easily."

"You want me to join you?" asked Chadrick, frowning but looking so hopeful that James nearly laughed.

Phoenix did laugh and Evandor looked thoughtful for a moment, turning his head from one side to the other before nodding.

Chadrick smiled, a wide, warm smile that went to his eyes and made James smile too. "I am honoured," Chadrick said, nodding at each one in turn.

"So what are we waiting for?" Phoenix picked up his sword which he had found lying in the grass, covered in blood. He wiped it with his cloak, but it had already dried and so it only flaked. He sheathed it and looked up, expectantly.

"Wait…" Anna said, turning to James. "You're Uringi now – whether you can call fire or not, you are our brother."

James's cheeks flushed and he stared at her, not sure what to say.

"Don't look so pleased with yourself, brother," Anna said, chuckling, "you're not going to like this next part." She held out her hand to him, motioning for him to take it, and he did. She turned his hand over and pulled up his sleeve, exposing his wrist. "The mark." She traced her finger along the smooth, soft skin. "You have earned it."

It was then that James realised what she was talking about. The mark of the Uringi – the one that marked them as such – he was the only one in the group without it. Anna was quiet for a few moments and he realised that she was asking for his permission.

He nodded.

"This is going to hurt," she said.

"Then why are you smiling?" asked Phoenix, laughing into cupped hands. She smirked in return and took her sword from its sheath.

"Woah – what are you…" James started but stopped when he saw what she was doing. She lifted her sword and then stabbed the ground, causing it to stand straight up on its own. She then took the butt in her hand and moments later lifted it again, exposing a red-hot glow from the heated metal. James then saw that it was the three lines that were so familiar to him that glowed red and his stomach sank.

"Hold him," she instructed the others, and Phoenix and Chadrick appeared at his side, each taking hold of an arm.

Evandor appeared holding a thick, wooden stick. "Bite down, it'll help," he offered, and James took it in his mouth.

"Are you ready?" asked Anna.

James nodded and a moment later, the butt of the sword was pressed into his arm.

For a few seconds, James felt nothing but the cold bite of steel and then he realised it wasn't cold but hot, and the pain followed. He screamed as he bit into the stick, involuntarily throwing himself backwards, but Chadrick and Evandor held him firm.

When Anna lifted the sword, three welts appeared.

"Keep it clean," Anna advised, and then sheathed her sword. "When it heals, we will mark it with ink and you will be a true Uringi."

James looked down at the mark again, turning his arm over, feeling a sense of pride well up and threaten to spill over in tears. He swallowed it back, shaking his head.

He looked up to find the others setting up the road.

"Into the field once more we go," shouted Phoenix.

"Ne'er to return, we heed Uriaha's call," called Anna.

"Take my place, brother, should I fall," said Evandor.

"Mors Vorcat, death calls to us all," Chadrick called back as he joined them on the road.

"Until we meet again," James heard a voice whisper to him from the black smoke that filtered out of the caverns. He turned quickly, expecting the fool to be standing behind him, but there was nothing there. The dead did not move. Nothing came out of the catacombs.

James hurried to catch up with the others, trying to convince himself that he was mistaken.

When he reached the others, he fell in line with them, keeping his eyes ahead on the road, towards Migdasha. Towards home.

*

It was two days later when James came downstairs and made his way outside to find Anna sitting at the breakfast table, a blanket wrapped around her shoulders, a mug of hot tea in her hands.

She greeted him with a smile. "Morning, James."

He nodded to her, pouring a mug of tea for himself and taking a sip. "I need to go back to Dasdaya, to fetch something," he said.

"Do you want some company?" she asked him.

He shook his head. "I know the way," he replied.

She nodded at this.

Once he'd had his breakfast, he packed his bags and said goodbye to Evandor and Chadrick. Phoenix was still sleeping by the time he'd left. Then he was setting down the road and breathing in the cold winter air as he followed, one foot in front of the other, back to Dasdaya.

*

When he arrived at his old room, he waited a few seconds before he opened the door, as if he needed some time to prepare himself. The room was dark, quiet, and everything was still where he'd left it the day he'd first left to Migdasha.

The bed was unmade and his wooden chest was still locked at the end of his bed.

He took a key from his pocket and slipped it into the keyhole. When the chest opened, he saw that the few items it held were all still there. He didn't know what he'd expected. He pulled out the small black-and-white portrait of young woman. She was smiling, her eyes cast downwards.

He put the picture back and pulled out a small compact mirror. Something rattled inside it when he shook it. He put it back and closed the chest. Then he picked it up, tucking it under his arm. He placed a few coins on the chair and left his key beside them. Then he took one last look around the room before he left, closing the door behind him.

TWENTY-ONE

PLAYING THE FOOL

"Keep still," the familiar voice whispered to him. James was lying in his bed in Migdasha and for a second, he thought he was still sleeping.

"What do you want?" James opened his eyes, but there was no figure looming over him like it had the first time it had come for him in the night. Instead, the figure was standing by the large glass doors that looked out over the hills surrounding Migdasha. The glass doors were wide open and cold air was filtering into the room, causing the last embers in the fireplace to die, leaving a wisp of smoke trailing behind it like a ghost. Winter was on its way.

The moonlight turned the figure into little more than a silhouette, but when it turned, James could see its pointed chin and much-too-long fingers that tapped at its thighs. James wondered where Humbert was. Wasn't he supposed to protect the house? How did the creature get in?

The fool seemed to be thinking, turning its head from side to side, watching James. "You buried her out there," the fool hissed, turning to the windows once more. James knew he was referring to Satria, who was now resting at the foot of the hills. Evandor, Phoenix and Chadrick had all helped to dig her grave, and Anna had wrapped her in a silken shroud. It was James who'd lowered her into the ground.

James could feel his hands clench and his fingers began searching for his dagger. The fool was wrapped in long robes that touched his fingertips and his ankles. It was strange that the robes did not look out of place. James wondered if he could kill the creature by putting the dagger through its heart.

"I warned you," the fool said. "I told you I would take your heart."

"I am going to kill you for what you did to her," James said, pulling back the covers to get out of bed. He realised then that he couldn't move.

"Don't you want to know why?" the creature asked. "Why she lied? Why she let them lure you into the cavern? Why she… *distracted* you until her brothers could join you?"

"She didn't know," said James stubbornly, but he didn't believe his own words.

"The dead are always innocent of their crimes," the creature said. "Well, I'll tell you a secret." It sidled up to James, close enough for James to feel its breath on his face. "She knew. Oh yes, she knew."

James fought against bonds he couldn't see.

"It is no use." The fool spoke, not looking at James. "The anger you feel will fade and you'll realise I did it for your own good. For them all." He made a broad gesture that James thought included the four companions that must be sleeping soundly in their beds.

"Release me and fight me," spat James, barely listening, trying to goad the fool, to draw him closer, aware of the ridiculous nature of his command.

The fool still did not look at him. "I have waited for too long. What a mess you have made of this world." The fool was talking as if to himself. "We have been silent for too long." James was trying to force his legs to move, force himself out of bed, but the power would not relent.

"You are too stupid to see through your rage," the fool said, and then he turned and moved towards James. In a moment, he was on top of James. His eyes were white, blind. He grabbed at James's wrists, but there was no need because James could only move his head. The creature's robes had lifted as he had reached out to grab James, and he saw that they were scarred with bright, thick red lines. It looked as though the creature had been chained at one point, chained by something that burned him.

"You will see James, you will see," it whispered, leaning in close to James.

"What are you?" James tried desperately to make his fingers work, to reach out and grab the robes of this creature. This question made the fool smile for the first time. It was a wide smile and it sent a cold wind through the room.

"You know me, James Fiddick," the creature whispered to him. "You know me, chained and forgotten," it said. "Now you will help the world remember again."

Anna burst into the room with Chadrick following right behind her. She was still in her nightgown and Chadrick was shirtless. The second the door opened, James could hear a siren, screeching, from beyond his room.

"James, what's going on in here? Humbert is tearing the house apart trying to get in here…" She stopped when she saw the creature looming over James. Both Chadrick and Anna threw themselves towards James, but they too found themselves unable to move after only a few steps.

James couldn't figure out what sort of creature had this sort of power, until he remembered the marks on its legs. The chains.

"You're a Weaver?" guessed James. And the fool began to chuckle, low, as if not to wake anyone in the house.

The most powerful creatures ever to have existed. That's how Anna had described them.

"You are opening your eyes," it hissed at him. "You are *seeing me now.*"

"Get away from him!" shouted Anna.

And then it was gone. The room was dark and empty. The glass doors that led to the room slammed shut and shattered, shards pouring down onto the floor.

If the Weavers are gone, we stand alone against an army, Evandor had said.

James found he could move again.

Anna rushed over to him, treading a careful path through the broken glass. "Are you okay? Did it hurt you?"

"A Weaver, Anna," James was saying. "It's a Weaver."

Anna's eyes were wide and the colour left her face.

Chadrick had a dark look on his. He had moved over to the large, glass windows and he was looking out.

Evandor and Phoenix ran into the room, and it took a couple of minutes for James to tell them what happened. Evandor grew quiet after James stopped speaking and Phoenix's eyes were wide.

"The fool is a Weaver?" asked Phoenix, confused.

"Perhaps he was never the fool," suggested Chadrick.

"Or perhaps he was both," added Evandor.

James shook his head, trying to make sense of it all, but it was no use.

"You were right," Phoenix said to Anna, but this time, there was no humour in his voice, only fear.

"Except I thought the Weavers would be on our side," said Anna.

We stand alone. James thought of what Evandor had said when they first spoke of what would happen if they didn't find the Weavers. *We are alone. Against the fool's army. Against the Weaver's army.*

"How can we fight him, Anna?" asked James, shaking his head. "How do we fight a legend?"

"There is only one way," said Anna, her face becoming hard. "We become one."

James frowned, questioning her. She smiled, and it brought some warmth into the room. There was safety in that smile.

"Boys, we're going to bind the fool."